Glass Warriors

Duncan Anderson

Glass Warriors

The Camera at War

Collins

First published in 2005 by **Collins**
an imprint of HarperCollins Publishers

HarperCollins Publishers
77–85 Fulham Palace Road
London w6 8jb
www.collins.co.uk

Designed by Mark Thomson
Typeset in FF Nexus

Printed and bound in Great Britain by
Clays Ltd, St Ives plc.

A CIP catalogue record for this book is available from
the British Library.

ISBN 0–00–720030–7

Contents

Introduction

In the century and a half since Roger Fenton set up his apparatus on a battlefield in the Crimea, every war has attracted cameramen. The very first – Fenton, Felice Beato, James Robertson – did not think of themselves primarily as war photographers. War was just one amongst many subjects on which they worked. But as early as the 1860s a subdivision was emerging within their ranks. Matthew Brady, Alexander Gardner and John Burke saw themselves as different from other photographers, in part because of their subject matter, in part because of the risks they ran in capturing it on film. The evolution of the war photographer paralleled that of the war correspondent. William Howard Russell's articles in *The Times*, describing the ineptitude with which the Crimean expedition was surrounded, triggered the despatch of Fenton to Balaclava because, unlike a journalist, a photograph couldn't lie, or so mid-Victorians believed, at least at the very infancy of the medium.

For a generation the war photographer and the war correspondent were complementary but different, until technology – the new light-weight cameras and dry developing processes of the late 1880s – allowed them to merge into a single entity, the photo-journalist. By the turn of the last century they had evolved a distinctive culture. Some, like Richard Harding Davis, Luigi Barzini, Jack London, Frank Hurley, Edgar Snow and Robert Capa, achieved immortality. Most are less well known, though their photographs would be recognised immediately.

Far more than any other profession, war photographers risk their lives. Fenton survived more by good luck than good management, driven by a desire to secure an action shot. As technology improved, the photographer could get ever closer to the action, in the belief that it was here that the reality of war would finally be captured. Robert Capa's pithy 'If your shots are no good then you aren't close enough' sums up this attitude. Capa always did get close enough – and was killed, along with hundreds of others, from Ridgway Glover, hacked to death by the Sioux in the Little Bighorn Mountains in 1866, to the dozens who have died so far in the early twenty-first century's 'War Against Terror'. When soldiers are taking cover, the photo-journalist is taking pictures – even platoon commanders on the Western Front in the First World War had a greater chance of survival.

Photographers want their pictures to have an impact. Sometimes they succeed, like the Somali cameramen whose pictures of the mutilated bodies of American soldiers being dragged through the streets of Mogadishu in October 1993 served to trigger a US withdrawal. But more often they do not. Far more significant than the immediate impact is the long-term significance. Human beings have visual memories. The moving image – either on film or television – is ephemeral; the still image, repeatedly published, and looked at again and again, attains iconic status. Our collective memories of conflict these past 150 years owe much to our ability to link these images into something like a B-movie that runs constantly in our memory banks. This book explores the creation of these icons.

Many people have helped with this book. I would like to thank Andrew Orgill and the staff of the library of the Royal Military Academy, Sandhurst, the best military history library in the English-speaking world, and the staff of News International's archives. The book was conceived by Philip Parker of Collins. Without his constant encouragement it would not have come to publication. Finally I should like to thank my wife Christine Gerrard, who interrupted her studies of the eighteenth century, to act as my first critic. The responsibility for errors and omissions are, however, entirely my own.

The War Correspondent
and the War Photographer

The meeting

Early in June 1855 a meeting took place between two men in the British lines in front of Sebastopol which was to be of enormous symbolic importance in the history of war reporting. The world's first war photographer, Roger Fenton, newly arrived from England, persuaded the world's first war correspondent, William Howard Russell, to pose for him. Russell, his by now full beard reaching down to his chest, his hair hanging over the back of his collar, sat in a camp chair, clasping his hands before him. Having come badly equipped for the campaign, he had begged and borrowed clothes from sympathetic officers. He wore a commissariat officer's cap, a rifleman's patrol jacket and a pair of cord breeches, which he had tucked into calf-high butcher's boots. Pictured with his eyes partly hidden in a shadow cast by the peak of his cap, Russell's expression is one of thoughtful contemplation, as though trying to make sense of all he had seen since the spring of 1854.

We have no idea how these men regarded each other. Russell made no mention of Fenton in his diaries, and Fenton made only the brief comment 'I have got W. H. Russell's likeness' in a letter to his sponsor, William Agnew. It was Russell's presence which had brought Fenton to the Crimea. From the late autumn of 1854 the journalist's despatches in *The Times*, exposing incompetence, mismanagement and corruption, had enraged the British public and contributed to the collapse of Prime Minister Lord Aberdeen's government. In vain the military authorities, from commander-in-chief Lord Raglan down, had complained that Russell's despatches were grotesque caricatures and over-simplifications. The problem was how to expose Russell's mendacity, because even his worst critic allowed that Russell's descriptive powers were of unusual acuity. There was simply no one who could write with the same force as *The Times*'s correspondent. The solution was not to attempt to match Russell with the written word, but to respond with a new technology then only 15 years old – the photograph – because everyone knew that the camera could not lie. Thus it was that, in their first campaign, the war correspondent and the war photographer were on different sides. More than a generation was to pass before new technology allowed the correspondent and the photographer to merge into a single being – the photo-journalist.

Back by Easter

The 34-year-old Russell had been working on and off for *The Times* for 12 years, when in February 1854 *The Times*'s editor John Thaddeus Delane offered him a chance to join the British expedition setting out to face down the Russians and force them to withdraw their troops from Russo-Turkish border provinces in the Balkans. Delane told Russell he would be travelling with the Guards, that he would probably not go further than Malta and that he would be back by Easter. But Delane was wrong. The crisis with Russia was ostensibly the result of a long-standing dispute over Russian claims to the guardianship of the holy places in Palestine, then a province of the Turkish empire. In October 1853, when Russian troops entered the border provinces of Moldavia and Wallachia, which formed a neutralised buffer between the Russian and Turkish empires, Turkey declared war. Six weeks later a Russian fleet had sallied forth from its naval base at Sebastopol on the Crimean peninsula and attacked and sunk the Turkish fleet at its base at Sinope, near Constantinople. Britain and France both had reasons for supporting Turkey: Britain to protect her line of communications with India, and France, now led by Napoleon III, grandnephew of the great Napoleon, anxious to avenge the defeat of 1812 and establish legitimacy for the new Bonapartist dynasty. Less than a month after Russell received Delane's request, Britain and France were at war with Russia.

Croakers

Russell quickly discovered that Delane had been over-optimistic in expecting the military to co-operate. *The Times*'s correspondent was not, after all, permitted to travel with the Guards (there was no space for him on the transports) but was forced to make his own way overland, joining up with the convoy at Malta. The British commander-in-chief, Lord Raglan, had served as Wellington's military secretary in the peninsula, and had lost an arm at Waterloo. Now 66 years old, and commanding an army in the field for the first time in his life, Raglan decided to treat Russell just as Wellington had treated observers at the front reporting back to the newspapers some 40 years earlier. Officers in Wellington's army had written to the newspapers on a regular basis, frequently complaining about the conduct of the campaign. Wellington had called them 'croakers', had ostracised them and then used political allies in London to marginalise and neutralise them. This media policy had served the duke well, and Raglan would do the same. He could not stop Russell coming, but he planned to ignore him. It was not that Raglan wished to be personally rude to Russell – he was, in fact, an extremely polite and courteous man – it was simply that he had no conception of the latent power of Russell's pen.

The expedition to the East was the largest force Britain had so far despatched in such a short space of time, dwarfing those sent to America in 1776 and 1812, or to the Iberian peninsula in 1808 and 1809. British administrative arrangements, perfectly adequate for the despatch of regiments and brigades to South Africa and India, quickly broke down when required to deal with divisions and corps. The French, who were used to operating at divisional level and larger, and had had recent experience of sending substantial forces across the Mediterranean to fight in

Algeria, coped far better. To Russell, whose knowledge of military affairs was confined to reporting a brief skirmish between the Prussians and the Danes in 1850, the contrast was all too apparent. Reporting on the landing at Gallipoli on 8 April 1854, Russell was impressed by the ceaseless activity of the French: '… the daily arrival of their steamers and the admirable completeness of all their arrangements in every detail – hospitals for the sick, bread and biscuit bakeries, wagon trains for carrying stores and baggage – every necessary and comfort, indeed, at hand, the moment their ships came in'. By contrast, the British

> … suffered exceedingly from cold. Some of them, officers as well as privates, had no beds to lie upon. None of the soldiers had more than their single regulation blanket. They therefore reversed the order of things and dressed to go to bed, putting on all their spare clothing before they tried to sleep. The worst thing was the continued want of comforts for the sick. Many of the men labouring under diseases contracted at Malta were obliged to stay in camp in the cold, with only one blanket under them, as there was no provision for them at the temporary hospital.

After several weeks based in Turkey, followed by deployment to Varna in Bulgaria, the expedition landed at Calamita Bay on the west coast of the Crimea, its objective to capture the Russian naval base at Sebastopol. Russell had already demonstrated a quite unusual ability to describe complicated events both vividly and with clarity, and was later to compare his eye to a lens and his pen to a camera. His description of the Anglo-French task force as it crossed the Black Sea evoked visions of a Turner seascape:

> No pen could describe its effect upon the eye. Ere an hour had
> elapsed it had extended itself over half the circumference of the
> horizon. Possibly no expedition so complex and so terrible in its
> means of destruction, with such enormous power in engines of
> war and such capabilities of locomotion, was ever sent forth by
> any worldly power. The fleet, in five irregular and straggling lines,
> flanked by men-of-war and war steamers, advanced slowly, filling
> the atmosphere with innumerable columns of smoke, which
> gradually flattened out into streaks and joined the clouds, adding
> to the sombre appearance of the well named 'Black' Sea.

Russell's descriptive ability, his status as a barely tolerated
outsider, and his lack of experience of British military operations,
gave his despatches an extraordinary power. Compared with
landings in the past, the disembarkation at Calamita Bay on 14
September proved unexceptional and was a good deal more
efficient, for example, than the landing of Wellington's army at
Mondego Bay in Portugal in 1809. But the inexperienced Russell,
unaware that physical discomfort and being soaked to the skin
are part and parcel of the soldier's condition, attributed all such
episodes to military incompetence. He vigorously complained
that

> seldom or never were 27,000 Englishmen more miserable. No
> tents had been sent on shore, partly because there had been no
> time to land them, partly because there was no certainty of our

being able to find carriage for them in case of a move. Towards night the sky looked very black and lowering; the wind rose, and the rain fell in torrents. The showers increased about midnight. And early in the morning fell in drenching sheets which pierced through the blankets and great-coats of the houseless and tentless soldiers.

When they eventually saw Russell's accounts in *The Times*, the veterans of Salamanca and Waterloo dismissed him as yet another 'croaker'. But hard on the heels of the Calamita Bay account came Russell's description of the Battle of the Alma, when the British army, ably supported by the French, drove the Russians from a naturally strong defensive position. Years later Russell described his feelings as he tried to make sense of his first big battle: 'My eyes swam as I tried to make notes of what I had heard. I was worn out with excitement, fatigue and want of food.' His Alma despatch did the British army proud, and heroised the commander-in-chief. 'The men halted on the battlefield … and when Lord Raglan was in front of the Guards the whole army burst into a tremendous cheer, which made one's heart leap – the effect of that cheer can never be forgotten by those who heard it.'

'The Thin Red Line'

The Alma Despatch established Russell's reputation for even-handed honesty. His criticism of incompetence was matched by unstinting praise for a good performance. A few weeks later, with the army established at Balaclava, the power of his pen was demonstrated with full force. On 25 October columns of a

Russian relief army overran the positions of Britain's Turkish allies, and bore down on the harbour. For the moment the only force which opposed the charging Russian cavalry was the 93rd Highlanders, commanded by Sir Colin Campbell. Watching from a nearby hill, Russell described the Highlanders as 'that thin red streak tipped with a line of steel', a phrase which was soon to enter British popular consciousness as 'the thin red line'. He continued, '… With breathless suspense everyone awaited the bursting of the wave upon the line of Gaelic rock; but ere they came within two hundred and fifty yards, another deadly volley flashed from the levelled rifle and carried terror among the Russians. They wheeled about, opened files right and left and fled faster than they came.'

A short time later Russell witnessed the Charge of the Light Brigade. 'A more fearful spectacle was never witnessed than by those who, without the power to aid, beheld their heroic countrymen rushing to the arms of death. At a distance of 1,200 yards the whole line of the enemy belched forth, from thirty iron mouths, a flood of smoke and flame, through which hissed the deadly balls.' *Punch* magazine depicted a father reading Russell's despatch in *The Times*, waving a poker in the air with enthusiasm, while his sons jump with excitement and his wife and daughters weep. The despatch became the basis of the Poet Laureate Alfred, Lord Tennyson's *Charge of the Light Brigade*, the single most famous description of a military action in the English language. It remains to this day the best-known 20 minutes in British military history. Without Russell's pen it would have been yet another minor military disaster, its details known only to a handful of specialists.

The Balaclava despatch turned Russell into a household name. His fame was reinforced by his subsequent description of the Battle of Inkerman, the bloody hand-to-hand conflict fought to prevent a second Russian relief effort on 5 November. Now a national celebrity, with an avid readership, Russell's despatches detailing the collapse of the British administrative system in the autumn proved deadly. By this time he had many friends in the army and they were all talking. He could assert that 'generals who passed their youth in the Peninsular war, and had witnessed a good deal of fighting since that time in various parts of the world, were unanimous in declaring that they never knew or read of a war in which the officers were exposed to such hardships'. Forty years later in his reminiscences Russell said he 'could not tell lies to make things pleasant'. The tents were sometimes a foot deep in water and

> ... our men had neither warm nor waterproof clothing – they were out for twelve hours at a time in the trenches – they were plunged into the inevitable miseries of a winter campaign – and not a soul seemed to care for their comfort, or even for their lives. These were hard truths, which sooner or later must have come to the ears of the people of England. It was right they should know that the wretched beggar who wandered the streets of London in the rain led the life of a prince compared with the British soldiers who were fighting for their country, and who, we were complacently assured by the home authorities, were the best appointed army in Europe.

Russell's despatches did produce reforms to the commissariat and the medical services, but it was too little too late. A political storm broke in Britain, which on 1 February 1855 swept away the fragile Aberdeen coalition, and paved the way for the premiership of Lord Palmerston. Discussions between the Duke of Newcastle, the secretary of state for war, and Prince Albert, the Prince Consort, who took a deep interest in military affairs, gave rise to the idea of producing an irrefutable photographic record which would show that the army in the Crimea was now well looked after. The Prince, a firm patron of the Royal Photographic Society, was impressed by the way in which a sequence of photographs could be arranged to tell a story. He had first seen photography's narrative potential in a display of more than 1,500 pictures at the Great Exhibition some four years earlier. He already knew Roger Fenton, the honorary secretary of the society, who had taken portraits of the royal family the previous year. Fenton, the son of a Lancashire MP, had studied art in Paris under Paul Delaroche, who in 1839 had become fascinated by the possibilities of the daguerreotype. Influenced by Delaroche, by the early 1850s Fenton was one of Britain's leading society photographers, a mid-nineteenth-century Cecil Beaton. He could hardly resist the challenge of a photographic expedition to the Crimea, a patriotic mission which might also prove a major commercial success.

Thus it was that Fenton arrived in Balaclava on 9 March 1855. His first impression was that 'everything seems in much better order than *The Times* led me to expect'. He reported to his wife that 'Lord Raglan was in town this morning with his staff. The soldiers have nothing but good words to say about him; one of them told me that when the weather was at the worst he was constantly sitting about amongst the men'. But this favourable impression was soon undermined when he tried to get his equipment ashore. Fenton was accompanied by his servant William, a handyman and cook, and Marcus Spalding, a former corporal in the Light Dragoons, who was a gifted photographer himself and was to write a manual on the subject in 1856. The expedition came with 36 large cases crammed with equipment. They had five cameras of different sizes, about 700 glass plates contained in grooved wooden boxes, several chests of chemicals and a still for distilling water. In addition, they had a wine merchant's van, which they had converted into a mobile dark room. Fenton discovered that the harbour was controlled by different agencies, all with different chains of command. He met officer after officer who tried to be helpful, but didn't possess the necessary authority to secure a crane or a barge or docking space or labour. Eventually Fenton went to the captain of the *Mohawk*, a transport already at a dock, who transferred Fenton's carriage and supplies by boat to his own ship, from whence it was cross-decked on to a landing stage. Fenton wrote that this was a 'glorious example of the successful working of private enterprise'. He was sure 'it would have taken a week before by Government aid I could have disembarked my van'.

Before leaving Balaclava for the encampments, Fenton got Spalding to paint the self-explanatory slogan 'Photographic Van' on the side of the carriage, to avoid the persistent questions of curious onlookers. Ironically the slogan attracted rather than deterred attention. Soldiers flocked round the van, demanding that Fenton take their picture. He wrote to his wife, 'Everybody is bothering me for their portrait to send home; were I to listen to them and take the portrait of all comers I should be busy from now to Christmas and might make a regular gold digging in the Crimea.' At the end of March Fenton took the van out of Balaclava to the camps of the Guards and cavalry, where he took portraits, groups and views for several days. It was then dragged by stages up to headquarters.

Letters of introduction from Prince Albert to Lord Raglan and other commanders made Fenton (unlike Russell) *persona grata* with the military. Invited to dine with the commander-in-chief, he was placed on Lord Raglan's right, while the beautiful Lady George Paget, just arrived in the Crimea, was on Raglan's left, so that Fenton 'had plenty of conversation with her'. Fenton was entertained in a similar fashion by various subordinate commanders, and the French generals, and for several weeks was virtually attached to General Sir John Campbell's headquarters as one of his staff.

Fenton's ambitions went well beyond panoramic and group shots. His correspondence was laced with attacks on the accuracy of conventional war artists from the *Illustrated London News* and other journals, whose sometimes fanciful depiction of events and scenes was the target of amused mockery from soldiers and officers. Satirical journalism also poked fun at the fashion for, but limitations of, the photographic medium. In 1854 *Punch* published a cartoon of a young lady writing to her fiancé in the Crimea. Gazing lovingly at his photograph she writes, 'I send you, dear Alfred, a complete photographic apparatus which will amuse you doubtlessly in your moments of leisure, and if you could send me home, dear, a good view of a nice battle, I should feel extremely obliged. P.S. If you could take the view, dear, just in the moment of victory, I should like it all the better.'

Although Fenton was constrained by the limitations of technology, he tried to transcend his medium by capturing action shots. After lunch on 15 April he set up his camera on Cathcart's Hill, one of the highest in the British lines, with his camera pointing towards the Garden fort, one of the Russian outposts to the south-west of Sebastopol. Thanks to his privileged position Fenton knew that the French had driven a mine under the fort, and were due to detonate it at 4pm Fenton wrote, 'I was ready with my camera at the precise time, but no event coming off I shut up, and it was soon announced that it was postponed till half past six.' A few days later Fenton set up his apparatus in a ravine nicknamed the 'Valley of the Shadow of Death', which, lying behind British batteries, was filled with Russian cannon balls which had overshot their targets. As he prepared to take the picture, a Russian ball came over the lip of the ravine,

... bounding up towards us. It turned off when near, and where it went I did not see, as a shell came over about the same spot, knocked its fuse out and joined the mass of its brethren without bursting. It was plain that the line of fire was upon the very spot I had chosen, so very reluctantly I put up with another view of the valley 100 yards short of the best point. I brought the van down and fixed the camera and while levelling it another ball came in a more slanting direction, touching the rear of the batteries as the others, but instead of coming up the road, bounded onto the hill on our left about fifty yards from us and came down right to us, stopping at our feet. I picked it up and put it into the van; I hope to make you a present of it.

Fenton did his best, but was unable to get the shots he craved – the exploding mine or the bouncing cannon ball. He could have taken some sombre and haunting pictures of the aftermath of battle, but as a photographer 'embedded' into the British military system he felt morally unable to do so. On 2 June he rode along the route of the Light Brigade's charge seven months earlier and 'came upon many skeletons half buried, one was lying as if he had raised himself upon his elbow, the bare skull sticking up with just enough flesh left in the muscles to prevent it falling from the shoulders; another man's feet and hands were on the ground, the shoes on his feet, and the flesh gone'. Conscious of his mission, he also avoided taking pictures of anything which would suggest mismanagement, such as the organisation of Balaclava harbour, about which he complained at great length in his letters.

Displayed at photograph exhibitions throughout Britain, and available as postcards and stereoscope images, Fenton's collection was designed as an antidote to Russell's critical despatches. As his correspondence shows, he often engaged in rigorous self-censorship. Popular expectations to the contrary, the camera could, and did, lie.

About the same time that Fenton photographed Russell, *The Times*'s correspondent had another visitor, a young, good-looking Indian gentleman named Azimullah Khan, a plenipotentiary for Nana Sahib, the Rajah of Bitpur. Khan had decided to visit the Crimea on his way back to India from London, where he had negotiated fruitlessly with the directors of the East India Company for the restoration of Nana Sahib's pension, which had been cancelled on the death of his father in 1851. Russell, loquacious and fond of brandy, talked at length with Khan about the nature of the British empire, and the systemic weaknesses of the British army, so much in evidence in the Crimea. Khan, who had hitherto believed Britain an invincible super-power, was soon regaling Nana Sahib in his palace at Cawnpore with these revelations.

There were other intimations of British weakness. On 26 November 1855 the British commander of the city of Kars in eastern Anatolia, General Sir William Fenwick Williams, surrendered to besieging Russians. Although the event is almost forgotten today, in late 1855 the British press regarded it as a major disaster, because of the impact the fall of the city would have on British prestige in the East. Editorials in *The Times*, the *Daily Telegraph* and the *Morning Post* predicted that Britain's failure to save the city from the Russians would lead to disturbances in the more disaffected frontier regions of India.

In the spring and early summer of 1857 some sort of trouble was expected in India. It came not, as expected, from the frontiers, but in the heart of Oudh, a province sprawling over the central plain of the Ganges, which had been under British control since the beginning of the century. On 10 May soldiers of the British East India Company's Bengal army based in Meerut, about 25 miles from Delhi, went on the rampage, killing their British officers and any European civilians they could lay their hands on, including women and children. What had gone wrong? For nearly a generation ship-loads of evangelical Christian missionaries had been arriving in India, preaching against Islam and Hinduism, religions which they dismissed as barbarous nonsense. At first the Indians ignored them, but soon evangelical policies were being introduced by the company, not just the abolition of suttee, the burning of widows along with their dead husbands, which many Hindus also opposed, but interference with the educational system, local systems of inheritance, and the social position of women. The sense that a sustained attack on their society was under way was reinforced in early 1857 by the introduction of the new Minie rifle, the loading of which involved the soldier biting down on a greased cartridge; the Hindus believed the grease to be the fat of the sacred cow, and the Muslims, the fat of the unclean pig. This violation of religious scruples was too much for 85 cavalry sepoys at Meerut who, having refused to obey orders to bite the cartridges, were tried by court martial and condemned to long prison sentences. It was the sight of these soldiers being led away in chains, together with the growing apprehension that British power was based on bluff, which led to the explosion of rage.

The following day mutineers crossed over the Jumna River on a bridge of boats and arrived in Delhi, where the garrison joined them in butchering all the Europeans they could find. The rebels declared as their new ruler the elderly Bahadur Shah, the hitherto powerless king of Delhi, last descendent of the Moguls, thereby transforming a military mutiny into a proto-nationalist uprising. Within the month the whole of the Ganges plain, from Delhi to the outskirts of Calcutta, was in rebel hands, with the exception of British garrisons which held out at Cawnpore and Lucknow, both deep in the heart of the most disaffected areas. At Cawnpore, Nana Sahib, who had been heavily influenced by Azimullah Khan, ordered his own small army to support the mutineers in besieging the residency, while he secured the surrender of the British with a promise of safe conduct downriver to Allahabad. On 27 June Nana's troops murdered the now disarmed men, and imprisoned the women and children, as they were embarking on river boats.

The first British counterattacks were now under way. In a series of astonishing forced marches, carried out at the height of the Indian summer in temperatures well over 100 degrees Fahrenheit, a column composed mainly of Highlanders under the command of Henry Havelock raced for Cawnpore, in what today would be called a hostage rescue mission. Smashing Nana's forces at Fatehpur on 12 July, and Anong on 15 July, the troops entered Cawnpore the following day to discover the bodies of British women and children prisoners hacked to death and thrown into a well by Nana's orders. Havelock, a fundamentalist Christian, and his now berserk Scots, swore vengeance on the heathen, and proceeded to hack their way through overwhelming rebel forces, fighting their way into Lucknow on 25 September, where they, too, were besieged. On 16 November, Sir Colin

Campbell led a second relief force into the city, which allowed the survivors to be evacuated safely to Cawnpore. Meanwhile, another column under John Nicholson reached and stormed Delhi, killing thousands of mutineers and capturing Bahadur Shah. By now avenging British columns were cutting swathes along the Ganges, executing all Indians who might remotely be associated with the mutiny, which usually meant all able-bodied adult males. It was said it was possible to follow the march of the British by the bodies hanging from trees. The Indians now had a name for the avenging British – the Devil's Wind.

Intimations of horror

Once again representing *The Times*, William Howard Russell landed at Calcutta on 18 January 1858, and immediately joined Sir Colin Campbell's army which was about to re-conquer the Ganges plain and extinguish the last embers of rebellion. This time Russell was thoroughly 'embedded'. He recorded Sir Colin saying to him, 'Now, Mr Russell, I'll be candid with you. We shall make a compact. You shall know everything that is going on. You shall see all my reports, and get every information that I have myself, on condition that you do not mention it in camp, or let it be known in any way, except in your letter to England.' About the same time, Felice Beato, a photographer of Italian birth who had filmed in the Crimea after Fenton had left, arrived in India with a commission from the War Office. Beato was primarily a photographer of architecture, who had worked around the Mediterranean, recording everything from the Borgias' palaces to Venetian fortresses. As areas were pacified the British wanted Beato to photograph the physical destruction of buildings, not just to maintain a record for its own sake, but to provide evidence of the effect of various types of shot against various types of masonry, an activity which is today called 'operational analysis'. Like Fenton in the Crimea, Beato had a mission, but this time the photographer and the journalist, though never in the same place at the same time, would work in tandem rather than in opposition.

At Cawnpore, Beato photographed the Bibighar, or 'House of the Ladies', the chambers where Nana Sahib had imprisoned the 206 women and children who had survived the massacre on the boats, before they too had been murdered. Beato chose an angle which cut out many of the Bibighar's windows and columns and, by concentrating on three small windows, a broken wall and a twisted tree, made the building look like a tomb. Even without knowing the history it is sinister, certainly not a place one would choose to spend the night. Russell also found it 'a horrible spot! Inside the shattered rooms, which had been the scene of such devoted suffering, are heaps of rubbish and filth. The entrenchment is used as a *Cloaca Maxima* by the natives, camp-followers, coolies, and others who bivouac in the sandy plains around it. The smells are revolting. Rows of gorged vultures sit with outspread wings on the mouldering parapets, or perch in clusters on the two or three leafless trees at the angle of the works by which we enter'.

On 16 March Campbell's army, now 30,000 strong, had reached Lucknow. Neither Russell nor Beato had expected such a large city, nor one with so many architecturally splendid buildings. Just days apart, both men climbed the same lofty minaret, so that they could describe the city in their different ways. Beato's photograph, skilfully composed, depicted Lucknow as a mid-Victorian eastern fantasy, a forest of marble domes, battlements and minarets. Russell, for once, felt overwhelmed by the scene. 'Alas, words! words! how poor you are to depict the scene which met the eye of the infidel from the quiet retreat of the muezzin! Lucknow, in its broad expanse of palaces, its groves and gardens, its courts and squares, its mosques and temples, its wide-spreading, squalid quarters of mean, close houses, amid which are kiosks and mansions of rich citizens, surrounded by trees, all lay at our feet, with the Dilkusha, and Martiniere, and distant Alumbagh plainly visible, and the umbrageous plains clothed in the richest vegetation, and covered with woodland, which encompasses the city. In the midst winds the Gumti, placid and silvery, though its waters are heavy with the dead.'

War photography's first controversy

Tasked with photographing the scenes of action, Beato made his way to the Secundra Bagh, a large palace on the eastern side of Lucknow which had been stormed by the Highlanders and Sikhs in November 1857. Here the British had taken heavy casualties, but had also killed more than 2,000 mutineers, whom they had buried in large pits. Beato's picture of the Secundra Bagh is his best known. The damage wrought by round-shot on the marble and masonry is clearly visible, and in the middle distance Beato has placed four Indians with a horse, to give a sense of scale.

The most controversial aspect of the picture is the dismembered skeletons which litter the foreground. This was the first time the dead had been shown after a battle, albeit one that had taken place four months earlier. When it was displayed in Britain the commander of the 93rd Highlanders, Colonel Maude, was surprised by the corpses, because 'every one was being regularly buried'. He presumed that 'the dogs had dug them up'. This led to the allegation that Beato had in fact arranged the bones in the manner of a still life to add to the composition. Another veteran of the battle, William Forbes Mitchell, flatly contradicted the colonel, writing that the British dead had been removed and buried in a deep trench, 'but the rebel dead had to be left to rot where they lay, a prey to the vulture by day and the jackal by night, for from the smallness of the relieving force no other course was possible'. It had taken just three years since Fenton set up his cameras in the Crimea for war photography to generate its first controversy.

The controversy would have been greater still if, like Russell, Beato had recorded everything he had seen. *The Times's* correspondent described in graphic detail the looting of the Kaiserbagh, a rambling palace which lay at the centre of the city. Beato photographed the exterior, but not the shambles which lay within. Similarly, Russell wrote movingly of the bodies of executed Indians which festooned trees all along the Ganges, many of whom, he suspected, were innocent men who happened to be in the wrong place when the Devil's Wind swept by. British officers, many of whom were accomplished sketch artists, drew pictures of trees with bodies hanging like over-ripe fruit. Beato, mindful of his mission, exercised considerable self-censorship, confining himself to a single photograph of just two Indians swinging from a gibbet, which suggested that the British had exercised commendable self-control.

When Russell left for Britain in March 1859, British columns had smashed the mutineers' main armies, and the conflict had entered a long 'mopping-up' phase. The British pursued Nana Sahib into the jungles of Nepal where the trail went cold, though for the next 30 years young British officers continued to arrest suspects. British agents traced Azimullah Khan to Calcutta, where he went to ground, emerging some time later in Constantinople. The Osama bin Ladens and Saddam Husseins of their day, Nana Sahib and Azimullah Khan became the embodiment of all that the British found dark in the Indian soul.

Bull Run Russell

On 16 October 1859, as the British continued their counter-insurgency campaign in India, a group of terrorists seized the United States' main arsenal at Harpers Ferry in Virginia, and captured local citizens as hostages. It was a classic example of what a hundred years later the Cuban revolutionary Che Guevara would call the 'Foco Theory', the idea that a dramatic action by a small group of determined men could plunge a society into crisis, and set in motion forces which would produce revolutionary change. The terrorists, only 19 in number, were led by John Brown, a fundamentalist Christian who believed that God had commanded him to bring an end to slavery in the United States through an apocalyptic uprising. Having succeeded in the first part of his operation, Brown issued a proclamation calling on the slaves of the south to desert their masters and come to Harpers Ferry, where they would be issued with arms. Few came, and a detachment of US Marines led by US Army Colonel Robert E. Lee soon captured Brown. He and six of his men were tried, convicted of treason and sent to the scaffold on 2 December. As far as the southern states were concerned the crisis was over, but it wasn't. The largest crowds ever seen in New York, Boston and Philadelphia gathered to register their protest against Brown's execution, for the great majority of the population in the north felt that Brown had been morally justified in what he had done and that his execution was judicial murder. The political knots which had kept the union together now unravelled at terrifying speed, leading to the election of Republican Abraham Lincoln to the Presidency on 6 November 1860, and to the secession of South Carolina on 20 December.

Russell arrived in New York in March 1861, by which time another ten states had seceded, though it was by no means certain that war was inevitable. Introduced to the president in the still-unfinished White House, Russell recorded that 'Mr Lincoln put out his hand in a very friendly manner, and said, "Mr Russell, I am very glad to make your acquaintance, and to see you in this country. *The London Times* is one of the greatest powers in the world – in fact, I don't know of any thing which has much more power – except perhaps the Mississippi. I am glad to know you as its minister."' The meeting had left Russell 'agreeably impressed with his shrewdness, humour and natural sagacity'.

Months before the meeting, Russell had been impressed with

a photograph of presidential candidate Lincoln, taken on 27 February 1860 in the Broadway studios of New York society photographer Matthew Brady. By constantly adjusting Lincoln's position, Brady had transformed the shambling unkempt backwoods lawyer, the first impression Lincoln often created, into a noble sage, whose eyes betokened humanity and wisdom, and it was this Lincoln that Russell met. On leaving the studio, Lincoln had gone to the Cooper Institute where he delivered a speech which established him as front runner for the presidency. Woodcut reproductions of Brady's portrait of Lincoln appeared in mass-circulation newspapers, while tens of thousands of photograph cards – known as *cartes de visite* – were printed and sold for about 25 cents each. Some time later, when asked if he knew Matthew Brady, Lincoln said that Brady and the Cooper Institute had made him president.

On the morning of 21 July 1861 correspondent and photographer were at last in the same spot at the same time, more or less. The war had begun three months earlier, when South Carolina had bombarded Fort Sumter, a federal fortification controlling Charleston harbour. Soon two volunteer armies had formed, one for the Confederacy to protect Richmond, the South's new capital, and one for the Union, to protect Washington. That morning the North's army set out for Manassas railway junction, where the Confederate Army had positioned itself along Bull Run, a small tributary of the Potomac River. Loading his apparatus into a carriage, Brady had left Washington before dawn. He set up his camera on a hill near the small town of Centreville, which afforded excellent views of Manassas, about six miles distant.

Here he was soon joined by the cream of Washington society, congressmen, senators, senior public officials and their wives. At first there were hundreds and then thousands, many equipped with picnic hampers and all set to enjoy the spectacle of the largest battle yet fought on American soil.

Russell had also tried to leave before dawn, but had been delayed by American reluctance to issue him with a pass. At about noon he reached Centreville. Russell reported that 'on a hill beside me there was a crowd of civilians on horseback, and in all sorts of vehicles, with a few of the fairer, if not gentler sex'. By now the battle was well under way: 'Clouds of smoke shifted and moved through the forest; and through the wavering mists of light blue smoke, and the thicker masses which rose commingling from the feet of men and the mouths of cannon, I could see the gleam of arms and the twinkling of bayonets.' Moving south to get a better view, Russell ran into a mass of wagons and men, all racing north. At first he thought they were returning to get more ammunition, but soon there was a mob: 'Emerging from the crowd a breathless man in the uniform of an officer with an empty scabbard dangling by his side was cut off by getting between my horse and a cart for a moment. "What is the matter, sir? What is all this about?" "Why, it means we are pretty badly whipped, that's the truth," he gasped.'

Russell was borne along on a human tide which carried all before it. 'The scene on the road had now assumed an aspect which has not a parallel in any description I have ever read. Infantry soldiers on mules and draught horses, with the harness clinging to their heels, as much frightened as their riders; negro servants on their masters' charges; ambulances crowded with unwounded soldiers; wagons swarming with men who threw out the contents in the road to make room, grinding through a shouting, screaming mass of men on foot, who were literally yelling with rage at every halt, and shrieking out, "Here are the cavalry! Will you get on?"' This portion of the force was evidently in discord.

As the mob swept past Centreville, it was reinforced by terrified senators and congressmen, whose carriages became part of the utter rout. Brady's carriage was overturned and he was found wandering in a confused state by some officers of a New York regiment who recognised him and gave him a sword. He made it safely back to Washington – he was never quite sure how – and the following day had his picture taken in what was then recognised as the photographer's dress uniform – long white dust jacket and broad-brimmed straw hat. He inscribed the picture 'Brady, The Photographer, returned from Bull Run. Photo taken July 22 1861' and used it as a publicity shot throughout the war. Russell sent his description of the Bull Run rout to *The Times* and then concentrated on other stories, as Northern panic subsided.

Four weeks later, when *The Times* 'Bull Run' edition arrived in New York, a storm broke over Russell. Americans had, of course, said exactly the same things, but in the interval rationalisations had been invented. Russell's story tore open a freshly healed wound. It would have been bad enough if an American had done this, but Russell was British. One by one his sources of information closed down, until he was left with no choice but to return to London.

Photographing Total War

The American experience, 1861–65

Even before Bull Run, Russell, who had toured the Confederacy, had confided to his diary that the Union 'will not have it over the South without a tremendous and long-sustained contest, in which they must put forth every exertion, and use all the resources and superior means they so abundantly possess'. The defeat at Manassas Junction convinced the North that it had to mobilise on the same scale as the infant French republic in 1792, and prepare to wage a war which would last years rather than months, and which might come to involve potentially hostile European powers like Britain and France. By contrast the Confederacy relaxed, being convinced by Manassas of its innate military superiority, and certain that Britain and France would have to intervene to secure supplies of cotton for the mills of

Manchester and Lyon.

To American photographers it was clear that the war would create a demand for images. Before Bull Run the pictures of one of Brady's former employees, George S. Cook, were on sale in New York. Cook, a southerner, had returned to New Orleans during the secession crisis, and had then travelled up to Charleston. At the beginning of April 1861, Cook had talked his way into Fort Sumter to photograph Major Robert Anderson, who had refused to surrender his garrison to the Confederacy. A few weeks later Anderson's card photograph was selling like hot cakes in New York, at 50 cents a copy, twice what Brady had got for Lincoln's photograph a year earlier. On 13 April, the day Anderson surrendered, southern photographers swarmed over the fort, taking dramatic pictures of battle damage, similar to those taken by Beato in India.

After this first splurge, however, Southern photographers quickly ran short of photographic materials, none of which were produced in the Confederacy. Moreover, unlike the cities of the North, which were utterly remote from the war, there was little demand for battle scenes in the South, where the reality of war came closer month by month. Southern photographers rationed their increasingly scarce stocks for the photograph which was always in demand, the portrait of the husband, father or son in the uniform of the Confederacy, taken before he left for war.

In the North, Brady had originally planned to produce a single volume of photographs, rather like Fenton's collection from the Crimea. As the conflict became increasingly total, Brady realised he would have to organise his photography on the same basis as other aspects of the North's war effort – its scale would have to be industrial. Brady began by hiring about 20 skilled photographers, assigned them to various units and spent about $100,000 paying for all their supplies and equipment. He took relatively few pictures himself, but was rather like the chairman of a photography industry, who was part entrepreneur, part director of photography, but also part artist. More than 300 photographers took pictures of various aspects of the American Civil War, about half of whom worked for Brady at one time or another.

Breaking the taboo

One of Brady's assistants, Alexander Gardner, a Scot who had emigrated to America in 1849, pushed the limits of what was thought acceptable in September 1862, by photographing the corpses of Confederate soldiers killed at Antietam. When the collection was displayed in New York about three weeks later it caused a sensation. An editorial in the *New York Times* thought that 'Mr Brady has done something to bring home to us the terrible reality and earnestness of war. If he has not brought bodies and laid them on our dooryard and along the streets, he has done something very like it ... It seems somewhat singular that the same sun that looked down on the faces of the slain, blistering them, blotting out from the bodies all the semblance to humanity, and hastening corruption, should have thus caught their features upon canvas, and given them perpetuity for ever. But it is so.'

Propelled by an apparently insatiable demand for photographs, Brady's empire expanded very rapidly, and then, like all such enterprises, began to fragment. Having already, thanks to Antietam, established a reputation as a daring and innovative photographer, Gardner broke away in 1862, and others soon followed. Competition between Brady's and Gardner's enterprises was intense. On 5 July 1863, Timothy H. O'Sullivan, a former Brady employee who had defected to Gardner, took the most famous photograph of the war, *The Harvest of Death*, an arrangement of enemy dead on the Gettysburg battlefield. Brady hurried to the battlefield but arrived too late. The Gardner team had ensured that, by the time Brady got there, all the best bodies had been buried.

Brady, Gardner and their teams were concerned not just with portraying the aftermath of battle, but with recording the process by which a society geared itself up for total war. They took pictures of American munitions factories working at full blast, of railroads moving ammunition and cannon, and of vast military encampments, where thousands of men drilled in serried ranks. They also catalogued a new type of war, though at the time they didn't realise what they were doing. Fenton and his successors had photographed the siege lines around Sebastopol, and American cameramen took pictures of trenches at Petersburg. In so doing they captured on film one of the consequences of industrial war. The trench systems in Northern Virginia in 1864 and 1865 were not concentrated around a single defended locality, but snaked for 10 and then 20, and then finally for nearly 30 miles, before the Confederacy ran out of soldiers to put in them.

Photographers also detailed the pulverising of the South. Seventy-eight years before Spaatz's and Eaker's B-17 bombers cut a swathe of destruction across Hitler's Third Reich, Sherman's cavalry columns had wreaked havoc throughout Jefferson Davis's Confederacy. Like the B-17 crews, who had to photograph the results of each mission, Sherman's cavalry was accompanied by photographers. One of the best known, the 23-year-old George N. Barnard, catalogued the results of Sherman's 'March to the Sea', the burning of Atlanta, the systematic destruction of the railway and telegraph system, and the razing of Columbia, Charleston, Richmond and many other Southern cities and towns.

Competing ruthlessly against each other, photographers strove to overcome the limitations of technology to produce the still-elusive action shot. On 8 September 1863, George S. Cook set up his camera on the ruins of Fort Sumter to photograph US monitors bombarding Fort Moultrie. Cook, in the direct line of fire, caught the warships at the moment of opening fire. One of the balls narrowly missed him, while another knocked one of his plate holders off the parapet into a rainwater cistern. During the Battle of Seven Pines, another of Brady's assistants managed to persuade Union gunners to stand still while they were actually repelling attacks by 'Stonewall' Jackson's soldiers, long enough for him to get an exposure. In 1899 Captain A. J. Russell recalled watching photographer T. C. Roche take pictures during artillery duels in the trenches before Petersburg in the autumn of 1864:

> He had taken a number of views and had but one more to make to
> finish up the most interesting views, and this one was to be from
> the most exposed position. He was within a few rods of the place
> when down came with the whirlwind a ten-inch shell, which
> exploded, throwing the dirt in all directions; but nothing daunted

and shaking the dirt from his head and camera, he quickly moved to the spot, and placing it over a pit made by the explosion, exposed his plate so coolly as if there were no danger, as if working in a country barnyard. The work finished, he quickly folded his tripod and returned to cover. I asked him if he was scared. 'Scared?' he said. 'Two shots never fell in the same place.'

By early 1865 Gardner was trying to overcome the limitations imposed by the long exposure time needed, by setting up several cameras in the same location to photograph the same predictable events – parades, funerals, executions and so on – at intervals of a few seconds. When arranged in chronological sequence, the photographs would tell a story visually. Like all great innovators he had foreseen possibilities – in this case the cinema – about 30 years before various technical developments would make it possible.

The Civil War photographers produced images on a scale which had been unimaginable only ten years earlier. In 1851 visitors to London's Great Exhibition had been astonished by a display of more than 1,500 photographs, more visual images than ever before had been displayed at one time and in one place. These images had been the product of scores of photographers hard at work over the preceding decade. We have no idea of how many photographic images were produced in North America between 1861 and 1865, though some estimates put it as high as a quarter of a million. When Gardner left Brady, for example, he took with him some of his best negatives, and in September 1863 started his own mail order business, 'Photographic Incidents of the War', which offered a customer a selection of nearly 600 images. Today, libraries and museums have catalogued more than 18,000, of which 7,000 have been attributed to the Brady organisation.

It is not just the sheer size of the Civil War photographic legacy, but the quality of many of the photographs, which continues to surprise and delight historians. Under the pressure of a war for national survival, and locked in a no-less-deadly struggle with their competitors, many of the photographers were able to produce images which were not to be equalled until the 1890s, when technological advances made photography increasingly foolproof.

Photographing Limited War – The European Experience, 1859–78
Between 1859 and 1878 Europe witnessed eight major conflicts. Two of these, the Franco–Austrian War (June – Oct 1859) and Garibaldi's invasion of Sicily and the Kingdom of Naples (1860 – 62), were part of the process by which Italy was to be unified. There were another three conflicts which involved the fragmentation of states and empires: Poland rose in bloody insurrection against Russia between 1863 and 1864; between 1874 and 1875 Spain lapsed back into civil war for the third time in the nineteenth century; and disturbances within the Christian Balkan provinces of the Turkish empire led to conflict with Russia (1877–78), and almost to a general European war. There were three further conflicts, a war between a German–Austrian coalition and Denmark over the border provinces of Schleswig-Holstein (1864), a war between Prussia and Austria to decide who was going to be

the leader of the Germanic world (1866) and a war between France and Prussia (1870–71) to determine which nation would be dominant in Europe. The last three conflicts were the classic 'Kabinet Kriegs' by which Prussian Chancellor Count Otto von Bismarck sought to effect the unification of Germany. Described as 'Froehliche Kleine Kriege' ('Jolly Little Wars'), there was nevertheless a danger that they could have developed into something very much larger.

The first of these conflicts was over almost before the rest of Europe realised what was happening. On 23 April 1859, in conditions of the greatest secrecy, a French army under the personal command of Napoleon III moved into northern Italy to support the proto-Italian state of Sardinia-Savoy against the Austrian empire. In a whirlwind campaign the French achieved crushing victories at Magenta on 4 June and at Solferino 20 days later, after which Austria sued for peace. Eight weeks was simply not enough time to mobilise correspondents and photographers, even if the French and Austrians had been disposed to offer them freedom of movement, which they were not.

Italian Pin-ups

Unlike the army of the Second Empire, Garibaldi's insurgents needed publicity, and courted newspapers and photographers. But this was only possible when they were in exile, not trekking in Sicilian mountains, so that most photographs of this period depict handsome, dashingly bearded Italian guerrillas in heroic poses. Photographs of Garibaldi and the insurgent poet Mazzini decorated the bedroom walls of thousands of middle-class young women in London, Paris and Berlin, in much the same manner that posters of Che Guevara would hang on the walls of their granddaughters' bedrooms 100 years later. The Polish insurgents who rose up against the Russian empire in January 1863 also wanted publicity, but western correspondents were forbidden entry into Russian territory, and Britain and France had to make do with reports produced by Polish exile groups. Nor could the Poles hope for sympathy from within the Russian intelligentsia; Leo Tolstoy, for example, who had served in the siege of Sebastopol, advocated crushing the Poles with extreme ferocity, advice which the Russian army followed with enthusiasm. The last embers of the revolt had been extinguished by the early summer of 1864.

On 1 February 1864, while Anglo-French attention was focused on America and on the Polish revolt against Russia, a largely Prussian Army, with some Austrian assistance, crossed the Danish border and struck into the disputed provinces of Schleswig-Holstein. The Prussians expected a quick victory, but on 15 March the advance was held up at the Danish fortress of Dybbol, on the Baltic coast of Schleswig, which the Prussians were forced to besiege. With sea lanes open, the Danes were able to communicate their stand to the rest of the world, which immediately began to side with the gallant 'David' resisting the overwhelming power of Prussia's 'Goliath'. By April 40,000 Prussians were concentrated against the fort, subjecting it to an average of 500 artillery rounds per day. The garrison, only 5,000 strong, was steadily whittled down. By the time the Prussians made their final successful assault on 17 April, more than 1,800 of the defenders had been killed or wounded. Dybbol became a national symbol to the Danes, and even today a tour of the ruins is an essential part of the education of Danish school-children. Because the army had been static for more than a month, photographers had ample opportunities to photograph the operations, and to capture the picture that every officer's mess in Prussia wanted, that of their men standing on the main redoubt, beneath the Prussian flag flying triumphantly in the breeze.

At dawn on 16 June 1866 Prussian columns struck into the Austrian province of Bohemia, and 17 days later inflicted a crushing defeat on the Austrian Army at Koeniggratz on the Elbe. William Howard Russell had arrived in Vienna just before the outbreak of hostilities, and covered the war from the Austrian side, reporting on Koeniggratz from the top of a church steeple. This was the biggest battle fought in Europe since Leipzig in 1813, with about a quarter of a million Prussians and some 215,000 Austrians and Saxons converging on an area of about 20 square miles. For once Russell felt overwhelmed by the task. He wrote: 'Nothing but a delicate and yet bold panorama on a gigantic scale could convey any idea of the scene, filled with over half a million of men, moving over its surface like the waves of the sea or as a vast driving cloud in a gale.' There were photographic teams chasing both the Prussian and Austrian armies, but added to the problems of lengthy exposure and smoke was the as yet insurmountable photographic obstacle of a battle fought in driving rain.

'Such horrible shapes'

In Bismarck's next war, the conflict with France he cleverly
provoked in the summer of 1870, William Howard Russell was an
honoured guest of the Prussian political and military hierarchy.
Bismarck, who, like Lincoln, recognised the power of *The Times*,
gave Russell detailed briefings in his excellent if accented
English. After some initial confusion Russell went on campaign,
embedded in the Crown Prince's headquarters. At the end of
August the Prussian armies, numbering more than 200,000, had
trapped the 121,000-strong main French army, commanded by
Napoleon III in person, at Sedan. High on the ridges overlooking
the city, the Prussians placed nearly 500 of their new Krupps-
manufactured breech-loading iron guns, which had a greater
range and a higher rate of fire than French artillery.

On the morning of 1 September the Prussian guns opened up
a bombardment which was the heaviest and most intense so far
experienced in the history of war. The French attempted to break
out, first to the north and then to the south, but their formations
were shredded by Prussian artillery fire. Standing on one of the
ridges overlooking the city, Russell had a ring-side seat. He wrote
that he 'could almost look into Sedan. I could see soldiers on the
ramparts, citizens in the street … It is not a pleasant thing to be a
mere spectator of such scenes. There is something cold-blooded
in standing with a glass to your eye, seeing men blown to pieces,
or dragging their shattered bodies to places of safety, or writhing
on the ground too far from help, even if you could render it'.
With his army in a hopeless position, that evening Napoleon III
capitulated.

Two days later Russell walked over the battlefield. The casualties, 17,000 French and 9,000 Prussians, were not as heavy as the casualties at Antietam or Gettysburg, but Russell realised that they had died in new ways. He reminded his readers that he had had 'many years experience of the work of war', but that he had 'never seen the like before'. There were mounds of Prussian corpses, their bodies riddled with bullets, who had been mown down by the French Mitrailleuse, a terrifying hand-cranked machine-gun. But the real horror had been produced by the sheer intensity of Prussian artillery fire. He 'had never beheld death in such horrible shapes – because the dead had on their faces the expression of terror – mental and bodily agony such as I never should have thought it possible for mortal clay to retain after the spirit had fled through the hideous portals fashioned by the iron hand of artillery. There were human hands detached from the arms and hanging up in the trees; feet and legs lying far apart from the bodies to which they belonged'. Russell's despatch was a warning of the reality of industrial war, where a gallant 'thin red streak tipped with steel' would be obliterated within seconds.

The Sedan Photograph

There was at least one photographer at Sedan, and a single photograph survives, which purports to show Prussian infantry attacking up a slope, supported by lines of infantry moving up in reserve. Unfortunately, the photograph has been heavily retouched. The Prussians in the foreground are standing far too nonchalantly for men who would have seen the effects of the Mitrailleuse. In addition, the men in the far distance would have had to be about 20 feet tall in order to be picked up at that range by any camera of the period, and were clearly a later addition, as were the puffs of white smoke which drift across the picture, apparently independent of any artillery. Had the cameraman been of the quality of Gardner or O'Sullivan, we might well have had a visual record of what Russell had seen, and it is less likely that his warning about the way in which war was changing would have been so soon forgotten.

Bismarck thought the war would end with the capitulation of Napoleon III, but the people of France thought otherwise. In Paris on 4 September a meeting of the National Assembly abolished the monarchy, inaugurated a new Republic (the third) and began forming massive citizen armies. By 19 September Prussian forces had encircled Paris, but the Prussian chief of staff, Helmut von Moltke, had no intention of playing to French strengths, and he therefore decided on a siege to starve the French into surrender. By this time camera teams from Berlin had caught up with their armies, but the surviving pictures, though few and far between, show pictures of French prisoners, gun batteries, the logistic system, and personalities, like von Moltke, the Crown Prince and Bismarck. Absent from the cannon were photographs of Prussia's major military concern at the time, the guerrilla war which *francs tireurs* were waging along their lines of communication, and which the Prussians were suppressing with ruthless severity. Beato had already taken a photograph of executed Indians in 1858, and Gardner had photographed the hanging of four people implicated in the conspiracy to assassinate Lincoln in 1865. There were numerous sketches of executions in the illustrated British newspapers, but German cameramen fought shy of recording these scenes.

With the beginning of the siege of Paris, the photographic record of the Franco–Prussian War, so sketchy for the first few weeks, suddenly becomes much fuller. Paris was the centre of European photography, second only to London in its number of photo studios. Photographers took pictures of the new armies forming, particularly the *gardes nationales*, the 300,000-strong radical militia formed from amongst the working-class districts of Paris. They also took pictures of fortifications, of gun batteries, of barricades being built in the streets, and of the hot-air balloons which were the only form of communication with the outside world. And when the German shells began crashing into the city on 5 January they recorded the destruction. Four days later from his quarters at Versailles, where he was staying with the Crown Prince's staff, Russell recorded in his diary 'Paris burning in three distinct quarters ... It was a calm, frosty night – moon shining, stars bright – lights in the windows of Versailles – noise of laughter and tinkling glasses. What a contrast to the tortured city beyond!'

'The Reign of Terror' – the Paris Commune, 18 March–28 May 1871
Paris capitulated on 28 January 1871, and on 1 March 30,000 troops of the new German Empire, the Second Reich, marched in a triumphal procession along the Champs-Elysées. A German photographer, positioned in the Luxembourg Palace, caught the imposing scene as horse artillery and infantry lined up in the Luxembourg Gardens, before beginning the parade. Russell

didn't enjoy the day. He had been seen in the company of Prussian officers, and when he left them to make his way to the Gare du Nord to catch a train for Calais to send his story to London he was accosted by bands of angry Parisians. Though very much *persona non grata* in the French capital, Russell returned to Paris to watch the Prussians withdraw.

Just two weeks later, on 18 March, the radical *gardes nationales* declared that they no longer recognised the authority of the Third Republic, and established a new form of government, a union of the various Paris communes, a Communard republic. There now followed a Communard reign of terror, in which enemies of the people, government officials, priests, police officers and so on, were tried before revolutionary tribunals and executed by firing squads. Because these events were dramatic and predictable, Parisian photographers took scores of pictures of firing squads and their victims, building on the pioneering work of Beato and Gardner. When the regular army of the Third Republic, re-armed and released from German internment, fought its way back into Paris between 21 and 28 May, the Communards burnt down the Hotel de Ville and other prominent buildings, all of which was captured on photographic plates. The French army then exacted vengeance on the Communards, using photographs of the firing squads to identify the guilty. All told, an estimated 30,000 Communards were put to death, many of whom were, in their turn, photographed before, during and after execution.

The Bulgarian Atrocities – the limitations of the camera

In September 1875 simmering resentment against Turkish rule in the Balkans boiled over into open revolt in parts of Bulgaria. Suppressed by the Turks during the winter, the revolt flared again in April 1876, and this time the Turks unleashed gangs of Bashi Bazouks, Kurdish and Chechnyan irregulars notorious for their cruelty. Rumours of massacres circulating in Constantinople led the *London Daily News* to commission a freelance American correspondent, Januarius Aloysius MacGahan, to go into Bulgaria to investigate. MacGahan's despatches, published in the *Daily News*, showed that a written story was still more effective than a photograph in conveying emotion. Rather than describing the scene, MacGahan imaginatively reconstructed the events which had led up to the scene. The result was reportage of unusual force:

> We were told that there were three thousand people lying in this little churchyard alone … It was a fearful sight – a sight to haunt one through life. There were little curly heads there in that festering mass, crushed down by heavy stones; little feet not as long as your finger on which the flesh was dried hard … little baby hands stretched out as if for help; babes that had died wondering at the bright gleam of sabres and the red hands of the fierce-eyed men who wielded them; children who died shrinking with fright and terror … mothers who died trying to shield their little ones with their own weak bodies, all lying there together festering in one horrid mass.

The Russian empire, the defender of Slavic peoples, was soon at war with Turkey. Knowing that the weight of European opinion was on her side, Russia opened the gates to foreign correspondents, and more than 80 accompanied the Tsar's Army on the campaign. The Turks were more circumspect, though a number of freelance journalists took their chances to report the war from the Turkish side, including Lt Horatio Kitchener of the Royal Engineers, who took leave from the British garrison in Cyprus to cover operations for *Blackwood's Magazine*. After some initial successes the Russian advance stalled before Turkish fortifications at Plevna, where they were held from July to December 1877.

In some respects conditions were now perfect for photographers, who could do their best work in relatively static situations like sieges, but if pictures were taken none have survived.

What is clear is that photography was common only in advanced industrial societies, and it was only when these societies were at war that photographs would appear in abundance. Hence the extraordinary variety produced by the American Civil War, and the sudden explosion of photographs in late 1870, when the Prussians reached Paris. When technically backward armies engaged each other a long way from the centres of the new industrial civilisation, the photographer was not to be seen. The irony is that although war in Europe was poorly filmed during this period, the armies of the British empire and the United States were carrying the camera to the remotest regions of the world.

Until 1865 the Great Plains region of the United States, an area of roughly one million square miles extending from the Missouri to the Rocky Mountains, was largely the preserve of America's Native American nations. It was true that since the 1840s whites had crossed in wagon trains but they had been in transit, travelling to Oregon, California, or the Mormon settlements in Utah. In the mid-1860s the railways and the telegraph came, and with them a growing white settlement. Driven from traditional territories, the Native Americans offered increased resistance. The result was a quarter-century of war between 1865 and 1890, a war which finally witnessed their destruction. But they put up a real fight: it took the US Army 12 campaigns and 943 actions before it won the West.

The conflict was characterised by rapid movement over a thinly populated area the size of European Russia, but within this vast area there were particular points of conflict. One of the earliest was Fort Kearny in Nebraska, which in the summer of 1866 was the railhead for the Union Pacific Line. Ridgway Glover, a photographer and artist contracted by *Leslie's Illustrated Newspaper* to depict the culture of the Native Americans, had more than he bargained for when his train was attacked by Sioux. Glover reported that he 'desired to make some instantaneous views of the Indian attack but our commander ordered me not to'. After establishing himself at the fort, Glover and a companion, refusing to heed warnings about the dangers, travelled with cameras into the Bighorn Mountains. When they failed to return, a search party was sent out, which eventually found their scalped and mutilated bodies. Their deaths would probably have happened in any event, but the presence of the camera would not have helped. The plains Indians were terrified of the apparatus, believing that it captured the spirits of men.

One of the first photographs of Native American depredations was taken a year later near Fort Wallace in Kansas, about 180 miles to the south-west of Fort Kearny. On 26 June 1867, a 45-man patrol of the 7th Cavalry clashed with a much larger force of Indians, and in a running battle managed to lose seven men. The following day, William Bell, a photographer employed in photographic survey work for the Kansas Pacific Railroad, took pictures of the corpses. One soldier, Sergeant Frederick Wyllyams, was found stripped naked, with five arrows protruding from him. A newspaper report detailed his injuries: 'He was scalped twice, and his brains knocked out, his throat cut from ear to ear, his heart cut out and carried away to be eaten, and his arms and legs slashed and gashed to the bone.'

A corrective to the Native American as irredeemable savage emerged from the reportage of the war with the Modoc, which was fought along the California–Oregon border between 1872 and 1873. The New York Herald sent Edward Fox, the paper's English-born yachting correspondent, to cover the war. At considerable risk Fox tracked down the Modoc, interviewed them and ensured that the Herald carried stories of mistreatment and broken promises. The Modoc were also fortunate in having the great innovative photographer, Eadweard Muybridge, record their war. Like Fox, Muybridge covered operations from both sides, capturing crouching Native Americans and cavalry in similar poses.

The most photographed US military operation of the period was Colonel George Armstrong Custer's expedition to the Black Hills of North Dakota in the summer of 1874. Custer's force was huge. It comprised ten companies of the 7th Cavalry, and 60 Indian scouts, with additional firepower being provided by three Gatling guns and a 3-inch cannon. Along with the military came scientists – geologists, palaeontologists, zoologists; practical men – surveyors, engineers, miners; newspaper men – at least a dozen correspondents from the major Eastern papers; and a photographer, W. H. Illingworth of St Paul, Minnesota. Custer's expedition had an important political purpose: it was designed to keep Custer in the limelight with a view to a political career after the army, and it was also designed to bolster the reputation of the incumbent president, General Ulysses S. Grant, whose son, Colonel Fred Grant, accompanied the expedition as a member of Custer's staff. Illingworth took hundreds of photographs – Custer in buckskins, Custer posing by a grizzly bear he had just shot, Custer parleying with the handful of overawed Indians they encountered.

The expedition discovered traces of gold in the Black Hills, news which hit the headlines of mid-Western journals late in August. A gold rush was soon under way, with whites flooding into an area which, under the terms of a treaty signed in 1868, was a preserve of the Sioux nation. After ineffectual attempts to prevent the influx, the US Army attempted to remove the Sioux to yet another reservation, which led to the largest Native American uprising of the nineteenth century. In the early months of 1876 a number of columns under the command of General Terry slowly converged on the Sioux, now joined by the Cheyenne. After crossing the trail left by the Native Americans, Terry ordered Custer and the 7th Cavalry to ride south as fast as they could to block what he thought was the Native Americans' retreat. On 25 June on the banks of the Little Big Horn River in southern Montana, Custer discovered a long, straggling Indian village. Dividing his command into three columns, each about 200 strong, Custer rode for the centre of the village, thinking that it must hold at most a few hundred warriors. In fact some 6,000 Indian braves had camped by the river, of whom about 4,000 rode out to meet him. It was all over in less than 30 minutes. Custer had a newsman with him, who died along with the others. Illingworth should have been with them, but in the summer of 1876 he was otherwise engaged. The following summer another photographer, S. J. Murrow, visited the Little Big Horn, and photographed the piles of bones which was all that was left of Custer's command.

Although the Plains Indians generally had a peculiar horror of the camera, in the American south-west the Apaches took to photographic technology with relish. After terrorising large parts of Arizona and New Mexico in the early 1880s, Geronimo, the most famous of the Apache leaders, was pleased to have his photograph taken several times during peace negotiations on 25 March 1886. Arizona's most famous photographer, C. S. Fly, took shots of Geronimo posing with his still heavily armed and not very sober war band. After his surrender, Geronimo became the centre of his own tourist industry, selling postcards of himself in various threatening demeanours for 50 cents a time.

By the late 1880s, as the Native Americans of the American West moved from being a terrifying presence to a tourist attraction, there was one last spasm of resistance. Amongst the scattered remnants on reservations there emerged a spiritual movement – a belief that if certain rituals were followed, all the warriors killed in battle with the whites would come back to life, along with the buffalo herds slaughtered to the point of extinction. Known as the 'Ghost Dance' movement, it was regarded as a significant threat by the US Army, who took steps to suppress it. Sitting Bull, the Sioux medicine man who had stirred up resistance in the mid-1870s, was killed in a skirmish on the Grand River in South Dakota on 15 December 1890. Five days later the Sioux fought their last battle, when 153 of their largest surviving war band was wiped out by the 7th Cavalry at Wounded Knee. The last gasp of Native American resistance was covered by probably the greatest of all Western correspondents, the writer-artist Frederick Remington, who sketched the Ghost Dance. It was also extensively photographed, particularly by J. C. H. Grabill, of Deadwood, South Dakota, whose picture showed frozen Native American bodies piled into a wagon, watched by victorious cavalrymen silhouetted against the skyline.

'Empiring it around the world' – the British experience

During the last 40 years of the nineteenth century, much of Asia and Africa was convulsed by conflict, as European nations transformed informal control to formal empire. Britain was foremost among the imperial nations, and British forces fought in over 30 major conflicts, which ranged from hostage rescue missions in Abyssinia, in 1867, to full-scale invasions of a country like Egypt, in 1882. The Royal Engineers had established a photographic unit in the early 1860s, but many British officers, particularly medical officers who understood the chemical processes better than most, were enthusiastic photographers. In addition, particularly in India and southern Africa, there was a growing number of commercial photographers. Together they would catalogue the expansion of empire.

After photographing the suppression of the Indian Mutiny, Felice Beato was attached to a shipment of reinforcements going to China. His mission was essentially the same as it had been on the Ganges plain – to catalogue the effect of artillery fire on fortifications. By the time Beato reached China, the Second Opium War was already in its fourth year. This war had been instigated by British attempts to impose free trade on Peking, which effectively meant defending the right of British merchants in India to export opium to China. In August 1860 a force of 11,000 British and Indian troops and 7,000 French landed at the mouth of the Peiho River near Tientsin, the port for Peking. Progress of the advance was blocked by the Taku forts, described by the engineers as formidable 'redoubts, with a thick rampart heavily armed with guns and wall pieces'. The approach to the forts was over open mud flats, which the Chinese had turned into a killing ground, 'with two unfordable wet ditches, between which and the parapet sharp bamboo stakes were thickly planted, forming two belts, each about fifteen feet wide, round the fort'. It was not an easy undertaking, but on 21 August 1860, under covering fire from gun-boats, the British Royal Marines and the soldiers of the 44th and 67th regiments, along with 1,500 French, stormed the fort, taking only about 400 casualties.

It was a far cry from the unsuccessful attack on the Redan just five years earlier. The attacking forces were undoubtedly skilled and ferociously brave – the British assault force earned five vcs – but Beato's pictures show that naval gunfire had had a devastating effect on the defenders, with the fortifications littered with bodies. This pattern was going to be repeated again and again during the next 40 years. Unlike the situation in India, when the British fought against soldiers they had armed and trained, they now had decisive technological and organisational advantages.

While the British were forcing yet another unequal treaty on China, a conflict of a very different sort broke out in New Zealand. The dynamics of the conflict were the same as those of the American West at that time – a land-hungry settler population dispossessing the native inhabitants. But the resistance of the Maoris was to prove more effective than that of even the most warlike of the Native Americans. In the early 1860s the British Army and colonial militias had the worst of the fighting, which was conducted in the rugged, heavily forested country of New Zealand's north island, ideal terrain for guerrilla operations. By the mid-1860s massive British reinforcements had arrived, including artillery and substantial numbers of Australian volunteer riflemen. The Maoris coped with increased British firepower by adapting their traditional pa, or fortress, to the requirements of war with an industrial power. Like the Viet Cong 100 years later, they dug deep trenches, bunkers and tunnels which allowed them to hold out against sometimes overwhelming British strength. At Orakau in 1863, for example, 300 Maoris held off 2,000 British soldiers for three days, and then escaped by charging through them into dense bush. British photographers, often medical officers, took copious pictures of the Maori fortifications and, when they negotiated an armistice, of surrendered Maoris.

Potentially the most difficult, but also the most brilliantly handled British campaign of the second half of the nineteenth century, was General Sir Robert Napier's expedition to Abyssinia in 1867. The world-wide expansion of British interests meant opening up legations in areas where European notions of diplomatic behaviour were not recognised. In 1864 Emperor Theodore of Ethiopia seized the British delegation and, despite protests and attempts at negotiation, refused to release them. Napier's expedition was a hostage rescue operation, and Napier, an engineer, was well placed to utilise all the advantages superior technology had conferred on Britain. The expedition's chief cameraman, Sergeant Harrold of the Royal Engineers, recorded the creation of an immense supply base on the coast, and the construction of a railway inland, which considerably reduced logistic difficulties. When the going became too rugged, Napier abandoned the technology of the nineteenth century, and used Indian elephants to haul artillery and ammunition, which had a considerable effect on the Ethiopians. With the British inexorably approaching Magdala, his capital, Theodore launched his warriors at them, saw them mown down by the aimed fire of Enfield rifles, and committed suicide. The expedition was astonishingly successful – even the hostages were released unharmed – and Sergeant Harrold managed to record much of it in temperatures and atmospheric conditions which would have defeated Fenton just 12 years earlier.

When the British treated their enemies with respect and utilised their technological and organisational advantages to full effect, the result was usually success. But apparently effortless superiority could breed complacency, and in January 1879 a British task force paid the price at Isandhlwanda, on the Natal–Zululand border. The conflict had been the result of yet another aspect of imperial expansion, the need to provide security for Natal, a colony of European settlement, from a militarily powerful Zulu kingdom. Like Custer two and a half years earlier, the British commander separated his invasion force into three columns, and then divided his central column in two, leaving a 1,600-man force camped at the base of a high kopje named Isandhlwanda, while he took the bulk of the force off in search of the Zulus. At about 11.00 hours on 22 January, the Zulu main army attacked and overwhelmed the camp, killing virtually all the British. The disaster was redeemed only by the extraordinary defence of the mission station at Rorke's Drift about 12 miles away, where 85 able-bodied British soldiers drove off six attacks by up to 4,000 Zulus which lasted throughout the night.

It was May before the British returned to the battlefield, accompanied by a photographer, Frederick Lloyd of Durban. He took pictures which showed why the British had lost, ammunition wagons still on their wheels with ammunition boxes still stacked up inside the wagons. If the British had been able to organise a proper defence, the wagons would have been tipped over on their sides to provide firing platforms, and the ammunition distributed amongst the men. Conversely, the pictures of Rorke's Drift show why the British held out – a completely walled location with clear fields of fire in all directions and, from the open boxes littering the ground, an almost unlimited supply of ammunition.

By the summer of 1879 British reinforcements and technology – artillery and Gatling guns – had redressed the balance. William Howard Russell arrived in Durban at the same time for what was his last campaign. He missed all the fighting but he heard of the aftermath, the massed slaughter of wounded Zulus, and was sickened by it.

The ultimate cause of so much of Britain's imperial expansion in the second half of the nineteenth century was the need to protect India. During this period Britain was almost constantly at war on India's north-west frontier, either suppressing tribal uprisings, or ensuring that Russia did not get too much influence in Afghanistan. These conflicts were a source of interest to the large English-speaking community in northern India, both British and Indian. There was a substantial English-language press, and some correspondents, for example the young Rudyard Kipling who joined the *Lahore Examiner* in 1882, were going to become internationally famous. There was, too, an increasingly large number of locally based photographers, many of whom, from time to time, worked for the army on temporary contracts. One of the best was John Burke, who recorded the successful British invasion of Afghanistan in 1879. After his arrival in Kabul in May, Burke photographed the negotiations between Afghan leader Amir Yakub Khan and the new British resident Sir Louis Cavagnari, who was to remain in Kabul after the British army withdrew and exercise control over Afghanistan's foreign policy. Burke's camera was the first Yakub Khan had seen and he took a close interest in the process. A little later, at a farewell dinner for Cavagnari which Burke also recorded, the British commander, Major General Frederick Roberts, felt unable to propose a toast wishing Cavagnari well. Roberts wrote, 'I was so thoroughly depressed, and my mind was filled with such gloomy forebodings as to the fate of these fine fellows, that I could not utter a word.'

Roberts was right. News that the mission had been murdered reached Simla on 5 September. Sweeping aside Afghan resistance, Roberts returned to Kabul at the head of 10,000 avenging British soldiers, and smashed an attempt by 100,000 Afghans to overrun him on 23 December. In the following summer, after the remnants of a detached column which had been all but wiped out at Maiwand managed to fight its way back to the temporary safety of Khandahar, Roberts marched to their rescue. The march from Kabul to Khandahar, 313 miles in blazing summer temperatures in just 22 days, became an epic of the Victorian Army. On 1 September 1880 Roberts once again defeated the Afghans, and then imposed upon them a ruler favoured by the British. Burke had accompanied the army, recording the campaign in images of startling detail. Reinforcing newspaper reports, Burke's photographs, reproduced as woodcuts in illustrated British journals, helped turn Roberts into a military superstar. In one of the photographs, widely reproduced as a postcard, a calm and unruffled Roberts, exuding an air of unquestioned authority, sits alone amongst a large group of ferocious-looking Afghan tribal leaders. Roberts understood the power of the technology better than many contemporaries and, throughout his later campaigns, pursued what would today be called a media policy.

Two years later the British obsession with the security of India led to another military operation. This time it was in Egypt, where nationalist uprisings threatened the smooth operation of the newly built Suez Canal, now widely seen as the jugular of the empire. In mid-July 1882 photographers of the Royal Engineers recorded the destruction wrought by the British naval bombardment of the formidable forts guarding Alexandria harbour, which extended for a distance of four miles and mounted over 180 guns. The 25,000 troops who now landed constituted the largest British expeditionary force between the Crimean War and the outbreak of war in South Africa in 1899, and were commanded by General Sir Garnet Wolseley, who was rivalled in fame only by Roberts. After a daring night march across the desert, Wolseley surprised and defeated a larger Egyptian Army of nationalist leader Ahmet Arabi at Tell el Kebir. Photographers took pictures along the trenches, showing some of the 2,000 Egyptian dead. With Egypt now under British control, tourists began to arrive and, along with pictures of the Pyramids and Sphinx, took shots of the Tel el Kebir battlefield, little changed from September 1882, except that the dead were now skeletons.

An unforeseen consequence of the British victory was a widespread Islamic fundamentalist uprising in the Egyptian-ruled Sudan. Forces inspired by the Sudan's spiritual leader, Mohammed Ahmed, known as the Mahdi, wiped out Egyptian armies at El Obeid and El Teb, disasters which led the British government to decide to cut its losses and order the complete evacuation of the Sudan. However, the officer ordered to organise the evacuation, the fundamentalist Christian General Charles Gordon, had other ideas. Ignoring instructions from London, Gordon allowed himself to be trapped in Khartoum, the Sudan's capital, where he and his garrison held out until 26 January 1885, when the Mahdi's forces finally broke in and massacred them all. A relief expedition under Garnet Wolseley, which reached Khartoum the following day, put about and steamed down the Nile for Egypt.

Few photographs survived of the dramatic events of 1884–85, partly because Royal Engineer camera teams perished at El Obeid and El Teb. But when the British returned to the Sudan in 1896, the situation was very different. Many officers now carried Kodak box cameras, which had been developed in the United States in the late 1880s. One particularly enthusiastic photographer, Lieutenant the Honourable E. D. Loch of the Grenadier Guards, kept his camera shutter going throughout the climactic battle of Omdurman, taking pictures of many incidents, including General Kitchener directing operations, and the Grenadier Guards waiting with fixed bayonets behind a thorn bush zariba, as the Mahedi's men rushed towards them. The slaughter was fearful – Lieutenant Winston Churchill of the 21st Lancers was appalled by the sight of bodies spread out as far as the eye could see – and Lieutenant Loch and other officers were ordered to carry out a count. Loch seized the opportunity to take pictures, but the Kodak camera proved unequal to the task. Using a tight focus Loch was only able to portray what looked like the result of a skirmish, not the result of 10,000 bolt-action magazine-fed rifles, Maxim machine guns and field guns firing shrapnel shells into a mass of men at point-blank range. Loch was an enthusiastic amateur; a professional photographer like Beato in the 1850s, Gardner in the 1860s or Burke in the 1870s and 80s would not have made this mistake. But the apparatus they used, of course, would not have allowed them even to have attempted the types of shots Loch was getting with a small hand-held camera. What was required to get the still-elusive action shot was for the professional photographer to begin using the small camera, even though this would mean sacrificing some quality. It was commercial pressure in the United States in the 1890s which was to bring this about.

The birth of the photo-journalist
1898–1914

William Randolph Hearst and 'yellow journalism'
Although illustrated newspapers had first been produced in the
early 1840s, they relied on either the sketches of artists, or on
woodcut reproductions of photographs. The development of the
half-tone process in the late 1880s allowed photographs to be
printed directly on to a news-sheet. Various American newspapers
experimented with this technique during the 1890s, a process
which culminated in 1897 with the *New York Tribune* illustrating
stories with photographs on a daily basis. As the *Tribune*'s
circulation soared, more and more papers joined in, including
Joseph Pulitzer's *World* and William Randolph Hearst's *Journal*,
a scandal-mongering sensation sheet that sold for a cent. Hearst's
unscrupulous tactics forced other papers to follow suit, giving

rise to 'yellow journalism', named after a popular comic strip character of the 1890s, the Yellow Kid.

'You furnish the pictures and I'll furnish the war'.
The competition created a demand for news and pictures of the news. New man-portable light-weight cameras were in general use in American newspaper offices by the mid-1890s, with journalists who were not only adept at taking pictures but typing a story to accompany the pictures. Pulitzer, Hearst and other newspaper barons knew that war sold papers, and by the mid-1890s were taking a close interest in a conflict then being waged in Cuba between nationalist guerrillas and the Spanish administration. Hearst sent Frederic Remington to Cuba to provide pictorial evidence of Spanish atrocities for the *Journal*. When Remington reported that Cuba was calm, Hearst is supposed to have cabled back 'You furnish the pictures and I'll furnish the war.' The Cuban guerrilla leader, Maximo Gomez, was also taking a close interest in American newsmen, because he realised that the fastest way to get rid of the Spanish was to encourage American intervention. Respected American correspondents like Richard Harding Davis described the Spanish execution of Cuban patriots, descriptions which were soon verified by the publication of photographs. In December 1896, for example, *Leslie's Illustrated Weekly* carried a picture showing the bodies of six Cubans lying on their backs, 'with their arms and legs bound and their bodies showing mutilation by machetes, and their faces pounded and hacked out of resemblance to anything human'.

On 15 February 1898 an explosion ripped through the American battleship *Maine*, while she lay at anchor in Havana Harbour, killing 260 of the crew, and injuring many more. American journalists descended on Havana, to photograph what was immediately assumed to be a Spanish-inspired outrage. James H. Hare, better known as Jimmy Hare, an English-born photographer working for *Collier's Weekly*, got pictures not just of the wreckage, but of the *Maine*'s chaplain comforting the wounded and identifying the dead. Hare's pictures, and those of many others, crammed the columns of American newspapers in the spring of 1898, accompanied by blazing headlines demanding that Spain be punished for the unprovoked attack. On 25 April Congress took heed and declared war.

In all some 500 correspondents were to cover American operations in Cuba, many of whom had cameras and were photojournalists. Burr William McIntosh, a society photographer and Broadway actor, had been about to appear in Lottie Blair Parker's 'A War Correspondent' when *Leslie's Weekly* hired him to cover the war. On 22 June as the American task force was preparing to land 17,000 troops at Daiquiri near Santiago on the south coast of Cuba, McIntosh and the other correspondents were told that they would not be allowed to accompany the landing. A few like Richard Harding Davis and Frederic Remington had managed to cultivate good relations with the task force commander, the enormously obese (he weighed 330 pounds) 63-year-old General William R. Shafter, and were allowed on to one of the boats. Not to be outdone, McIntosh tried to pass himself off as a soldier and filed onto a boat, but was quickly discovered and sent back. In desperation, McIntosh gave his camera and negatives to a soldier he had befriended, slipped over the side of the ship, and swam for the shore, about half a mile distant. Beating most of the boats, he retrieved his camera, and managed to photograph the landing.

Two days later McIntosh reached Las Guasimas on the road to Santiago, where there had been a clash between the Spanish and American forces, including Theodore Roosevelt's Rough Riders, composed almost entirely of the sons of New York's social elite. Here McIntosh discovered the bodies of his friend, Hamilton Fish, and another Rough Rider, roughly covered by blankets. A deeply shaken McIntosh was taking a picture when he heard laughter nearby, and saw a group of correspondents and officers, including Theodore Roosevelt, sharing a joke. McIntosh later wrote, 'I took a photograph and then another to show the distance from the two bodies. The photographs were taken with a heart filled with resentful bitterness … I felt a resentment toward certain of those men, who were joking with that boy's body lying within a few feet of them – a resentment which I never expect to be able to overcome.' McIntosh could have damaged Roosevelt's career, but decided to send only the first photograph to New York for publication. It appeared with the caption 'Rough Riders as they fell in the bloody engagement of June 24th – Hamilton Fish to the left – They died for humanity's sake.' Newspapers also juxtaposed the picture of the swaddled corpses with studio photographs of the handsome Fish, a study of youthful idealism and confidence. Fish became the first hero of the war – indeed *the* hero of the war – a symbol of the price America had paid to liberate Cuba from bondage.

Roosevelt, too, was to become a hero. On 1 July 1898 the Americans attacked Spanish positions on Kettle Hill, a spur of the San Juan Ridge, which dominated the road to Santiago. Many units were involved in the assault, but only one became famous. Mistaking Kettle Hill for San Juan Hill, Richard Harding Davis sent pictures of the first stages of the Rough Riders' attack back to the *New York Herald*, accompanied by a stirring account. 'Roosevelt, mounted high on horseback, and charging the rifle pits at a gallop and quite alone, made you feel that you would like to cheer. He wore on his sombrero a blue polka-dot handkerchief … which, as he advanced, floated out straight behind his head … No one who saw Roosevelt take that ride expected he would finish it alive.' Davis's report and photographs made clear that only Roosevelt was on horseback, but American illustrators soon depicted the Rough Riders' attack up 'San Juan' Hill as a full-bodied cavalry charge. The fact that other American units were also involved in the attack was also edited out of the popular consciousness. Now a military hero, Roosevelt was chosen for the vice-presidential slot in William McKinley's successful bid for the presidency in November 1900, and succeeded to the presidency when McKinley was assassinated in September 1901.

Boer War, 1899–1902

The United States had been propelled into war with Spain as the result of a cleverly orchestrated press campaign, which asserted that it was America's duty to liberate the people of Cuba from Spanish oppression. An apparent terrorist incident, the destruction of the USS *Maine*, had provided the *casus belli*. The war was immensely popular throughout the United States, with virtually no significant opposition. When Britain went to war with the Boer republics of the Orange Free State and Transvaal in South Africa in October 1899, the ostensible cause was as idealistic as that of America's conflict with Spain. Despite repeated British protests, the Boers had denied political rights to British settlers in the Free State and the Transvaal, where they were known by the Afrikaans word 'Uitlanders' (outsiders). In fact, all classes of political opinion regarded London's concern for the Uitlander as little more than a fig-leaf to mask the real intention – for British mining and banking interests to secure control of the Witwatersrand in the Transvaal, the richest reef of gold in the world. When Britain ignored the Boer republics' demand to halt military build-up in South Africa, the result was a Boer declaration of war, and an invasion of British colonies in South Africa, Natal and the Cape. The war did have considerable support in Britain and throughout Canada and Australasia, but there was also significant opposition, particularly from radical working-class movements and the newspapers they supported, such as the *Manchester Guardian* and the *Sydney Bulletin*. The mismatch in power was so great – the largest and most powerful empire the world had ever seen going to war with two republics of God-fearing Dutch farmers fielding only 80,000 men – that public opinion in Europe and in the United States quickly swung behind the underdog.

The Boers had no real appreciation of what a powerful ally they had in world public opinion, and no conscious effort was made to exploit it. A very effective media campaign did emerge, but it was more by accident than by design. By contrast, the British were well aware that the weight of world sentiment was against them, and attempted to control the flow of information by the most rigorous military censorship they had yet imposed. During October and November correspondents from France, Germany and the United States reached Pretoria, Johannesburg and Bloemfontein from Lourenco Marques in the Portuguese colony of Mozambique. The Boer republics were anxious to portray themselves as proper nations, with civil servants, police forces and uniformed armies, and set up convenient photo opportunities so that this image could be broadcast to the world. The correspondents weren't interested. Their imagination was gripped by the image of the Boer farmer volunteering to defend his homeland, going to war in his homespun clothes with his horse and rifle, his body festooned with bandoleers of ammunition. Richard Harding Davis, though an Anglophile American, nevertheless felt compelled to cover the war from the viewpoint of Britain's enemies. The Boer riflemen reminded him irresistibly of the Minutemen who had assembled to defend their homes against the British in 1775, a sentiment which was widely shared, even in Britain and her colonies of settlement. The Irish–Australian journalist Arthur Lynch, who had travelled to Pretoria to cover the war for the Paris-based *Le Journal*, was so moved by the sight of the Boer riflemen preparing to do battle with the British empire, that he volunteered for service and was appointed colonel of an international company. The British hit back, publishing these pictures with captions which invited the reader to ponder the rough and uncivilised nature of the

Afrikaaner. Some even suggested that students of physiognomy should study the photographs closely, with the unspoken implication that they would find evidence of inbreeding, or of contamination with African blood.

For six months, from October 1899 until April 1900, the Boers astonished the world. Their columns cut into Natal and the Cape, driving the British back, and besieging them in Ladysmith, Kimberley and Mafeking. The Boers went to great pains to show they were a high-technology army, encouraging correspondents to photograph the modern French and German artillery with which they were bombarding the British. They also made sure that the arrival of each trainload of British prisoners at Pretoria in transit for the prison at Waterval was fully photographed, and took pictures of disconsolate groups of prisoners, including war correspondent Winston Churchill. And they also took pictures of British dead. The single most evocative picture of the war was taken by a Boer cameraman on 24 January 1900, of the trenches of Spion Kop in Natal, crammed with the bodies of British soldiers who had fallen victim to superior Boer marksmanship and artillery fire.

The initial British reaction to the flood of images emerging from the Boer republics was to denounce them as fakes, or to argue that they testified to the brutal and uncivilised nature of the Boers. But as the news became ever worse, the British public, and those of Canada and Australasia, swung increasingly behind the war, as the realisation sank in that the situation was truly serious. Some of the best photographs of this period were taken not by correspondents with the Boers, but by a professional from

Johannesburg, Horace H. Nicholls, who joined the British retreat to Ladysmith in Natal. Nicholls' pictures show the army trudging through pouring rain, abandoning equipment as it went, with sick and tired men sitting by the roadside. The viewer was invited to think of earlier retreats – of Moore to Corunna in the winter of 1808–09 or of Wellington from Burgos to Portugal in December 1812 – and to remember that these were the prelude to great victories.

Over Christmas – New Year 1899–1900 reinforcements poured in from Britain and India. Throughout the empire tens of thousands of men volunteered from the Imperial Yeomanry, units of mounted infantry like Roosevelt's Rough Riders, who would be able to match the mobility of Boer riflemen. In previous campaigns only the officers had their own cameras, but the arrival of thousands of middle-class volunteers, most of whom had purchased Kodaks before leaving for South Africa, meant that by the end of the war Britain was going to be awash with photographs. In addition to the reinforcements, British papers sent out more than 300 correspondents, among them internationally renowned authors like Rudyard Kipling, Arthur Conan Doyle and Edgar Rice Burroughs. British papers like *Black and White* and the *Daily News* now had as many photographs as their American counterparts, while many of the British dailies published special weekly supplements of photographs of the war.

British proprietors, realising that disaster sold newspapers just as well as success, gave full coverage to British defeats like Stromberg, Magersfontein, Colenso, Spion Kop and Vaal Kranz. These setbacks, however, were balanced with an almost obsessive coverage of the three sieges where forces continued to hold out against superior Boer forces. Papers published letters and despatches from Kimberly, Ladysmith and Mafeking on an almost daily basis, and printed photographs connected with the sieges, whether British or Boer, as soon as they arrived in England. Thus pictures of 'Long Tom', a heavy Boer gun which bombarded Mafeking, appeared in newspapers and then on postcards, achieving an almost iconic status. As relieving forces began to advance, editors cleverly suggested that they might arrive too late, thus building up enormous tension in a public who had achieved mass literacy only in the preceding twenty years, and who were still relatively unsophisticated in the face of media manipulation. The relief of Kimberley on 15 February, and of Ladysmith two weeks later, produced widespread demonstrations of patriotic enthusiasm. In Mafeking the commander, Colonel Baden Powell, sent out reassuring messages as to the ineffectiveness of Boer shelling, which the British public, already aware of the power of Boer artillery, chose to believe were stiff-upper-lip understatement. When news of the relief of Mafeking reached Britain on 19 May, the country was convulsed with an explosion of rejoicing which went on for five days, far eclipsing the demonstrations which greeted victories in 1918, 1945 and 1982.

As in all previous wars, photographers tried for action shots, and sometimes managed to get pictures of troops about to go into battle. Much of the combat, however, was conducted at ranges of a third of a mile and more. There were many pictures of guns firing, and of shells detonating in the far distance, and occasionally there were pictures of the results. On 28 February

1900, for example, British cameramen photographed the wreckage of the Transvaal General Piet Cronje's encampment at Paardeberg, which had been shelled into surrender over the previous eight days. The British wanted the world to know that they were winning. After the initial disasters, Britain had sent Field Marshal Lord Roberts to command its forces, with General Kitchener as his chief of staff. Roberts, whose reputation had been made in Afghanistan 20 years earlier, understood the power of the photograph. He delayed the victory parade following the capture of Bloemfontein in mid-March 1900 until an army of newsmen with dozens of cameras could record the event properly. He did the same when he captured Pretoria on 5 June. With the enemy capitals under his control Roberts decided the war was over and returned to Britain, leaving the mopping-up operations to Kitchener.

But the war was far from over. Defeated in conventional operations, the Boer armies now broke up into independent commandos, and began guerrilla operations against the British. In this new phase of the war, the supply of photographs from Boer sources quickly dried up, while the British tried to photograph a counter-insurgency campaign. In order to inhibit the Boer's mobility, the veldt was broken up by barbed wire fences, covered at intervals of several miles by blockhouses. Columns of mounted infantry then swept the veldt, driving the commandos into the wired and fortified zones. That, at least, was the theory. In practice it was more difficult, with the commandos being supplied by the civilian population and occasionally melting into it.

Kitchener's solution was to remove the civilian population from the veldt and concentrate them in camps in secure areas. Between late 1900 and late 1901 approximately 120,000 Boer women and children, along with approximately the same number of Africans, were forcibly removed from the countryside and relocated in camps. Unused to living in such close proximity, and with inadequate water supplies, epidemics swept through the camps killing 28,000 Afrikaaners and 13,000 Africans in a little over a year. The process involved the tightest military censorship Britain had yet enforced. Emily Hobhouse, a Quaker who had formed the South African Conciliation Committee, was forcibly prevented from landing at Durban on a fact-finding mission, while Kitchener's command issued photographs showing well-fed women and children. In fact, thanks to the Kodak there were many pictures of conditions in the camps, some of which were published in European newspapers, while others formed the basis of collections in which the dead were memorialised after the war. Photographs of concentration camps were a potent weapon, which could not be denied. A report of a parliamentary committee on the camps identified appalling neglect and incompetence, and led to their improvement, but not until more than 40,000 women and children had died.

Boxer Rebellion, June–August 1900

The war in South Africa was beset by moral ambiguity, with the British empire and the Boer republics using photographs to sway world opinion. No such ambiguity complicated the response of the great powers to the increasingly widespread attacks on their citizens by mobs throughout northern China. Intelligence reports suggested that the trouble was being orchestrated by a fanatical secret organisation, the Society of the Righteous Harmonious Fists, which was dedicated to driving foreigners, and foreign influence, from China. British and American reporters, incapable of taking Chinese nomenclature seriously, nicknamed the organisation the 'Boxers'. Western legations in Peking demanded that the government of the Dowager Empress Tzu Hsi suppress the movement, but she professed her powerlessness to do so. In fact, it was widely understood that Tzu Hsi was actually inciting and supporting the Boxers.

By the summer of 1900, with western warships gathering in Tientsin, small military detachments from several nations (the total strength was only 485) arrived in Peking to reinforce their legations. On 10 June a larger Anglo-American force of some 2,000 sailors and marines began the march on Peking, but were repelled by a Chinese army at Tang Ts'u, losing 300 men. The news of a Chinese victory reached Peking on 20 June and set off mob violence. Many foreigners were murdered, including the German ambassador, and Chinese Christians were hunted down and crucified. Some survivors made their way to the British legation, which the diplomatic staffs and their small military contingents had fortified. Others, mainly Chinese Christians, made their way to the P'ei Tang, the compound of the Catholic cathedral, where 40 French and Italian marines, and a handful of priests and nuns, had set up a defence. Both compounds expected to be overrun in a matter of hours, but rifle and machine-gun fire broke up attack after attack of the enthusiastic but undisciplined Boxers.

The world had seen the relief of many besieged garrisons in previous decades, but one had to go back to Lucknow, more than 40 years earlier, to find an emotional mix of equal potency. Like the defenders of Lucknow, the defenders of the Peking legation and the cathedral compound included women and children, and all in the West knew the fate which would befall them should the Boxers succeed. With an expeditionary force forming before Tientsin, the newsmen began arriving. The Americans, who had been covering the suppression of the insurgency in the Philippines, and the Japanese, were quickly on the scene, to be followed by the Europeans and finally some of the British, who had quit South Africa for this much more dramatic story.

Although the Americans eventually numbered only 2,500 out of a force of more than 18,000, they played a leading role in operations. The US 9th Infantry Regiment spearheaded an assault on Tientsin on 23 July, taking heavy casualties. On 14 August, with the relief force outside the walls of Peking, the Americans once more played a major role, the US 14th Infantry successfully assaulting the north-eastern corner of the wall, and driving off the defenders. Once the legation and the cathedral compound had been relieved, American field artillery blasted open the main gate to the Imperial city, in order to overawe the Dowager Empress.

American photographers took some pictures which suggested the presence of allied forces, but their emphasis was resolutely on the United States' contribution. The newsmen of other nations were outnumbered, and had to match quantity with quality. Amongst the assembled correspondents was a 26-year-old Italian,

Luigi Barzini, who had just joined the staff of Italy's largest newspaper, Milan's *Corriere della Sera*. Like Jimmy Hare and Burr McIntosh, Barzini was a photo-journalist, equally adept at using the camera or the typewriter. Like his countryman Felice Beato in India 40 years earlier, Barzini recorded the suppression of a rebellion. A particularly grisly sequence – a before, during and after sequence of the beheading of a Boxer insurgent – was widely published in European papers because the executioner and the victim were both Chinese, and because it suggested that the Allies were behaving with constraint. Like Beato in India, Barzini decided to exercise self-censorship, and chose not to photograph the piles of Chinese corpses which indicated the fate of most Boxers who fell into Allied hands.

The Russo-Japanese War, 1904–05

A little over three years later north-east Asia was again the centre of international attention. In its long-term search for a warm water port, the Russian empire had began to penetrate Manchuria and Korea, territories which Japan felt belonged in her sphere of influence. Sensing impending trouble, the first of some 500 newsmen began arriving in Tokyo early in 1904, while a very much smaller number hung around St Petersburg, seeking permission from the Tsarist authorities to commence the journey eastward across the almost-completed Trans-Siberian railway. Amongst the early arrivals in Japan were the veteran Richard Harding Davis, rapidly becoming the doyen of American photo-journalists, and the 28-year-old novelist Jack London, who had been hired by Hearst to report for the *New York Journal*. An improbable but very real friendship had developed between the patrician Davis and London, who had been brought up in poverty, had been a prospector in the Klondike, and had sailed the world as a deckhand, a background which would make him an American archetype. Davis, London and the other correspondents found themselves confined to the Imperial Hotel in Tokyo, a luxury establishment where Japanese officials could keep an eye on the correspondents and control the flow of information. Many were prepared to accept this pleasant confinement, at least initially, but London knew that his future employment depended on getting the photographs and the story that the *Journal* demanded. He slipped away, attempting to get a passage to Korea, and was arrested while taking photographs of the movement of troops to ports in western Japan.

London had found his story – he had witnessed Japan's preparations for the surprise attack on the Russian naval base of Port Arthur which took place on 8 February – but he could do little with it. Richard Harding Davis used his influence in Tokyo to secure London's release, and, of equal importance, to get the Japanese to return London's camera, though the film had been confiscated. With the other correspondents still confined to Tokyo, a few weeks later London hired a junk which he himself sailed up the western coast of Korea to Inchon, where he joined up with General Tamesada Kuroki's First Army, which was advancing northwards to Manchuria. Arrested once again thanks to the machinations of jealous rivals in Tokyo but soon released, on 1 May 1904 London covered Kuroki's crushing victory over a much smaller Russian army on the Yalu River, the border between

Korea and Manchuria. London's photographs, despatched via Tokyo and published in the *New York Journal*, were the first pictures of the conflict seen in the west. As the Japanese advanced into Manchuria, London found their censorship increasingly stifling. He had already asked Hearst to transfer him to Russia, when he got into a fist fight with a Japanese soldier, and was again arrested, this time facing a court-martial for which the penalty for a guilty verdict could be death. Richard Harding Davis again came to the rescue, asking his friend President Theodore Roosevelt to intervene directly. The Japanese quickly released London, but on condition that he leave Japan and its territories.

Jack London's experiences were extreme, but the frustrations he experienced were universal. Correspondents rubbed up against Japanese censorship on a daily basis, and one by one they shipped out, some to attempt the long journey through the Tsar's empire to get the Russian side of the war. By 1905 virtually the only foreign correspondent who remained with the Japanese was Luigi Barzini, who became increasingly embedded with the Japanese armies. In March, Barzini covered almost the entire 40-mile front of Japanese positions before Mukden, where 620,000 men fought for 17 days in what was the largest battle fought up to that time in human history. Barzini took pictures of the trench systems which snaked seemingly endlessly across the rolling, open hills of central Manchuria, and photographed enormous guns firing from sand-bagged bunkers. He also photographed the aftermath of frontal attacks against positions protected by barbed wire and defended by machine guns, showing shell craters filled with piles of corpses. At the very

point that professional military observers were writing about
the importance of willpower in enabling men to advance through
a curtain of fire, Barzini produced a heavily illustrated book
The Battle of Mukden, which argued that the advantage in war
now lay massively with the defence.

1905 Russian Revolution

If Barzini's interpretation of the Russo-Japanese War pointed
with unerring accuracy to the trench systems of November 1914,
his former colleagues travelling through Russia recorded the first
intimations of the convulsion which was to destroy the empire
just 12 years later. The defeats at the hands of the Japanese
inflamed Russian opinion, and emboldened various reformist
and radical movements to demand change. On 22 January 1905
photographers outside the Winter Palace in St Petersburg caught
the beginning of a demonstration of workers and their families
led by Father Gapon carrying a petition to the Tsar. Other
cameramen photographed the aftermath, with more than 100
bodies lying in the snow, after Cossack guards had shot them
down. Riots broke out across Russia, with people venting their
frustration and anger against symbols of authority or unpopular
minorities. In the Ukraine mobs of peasants attacked Jewish
villages, burning them to the ground, and beating to death those
they could lay their hands on. These outbreaks of atavistic murder
– pogroms – had occurred many times before, but this time they
were caught on film. In Moscow on 17 February a teenage terrorist
threw a bomb filled with nails into the carriage of the Grand Duke
Sergei, Tsar Nicholas II's uncle, as he passed through the gates of

the Kremlin. The bomb detonated, shredding the Grand Duke into hundreds of unrecognisable pieces of flesh. The immediate aftermath was captured on film by an American photographer who was waiting in Moscow for clearance to join the armies in Manchuria. The most famous picture of the 1905 revolution was of the battleship *Potemkin*, the flagship of the Black Sea fleet, the crew of which mutinied on 17 June when they heard that the Russian fleet had been all but destroyed in battle with the Japanese navy in the Straits of Tsu Shima, between Korea and Japan. Other sailors followed the lead of the *Potemkin*'s crew, which signalled the Tsarist military and administrative system was about to unravel. As a consequence Russia was forced to make peace with Japan, just at the point when the land situation in Manchuria was becoming more favourable.

Italo-Turkish War, 1911–12

The Tsar's empire was not the only one tottering towards collapse. Russia's old enemy, the Turkish empire, was beset by national movements in Armenia, Kurdestan, Mesopotamia, the Hejaz and the Balkans. About the only part of Constantinople's domains which was relatively quiet was the province of Libya, but it was here in the summer of 1911 that an assault came which set in motion the collapse of the Ottoman empire. For 30 years a newly united Italy had watched with growing dismay as the southern shore of the Mediterranean was divided up between the French and British empires. The Turkish-controlled province of Libya, wedged between French North Africa and British-dominated Egypt, seemed ripe for the picking. Italian settlers in Cyrenica had been abused, an Italian priest in Derna, Father Giustino, had been murdered, and 'even the uncomplaining, fatalistic Arabs bitterly resented the neglect and utter stagnation into which Turkey had allowed the country to relapse', or at least so claimed Tuillio Irace, the Italian arch apologist for annexation.

In early October 1911, after a bombardment of Tripoli, Italian forces landed at several points along the coast, quickly securing the major towns and cities. The Turkish commander, realising he was outgunned and outnumbered, distributed arms to the Arab population, and withdrew his regular forces to inland oases. Within days of landing, Italian troops were being sniped at by guerrillas, who did not see them as liberators from Turkish oppression. The Italians reacted vigorously. Arab suspects were rounded up and executed by firing squad. Arab guerrillas hit back, attacking isolated Italian positions, and hideously mutilating the Italian dead. In Britian, the liberal newspaper proprietor William Thomas Stead, started a campaign to rouse public opinion against Italian aggression. British correspondents in Libya, Ellis Ashmead Bartlett for Reuter's, and Frances McCullagh for the *Daily News*, photographed hapless suspects being led to execution, and of the victims of Italian massacres. McCullagh questioned the accuracy of Luigi Barzini's reporting of glorious Italian victories. Comparing Barzini's account of the fighting in Tripoli with the wild and inaccurate shooting he had experienced, McCullagh wrote that 'the non-Italians who were present could hardly persuade themselves that the proceedings at which they were assisting constituted real war, and not comic opera or some Christmas pantomime of an excruciatingly funny sort.'

Barzini hit back, leading a delegation of Italian journalists into the British consulate in Tripoli, demanding that defamatory stories about Italian atrocities be officially denied by London's man on the spot. But much more effective than outright denials were accounts and photographs of Arab atrocities, if possible from British sources. Bennett Burleigh of the *Daily Telegraph*, for example, described finding five Bersaglieri who had been tied to a wall, crucified as on a cross, and afterwards riddled with bullets. Burleigh felt it was 'needless to dwell upon the nature of the further atrocities which savage Muslims invariably practise on the bodies of Christians. A sergeant had also been crucified, but with the head down, and in the hands and feet were still left enormous nails.' Like McCullagh, Burleigh backed his essay with photographs, the most shocking of which showed a soldier named Libello, of the 11th Bersaglieri, who before being crucified, had had his upper and lower eyelids perforated and laced with tightly tied coarse string. 'Each eyelid was then pulled, and the cord being pulled behind his head, the eyes were held wide open, and could neither be blinked nor closed in life or merciful death. Flies and insects abounded. The look of unutterable horror on the strained face of Libello will remain fixed forever before me.'

The Balkan Wars, 1912–1913
Italy had expected a quick victory, but a year after the landings found herself tied down by an increasingly vicious resistance movement. Fortunately for Italy, three Balkan nations, Bulgaria, Serbia and Greece, decided to take advantage of Turkey's preoccupation with Libya, and drive the Turks back into Asia.

Turkey hurriedly made peace with Italy on 15 October 1912; two days later her armies in the Balkans faced a Bulgarian thrust into Thrace and an assault on the Vardar valley in Macedonia, with the Serbs coming from the north and the Greeks advancing from the south. A flood of correspondents descended on the Balkans. British correspondents, many of whom sympathised with Greece, went to Athens, where they photographed a smart and reasonably well-equipped Greek army marching towards Salonika. German correspondents went to Bulgaria, where the Bulgarian King Ferdinand had marked pro-German leanings. The Russians and the French went to Serbia and Macedonia, where they captured the eternal reality of war in the Balkans, the wild-looking hill men, and the Turkish irregulars, the Bashi Bazouks.

The greatest number of correspondents by far, however, went to Constantinople, from where they were provided with a press train to move up to the headquarters of the Turkish army. Herbert Baldwin, a British photo-journalist, took the opportunity of a delay caused by a derailment to photograph columns of Turkish refugees streaming eastward. He found 'the spectacle of silent, sad eyed women, many of them bare-footed, many carrying tiny children in their arms, plodding wearily through the mud and filth ... a vivid reminder of what war means to the common people, the innocent victims of intrigue and maladministration.' Baldwin, who was careful to keep his camera well out of sight, avoided the fate of a less-careful colleague, who had his camera snatched from him and thrown into the mud by Turkish soldiers, furious at the insult which had been afforded Turkish womankind.

Although he had not yet realised it, Baldwin was watching the beginnings of the disintegration of the Turkish front. He later wrote that the photographer who films an attack which is successful is soon left behind; better by far to be with an army which is defeated, because the cameraman has to do very little, other than to find a vantage point on the line of retreat and begin snapping. Baldwin, who was working for the Central News Agency, and his colleague Bernard Grant, who represented the *Daily Mirror*, set themselves up overlooking a humpback bridge at Karishtiran. From here they filmed a panic-stricken mass, demoralised by Bulgarian artillery, pushing and clawing its way to safety. Most of Baldwin's shots were ruined by a technical failure, but Grant's appeared in special supplements of the *Daily News*, and confirmed British opinions about the degeneracy of the Turks. Baldwin had better luck a few days later, when he snapped a straggler who seemed to embody the whole spirit of the beaten and broken army. Baldwin recalled, 'He spoke no word, but he accepted the little food I was able to offer him with tears of gratitude that said more than any words could have done, and I felt glad that it had been in my power to help him on his way. I took a photograph of the old fellow as he resumed his journey, and I sent it home with the title "Beaten!" appended to it.' Other journalists, like the *London Daily Chronicle*'s Martin Donohoe and the *Daily Telegraph*'s Ellis Ashmead Bartlett, transmitted stories which provided a context for the photographs, and created the sense in Britain that Turkey was hopelessly degenerate.

Nothing comparable emerged from the Bulgarian side. They had the services of one of the finest photo-journalists of the period, Jimmy Hare, but kept him confined to a press pool, many miles from the action. The Sofia correspondent for the Berlin *Reichspost*, Hermenegild Wagner, complained that 'the official regulations for war correspondents clearly showed how closely the Bulgarian staff had followed the Japanese precedent in imposing fetters on the journalists at the seat of war.' Wagner then listed myriad regulations and concluded that 'it was categorically forbidden to send any news that was at all worth knowing, or to take any steps by which one could get possession of any such news.' Jimmy Hare put up with it for three months, and then decided to cover the war from Serbia.

The Times's correspondent in Constantinople, Walter Crawfurd Price, was able to cover the war from both sides by remaining behind in Salonika after it fell to the Greeks on 9 November 1912, one day before the Bulgarians reached the city. A Hellenophile, Crawfurd Price heroised the Greeks, who were 'in excellent condition, happy and bright, as befits conquerors, well clothed, booted and equipped.' The great majority of the population regarded them as liberators, shouted themselves hoarse, tore the hated fez from their heads, 'and shred them to ribbons.' When they entered the city the Bulgarians behaved very differently, looting and pillaging.

By mid-November Bulgarian armies were also closing on Constantinople, where Herbert Baldwin photographed scenes of increasing panic. On 23 January 1913 the Young Turk nationalist movement, led by Enver Bey, overthrew the Sultan and vowed to fight on, though the damage was now irreparable. Adrianople fell on 26 March, followed by Scutari on 22 April. The Great powers imposed an uneasy peace on the combatants, reducing Turkey's European possessions to the area immediately contiguous to the Dardanelles.

With Turkey gone the members of the Balkan league now fell out. Tension had reached fever pitch in Salonika where King George of Greece had been assassinated on 18 November 1912, mercifully by another Greek, though many in the city suspected a Bulgar plot. In May heavy street fighting broke out between Greek and Bulgar forces, the aftermath of which was photographed by Crawfurd Price. Joined by the Serbs, the Greeks checked the main Bulgar advances in heavy fighting in June. A month later Rumania and Turkey intervened, the Rumanians advancing on Sofia while the Turks retook Adrianople. Bulgaria eventually signed a peace treaty in Bucharest on 10 August 1913, which stripped her of virtually all the territory she had gained in the first conflict.

The war was marked by atrocities on all sides, though the Bulgars were the worst, killing Turks, Serbs and Greeks with equal enthusiasm. Photographs of destroyed towns like Serres taken by Baldwin, Crawfurd Price and others were used in the compilation of a report sponsored by the Carnegie Endowment for International Peace, which sought to use worldwide exposure to shame the combatants into adopting civilised norms, and of substituting 'justice for force in the settlement of international differences.' The journalists also reflected on the way the war was fought. Baldwin had been convinced of the primacy of artillery, but Crawfurd Price felt that the war 'will ever be distinguished by the great part played by the bayonet in the various combats.' He wrote this in the spring of 1914.

In South Africa, Manchuria, Libya and the Balkans, photographers had been constrained by military censorship. Even in Cuba, the military sometimes withdrew co-operation. But insurgent forces and resistance fighters – whether they were Garibaldi's Red Shirts, Geronimo's Apaches, or Gomez's Cuban guerrillas – recognised that the camera could publicise their cause. In 1910 Mexico collapsed into chaos, with several armies competing for power. In the north-western state of Chihuahua a 31-year-old bandit, Pancho Villa, transformed himself into a revolutionary, and set about breaking up the vast land holdings of local *hacendados*, and parcelling them out to his followers. A charismatic figure, his movement soon grew to thousands. Always in search of publicity, on 3 January 1914 Villa signed a contract with the Mutual Film Corporation of Hollywood, which agreed to pay him 25,000 dollars and a 50 per cent royalty of the profits earned by its newsreels, in exchange for the exclusive right to film his battles. Villa agreed to fight as often as possible in daylight, his men negotiating special rates as the danger increased.

Villa's movement was soon known throughout the United States. Photo-journalists flooded into Mexico, including Jimmy Hare and Richard Harding Davis. The man who really created Villa, however, was John Reed, a 26-year-old Harvard graduate, who was reporting for the *Metropolitan* and the *New York World*. Like hundreds of young Americans Reed joined the rebel forces and rode with them through four months of battles. In 1914 he collected his articles and essays into a single volume which he published as *Insurgent Mexico*, which imposed on Villa and his movement a Marxist consistency which it is doubtful Villa ever subscribed to.

With conflict raging along its southern border it was inevitable that the United States would be dragged into Mexico. In April, following the arrest of unarmed US sailors in Tampico, American naval and land forces shelled and occupied Vera Cruz. Worse followed two years later when Villa raided across the US border and attacked the town of Columbus in New Mexico, killing 14 soldiers and 10 civilians. On 15 March 1916, 10,000 troops under General John J. Pershing moved south of the border, and for 11 months swept northern Mexico in a vain attempt to hunt Villa to earth. Pershing did all in his power to reduce Villa's influence. He imposed strict military censorship, which was designed to dry up the publicity on which Villa thrived. Though he did not have the critical terminology, Pershing realised instinctively that photographs of Villa had an iconic status. He therefore insisted that all pictures carried a large US Army Censor's stamp mark, which soon reduced their usefulness. The Army Signal Corps took its own pictures, which it released to magazines and newspapers. Though nearly caught on several occasions, Villa escaped capture, becoming a symbol both of Mexican resistance to the United States, and of radical working-class resistance to capitalism.

In the period 1898 to 1914 photo-journalism came of age. Thanks to improved cameras and newspaper-printing technology, Jimmy Hare, Burr McIntosh, Luigi Barzini, Jack London, Herbert Baldwin, John Reed and all the others are much closer to the world of the early twenty-first century than they are to the world of Roger Fenton, Felice Beato and Matthew Brady. The photo-journalist had established a distinctive culture, which was expressed in a code of conduct which verged on the swashbuckling. Like Burr McIntosh in Cuba and Jack London in Manchuria, they were prepared to go to enormous lengths and risk their lives in order to get a good picture. By 1914 distinct subdivisions had emerged in the genre of war photography. Most controversial were pictures of the dead. Gardner's artfully arranged corpses in the Harvest of Death had been superseded by piles of corpses in the trenches at Spion Kop and Mukden. Beato's understated study of the hanging of two sepoys in 1858 had given way to Barzini's before, during and after shots of the beheading of Boxers in 1900. There were also pictures of the victims of war – Boer women and children in concentration camps, long columns of refugees in the Balkans, and butchered Arabs and gruesomely tortured Italians in Libya. All these subjects would be revisited again and again in the century which lay ahead. And there was the still-elusive action shot. Pictures of the Rough Riders on Kettle Hill had come close, but between 1914 and 1918 photo-journalists were to have more than enough opportunities to get this one right as well.

Photographing Armageddon

Just another Balkan assassination

On 28 June 1914 the city of Sarajevo in the Austrian province of Bosnia was swarming with photo-journalists from the major Vienna papers, who had come to cover the visit of the Archduke Ferdinand, the heir apparent to the throne, and his wife Sophia. When Gavrilo Princip, an 18-year-old Bosnian Serb student, stepped out of the crowd and fired two bullets, photographers were on hand to snap his arrest. In Vienna there was outrage and demands that Serbia, widely believed to be supporting Bosnian Serb terrorists, be punished. In desperation, Serbia appealed to Tsar Nicholas II of Russia, the self-appointed protector of the Slavic people. When Austria finally declared war on Serbia on 28 July, the Tsar ordered a partial mobilisation of the Russian army, in order to fire a warning shot across Austria's bows.

Over the abyss

Until this point the Austro–Serbian dispute had seemed just another Balkan problem, but now Europe's complex alliance system was activated. On 30 July Germany demanded that Russia cease mobilisation, and sought an assurance from Russia's ally, France, that she would not mobilise. When Moscow and Paris refused to comply, Germany mobilised in accordance with her long-term strategic scheme, the Schlieffen plan, which sent her forces through Belgium to attack and defeat France, before redeploying to defeat Russia. To the astonishment and annoyance of the Kaiser, Britain responded to the invasion of Belgium by declaring war on Germany, and a little later on Austria-Hungary. Newspapers for the week 28 July to 4 August, whether in St Petersburg, Vienna, Belgrade, Berlin or Paris, carried essentially the same picture – hysterically cheering crowds seeing their differently uniformed young men off to war. Only in London was there a slightly discordant note, with a large peace rally in Trafalgar Square, which was quickly edited out of history as crowds responded to Kitchener's call for volunteers. More and more countries joined in. Some, like Turkey and Bulgaria, sided with Germany and Austria. Others, like Japan, Italy and Rumania, threw their lot in with Russia, France and Britain. The only large, powerful neutral left by 1916 was the United States, and Britain and France were doing all in their power to bring her into the war as a co-belligerent.

'The Bestial Hun'

All the major powers had contingency plans for 'Armageddon', the great battle which would sort out European power politics. Bureaucratic procedures had been set up to censor the news media, and to control the access of correspondents to armies. But the war had come so suddenly that at first near chaos reigned on the battlefronts. As the Germans advanced through Belgium and northern France, British and French photographers filled the picture supplements of the daily newspapers, and of the new journals designed specifically to cover the war, with images of burning cathedrals and libraries, and stories of raped nuns and mutilated children. One enterprising American photo-journalist, UPA's William Shepherd, scoured Belgium but couldn't find atrocities. 'I offered sums of money for photographs of children whose hands had been cut off or who had been wounded or injured in other ways. I never found a first-hand Belgian atrocity story: and when I ran down the second-hand stories they all petered out.'

Controlling the Press

None of the belligerents was prepared to tolerate the free-wheeling style of a Jimmy Hare or Jack London. Britain, thanks to the new Secretary of War Lord Kitchener, who loathed the press, imposed truly draconian regulations. By the summer of 1915 all correspondents found themselves corralled and controlled to a near intolerable level, far worse than the limits imposed by the Japanese and Bulgarians in previous wars. Jimmy Hare, who had left Bulgaria in disgust in 1912, felt his freedom similarly curtailed in Britain three years later. He wrote that 'to so much as make a snapshot without official permission in writing means arrest.' By contrast, Germany and Austria–Hungary adopted much more press-friendly regimes, taking correspondents on regular guided tours to various battlefronts, and imposing many fewer restrictions.

The Schlieffen Thrust

Throughout the war, the belligerents reprinted each others' pictures, sometimes with misleading captions. Late in 1914, for example, British journals showed German troops marching through Brussels, and what seemed to be Germans rounding up Belgian civilians at bayonet point. In early November a picture appeared of masses of German infantry advancing through the dust and heat haze of late August, as they attempted to march to the west of Paris to effect von Schlieffen's great battle of encirclement. British papers hinted that it had been taken by Allied soldiers, just as they opened fire. Few pictures of the retreat from Mons passed the censor, though British and French papers printed numerous photographs of Paris taxi cabs rushing reinforcements to the Allied armies to deal a major blow to the Germans on the Marne. Unsurprisingly German papers scarcely mentioned this reverse, but filled their pages with pictures showing immense numbers of Russian prisoners, proof that Tannenberg had been a mighty victory. The same images did not appear in London or Paris until late spring of 1915, when they were used as evidence of the inexhaustibility of Russian manpower.

Because photographers had increasing difficulty in getting to the scene of action, much of the early visual material concerned the home front, particularly mobilisation and the production of munitions. France, Germany and Austria had been invaded, and all three nations devoted considerable attention to the plight of their refugees, the unfortunate inhabitants of Picardy, East Prussia and Galicia. Russia and Britain were more fortunate, so Petrograd's journals carried pictures of murdered Serbs, while British papers brimmed over with images of Belgian refugees. The week before Christmas, Scarborough and Hartlepool swarmed with correspondents, taking pictures of the damage caused by the German navy's bombardment of the towns on 16 December. This example of 'Hun frightfulness', the censors felt should not be suppressed. The same motive impelled the censors to allow maximum coverage of the damage wrought by the first Zeppelin raids at the end of January 1915.

Governments could control correspondents, but tens of thousands of soldiers, at least in the western theatre, took their own cameras on to the battlefield. All armies had regulations in place but they were unenforceable, particularly when senior officers were often the worst offenders. In Britain publications like the *Illustrated War News*, the *Daily Mirror*, the *Sphere*, and *War Illustrated* urged soldiers to send them their pictures, and offered prizes for the best shots in a variety of categories. As the war of movement ended in October 1914, pictures of life in the trenches filled the papers. Censors were content that the public should see pictures of their soldiers suffering privations on their behalf;

indeed, the worse the privations – standing knee-deep in mud in chilling autumn rain, for example – the better.

Soldier photographers

Editors had hoped that soldiers carrying pocket cameras would flood the press with images of combat. Overall the results were disappointing. On 14 November *War Illustrated* told its readers that '… modern warfare lacks much which the battlefields of the past provided. Soldiers today are fighting enemies on the continent whom they never see … For this reason the great mass of photographs which reach us do not show actual hostilities in progress.' But there were exceptions. Only a week later *War Illustrated* published a picture snapped by an officer of the Royal Horse Artillery, probably during the retreat from Mons, at the very moment an enemy shell exploded by his battery. He caught some men crouching down, others being blown sideways and terrified horses rearing up and straining at their traces. In early 1915 Private F. A. Fyfe of the Royal Highland Fusiliers, a former press photographer, snapped an equally impressive shot of the British attack at Neuve Chapelle on 10 March 1915. Troops with bonnets and caps missing, their faces screwed into intense concentration, are crawling forwards through a tangle of barbed wire to a sandbagged parapet, probably the forward German trench. In the background a banner has been unfurled, probably a marker to indicate to British artillery observers the forward position of their own troops.

Christmas truce

Vicarious exposure to the realities of combat could fascinate, but so too could more peaceful encounters with the enemy. In mid-January 1915 the first photographs were published of a spontaneous Christmas Day truce between British and German soldiers manning the front-line trenches. In a letter home Private J. Selby Grigg of the London Rifle Brigade, who was based near Armentières, wrote that he and some friends 'found a crowd of some 100 tommies (sic) of each nationality holding a regular mothers' meeting between the trenches. We found our enemies to be Saxons ... I raked up some of my rusty German and chatted with them. None of them seemed to have any personal animosity against England and all said they would be jolly glad when the war was over. Turner took some snaps with his pocket camera.'

War at sea

In 1914 all great powers used photographs of their warships to symbolise their potency, which raised the problem of how to handle pictures of ships going down. On 22 September the U9 sank the cruisers *Aboukir*, *Hogue* and *Cressy* with the loss of 1,400 lives off the Dutch coast. With bodies and wreckage washed up on the North Sea coast, and German papers celebrating the success, denial wasn't an option. Instead the British reprinted German coverage, juxtaposing the pictures of German celebrations with photographs of wreckage, making the point that the Hun was just as murderous at sea as he was on land. A little over a month later, on 27 October, the new super-dreadnought *Audacious* struck a U-boat-laid mine off the coast of Ulster, and sank in full view of other warships, whose sailors lined the decks to take photographs. This time the Admiralty imposed censorship; film was confiscated, eyewitnesses reminded of the disciplinary code to which they were subject and, although rumours abounded, the secret was kept until after the armistice. On 1 November the Royal Navy lost yet more ships, two heavy cruisers sunk by the German Pacific Squadron off the coast of Chile, although this time there were no photographs.

German success at sea in the first months of the war created a demand for images which would remind the British public, and the world at large, that it was Britain who still ruled the waves. On 9 November the Australian cruiser *Sydney* trapped the German cruiser *Emden* while at anchor off South Keeling atoll in the Indian Ocean, and smashed her into scrap metal. A month later Admiral Sturdee's battlecruisers ambushed von Spee's squadron off the Falkland Islands, sinking four of his five ships. Pictures of the wreck of the *Emden* appeared in British papers in the week after Christmas, a present from the infant Royal Australian Navy to Britannia. Three weeks later a dramatic picture from the South Atlantic reached Britain, which showed the ocean filled with bobbing heads and lifeboats, the survivors of von Spee's squadron. The most dramatic picture of this period was of the heavy cruiser *Blucher* capsizing, with hundreds of her crew standing along her keel, after she had been hit 75 times by the 11- inch guns of Admiral David Beatty's battlecruisers in an action off the Dogger Bank on 24 January 1915.

Gallipoli and the ANZAC legend

In the spring of 1915 Britain launched the largest amphibious operation hitherto undertaken to seize the Dardanelles and force Turkey from the war. The mood was light-hearted – British perception of Turkish power was based on their dismal performance in the Balkan Wars. As ever, Kitchener was opposed to allowing photographers on the expedition. The land force commander, General Sir Ian Hamilton, 'begged hard for Hare and Frederick Palmer, the Americans, knowing that they would help us with the Yanks', but to no avail. The Chief Naval Censor, Admiral Sir David Brownrigg, appealed to Churchill, First Lord of the Admiralty, himself a former journalist. In the teeth of Kitchener's opposition he managed to secure the appointment of Ernest Brooks, a former *Daily Mail* photo-journalist, as an official photographer. The Australians, too, had an official correspondent, Captain Charles Bean, who had been a journalist with the *Sydney Morning Herald*, and had already taken hundreds of pictures of the embarkation and training of the First Australian Imperial Force.

The Dardanelles was a disaster. The Turks did not run away, but fought back with determination. Six battleships were lost trying to force the straits without land-force support. When the British and French came ashore on 25 April the Turks, now alerted, pinned them in three separate beachheads, and counterattacked vigorously. The record, both photographic and written, did not underplay the setbacks. Rather, it suggested heroism on a scale which suited the magnitude of the enterprise. For example, the *River Clyde*, the British transport run ashore at

Cape Hellas to give cover to assaulting infantry, was widely hailed as a twentieth-century Trojan Horse. Aptly, the operation had taken place only a few miles across the Dardanelles from the site of Homer's epic siege. At Anzac Cove, Brooks and Bean captured the dominion troops clinging on to a cliff face, an evocation of courage and resolution in the face of almost impossible circumstances. The broad-brimmed felt hats of the ANZACS were particularly photogenic, suggesting that these men were not really soldiers, but farmers, drovers and cattle-ranchers, men of the great outdoors, who, thanks to healthy diets and healthy living, were taller and stronger than the urban populations of Europe. These men were in fact natural soldiers – they had been brought up with rifles and didn't have to be bullied and drilled like Europeans – and they had volunteered to do an unpleasant but necessary job. Pictures of the ANZACS were well received in the United States (Americans could draw all sorts of correspondences), and in Britain by the summer of 1915 they were being captioned 'ANZAC Supermen'.

Gallipoli was presented as a justified gamble but it ended many careers. The most notable was Sir Ian Hamilton, a good soldier with an impossible task. Winston Churchill also appeared washed up following his resignation from the Admiralty, but he fought back, redeeming himself by serving on the Western Front, and making sure he was photographed doing so. The greatest beneficiary of the Gallipoli campaign was an obscure Turkish officer who had commanded an early counter-attack against the ANZAC position. Mustapha Kemal courted the press in Constantinople, was photographed time and again in various striking poses and become the best-known Turk in the west, eclipsing by far the leader of the Young Turks, Enver Pasha.

Verdun – the battle of attrition

A little over a month after the last troops evacuated Gallipoli, France was engaged in a desperate battle of attrition with the German army at Verdun. Pictures emanating from the battlefield showed immense artillery parks, piles of munitions, and the devastation following bombardments of unprecedented violence. Pictures of the almost-obliterated outline of Fort Doumont, which was captured and recaptured many times, came to symbolise the nature of this struggle. Both nations tried for action shots, the German press publishing an extraordinary photograph of a French officer shot as he led his men in a counter-attack. It served its purpose in Germany and Austria-Hungary, but was ignored by the Allied press.

Easter Uprising

On 24 April 1916 the Irish Republican Brotherhood (IRB) attacked British units scattered throughout Dublin and seized many of the public buildings in the centre of the city. Padraic Pearse, the self-styled commandant general of the IRB, stood in the portico of the Post Office and proclaimed the birth of the republic of Ireland. But the population of Dublin did not flock to them. Instead, British troops sealed off the centre of the city, while Royal Navy gunboats sailed up the Liffy and shelled the republicans into submission. Tried by military courts over the next few weeks, fifteen of the leaders were executed. Irish newsmen photographed the entire uprising, which the British did very little to censor. In England public opinion was outraged by what was considered an act of treachery, and even in the United States there was widespread disapproval, particularly when the extent of German involvement became clear.

The Somme

During the early summer, as Britain's new volunteer divisions began arriving on the Western Front, the cabinet overruled Kitchener and approved the appointment of official photographers, who soon filled the press with pictures of cheerful 'New Army' units. On 1 July 1916 these men assaulted 17 miles of the German positions near the river Somme. Some, like the 18th and 36th Divisions, which managed to stay close to the artillery barrage, or who attacked as mines dug under the enemy's trenches exploded, managed to achieve most of their objectives; others, like the 31st Division, were all but wiped out. On the first day of the battle the British suffered 20,000 dead and 40,000 wounded. The first pictures of the Somme, published on Sunday 2 July, showed smiling New Army soldiers waving to the cameras as they marched to the start line, images of particular poignancy as many of these men were already dead.

Haig wanted a breakthrough, not a battle of attrition. For this reason he kept a large force of cavalry just behind the front, which he intended to release at the right moment. As the battle dragged on he was subject to increasing criticism, particularly from the new Secretary of State for War, David Lloyd George, who was to replace Asquith as Prime Minister in December 1916. After the war, Lloyd George caricatured Haig as a stupid, technophobic cavalry officer, criticism which Churchill endorsed enthusiastically. In fact, Haig introduced new technology as soon as it was available. At Flers on 15 September 1916, for example, he used all the tanks he had available and pleaded for more. Haig also wanted more aircraft – as many as industry could deliver. By the time the Battle of the Somme was fought, war had already developed a vertical dimension. Reconnaissance aircraft played a vital role in directing and controlling artillery. Increasingly sophisticated fighter aircraft had been developed to shoot down enemy reconnaissance aircraft and to protect their own. Aircraft were also being used to attack troops on the ground.

The 'Baby Killers'

For the British people, the most important type of aircraft were those which bombed them. In late October 1915 photographers in London managed to get a series of spectacular shots of Zeppelins lit up by searchlights, and in mid-September 1916 of a Zeppelin on fire, falling out of the night sky like a flaming torch. The officer who shot down the Zeppelin, Lieutenant William Leese Robinson, became a national hero, his photograph appearing in newspapers on an almost daily basis. Within a few weeks he was joined by Captain Ball, the Royal Flying Corps top scoring ace in France. All belligerents did the same thing, as though there was a collective need to re-establish the importance of the individual warrior at the very time the war of attrition was reducing human beings to cannon fodder. For a time air aces became as revered as football stars, their pictures appearing on cigarette and post cards. Only one has survived into the twenty-first century as a household name, the German flying ace, Count von Richthofen. The Zeppelins were soon replaced by the Gotha, the world's first twin-engine strategic, which in turn gave way to the Stakken V, a four-engined monster with a bomb-load of four tons. On 21 July 1917 the London press printed a remarkable picture of 22 Gothas in formation flying over the city, an intentional scare tactic to hasten the formation of an improved aerial defensive system for the capital.

Total War

By late 1916 all the major belligerents had moved to something approaching the total mobilisation of the population for war. Photographic essays filled magazines, extolling the role women were now playing in heavy industry and in offices, where they had been excluded from high-prestige 'white-collar' jobs, such as those of secretary and typist. This mobilisation placed a particular strain on the less-developed economies. The conscription of male peasants from labour-intensive agriculture in central and eastern Europe drastically reduced food production, and led to a crisis during the particularly severe winter of 1916–17, known in Germany as the 'turnip winter'. Conditions in Russia were extremely bad, owing in part to the breakdown of rail transport throughout much of Belorussia and the western Ukraine. This reduced the flow of already-limited foodstuffs into cities like Petrograd and Moscow, their populations swollen to about three times those of 1914 by the influx of hundreds of thousands of female peasants to work in the new factories. In February 1917 food-riots in Petrograd got out of hand, and the result was the abdication of the Tsar and the formation of a new government on 20 July under Alexander Kerensky.

Britain and France had received relatively few pictures from Russia since 1914. Those which were published evoked the stoicism of the Russian peasant soldier. A particularly striking picture of a dead Russian soldier hanging over barbed wire appeared in the western press in late 1915, which seemed to suggest that despite huge casualties Russia's will was indefatigable. In the summer of 1916 an initially successful offensive was hailed as the emergence once more of the Russian steamroller, and the British and French papers carried pictures of long columns of Austrian prisoners. But the offensive had petered out, and Rumania, which had joined the Allies in the expectation of its success, was soon overwhelmed by a violent German onslaught. In the West the revolution was seen at first as a positive development. The Tsar and his corrupt and incompetent administration had gone, and from the chaos a reinvigorated Russia would emerge.

French Army Mutiny

The apparent revitalisation of Russia had come just in time. On 16 April 1917 the French army's huge spring offensive, involving 1,200,000 men, 7,000 guns and hundreds of tanks, had been smashed virtually at its start-line. The French lost 120,000 men in four days, the order of casualties they had been able to sustain at the beginning of the war, but not as they neared the end of the third year. The failure of the offensive broke the heart of the French army. Within days soldiers were refusing to obey orders to attack, and by the end of April a large part of the army was in a state of mutiny.

By the spring of 1917 Germany had bested two of her adversaries. The third, Great Britain, had proved more difficult. After the naval actions of 1915, the German High Seas Fleet had tried to lure the Grand Fleet into a submarine ambush off the Jutland Peninsula in early June 1916. The German plan didn't work, but nor was it a British victory. Cameramen caught British battlecruisers exploding and sinking, which led Admiral Sir David Beatty, the battlecruiser commander, to comment, 'There's something wrong with our bloody ships today!' None of the pictures was released. The British diverted public attention by heroising a boy sailor, John Travers Cornwall, who had continued to man the gun in the forward turret of HMS *Chester*, even though the rest of the gun crew were dead or wounded. Cornwall's boyish face looked out from the pages of newspapers, sometimes accompanied by accounts of Lady Beatty's intention of setting up a fund in his memory, or pictures of her husband posing heroically on the bridge of a destroyer. Soon Beatty's *persona* became inextricably linked in the popular imagination with that of young Cornwall. Poor Admiral Sir John Jellicoe, the cautious, camera-shy commander of the Home Fleet, didn't stand a chance against such photogenic competition. Beatty replaced him, celebrating the event by being photographed with his cap at a rakish angle.

'The Yanks are coming!'

Having failed to destroy the Grand Fleet, Germany now had to consider the wisdom of resorting once more to a submarine campaign against British merchant shipping. The first, launched on 4 February 1915, had culminated in the U-20 sinking the liner *Lusitania* with the loss of 1,198 lives, including 124 Americans, off the Irish coast on 7 May. Photographers crowded into Queenstown as survivors and bodies were brought ashore. One of the more evocative images, particularly effective in the United States, was of coffins draped in the Stars and Stripes being loaded into a mass grave. On 19 August a U-boat sank the liner *Arabic*, with the loss of four more American lives. Two weeks later photographs taken from one of the lifeboats appeared in British and American newspapers showing the mighty liner going down by the stern, evoking memories of the *Lusitania*. American reaction was now so hostile that Germany announced on 1 September the cessation of unlimited submarine warfare. After a lull of five months, Germany launched a new campaign, sank yet another British liner with the loss of more Americans and again suspended operations. In early 1917 Germany believed some of her opponents were so close to defeat, that the risk that a new submarine campaign would bring in the United States was worth running. On 31 January Berlin announced the recommencement of unrestricted submarine warfare, which led to the USA severing diplomatic relations 72 hours later. Germany decided that the best way to handle mounting American hostility was to try to intimidate the United States by negotiating an anti-American alliance with Mexico and Japan. It was a huge mistake.

Uncovered by British intelligence, and passed on to the United States, these German plans led to an American declaration of war against Germany on 6 April 1917.

Passchendaele

German defeat was now inevitable, unless Germany could force a decision in Europe in the next 12 to 14 months, before overwhelming American strength could be deployed. Deciding to concentrate on destroying the Russians, German forces withdrew several miles on the Western Front to a zone of strongly constructed defences, the Hindenburg Line. The British moved forward, and on 31 July launched a now very experienced and well-trained army into a major offensive in Flanders, in the direction of the Belgian town of Passchendaele. For nearly 50 years after the war, until it was eclipsed in the mid-1960s by evocations of the first day of the Somme, Passchendaele was synonymous with the apparent futility of the strategy of attrition. Part of the reason was that the offensive began so promisingly. The semi-trained divisions of the summer of 1916 had become hardened professionals, and for the first day or so cut through the German defences. But the land was low-lying, the heavy bombardment had smashed a drainage system constructed over centuries and then rain began to fall. The offensive literally bogged down in a sea of mud.

The second reason that it passed into the collective consciousness of the British people was that there were so many good photographers at Passchendaele. The Germans used mustard gas for the first time on 20 September. Brooks snapped a photograph of temporarily blinded men moving back to a casualty clearing station to have their eyes washed, a photograph which was to inspire the American artist John Singer Sergeant. William Rider-Rider, in peacetime a photo-journalist from the staff of the *Daily Mirror*, was selected by Lord Beaverbrook to act as Canadian official photographer and arrived in France in June 1917. Six weeks later Frank Hurley, the Australian cameraman who had filmed Shackleton's epic voyage to Antarctica, arrived in Flanders as Australian official photographer. Together, Brooks, Rider-Rider and Hurley produced images of men living and fighting in a sea of mud which were to prove iconic. Brooks and Rider-Rider were content to operate within technical constraints but Hurley railed against them. He confided to his dairy, 'None but those who have endeavoured can realise the insurmountable difficulties of portraying a modern battle by the camera. To include the event on a single negative, I have tried and tried but the results are hopeless. Everything is on such a vast scale. Figures are scattered – the atmosphere is dense with haze and smoke – shells will not burst where required – yet the whole elements of a picture are there could they but be brought together and condensed.' Hurley, who wanted to doctor photographs, better to capture the reality, clashed with Charles Bean, who wished to be true to the camera lens. Eventually Bean agreed to a small number of composites which appeared in an exhibition of Australian war photography in London in the spring of 1918.

The Bolshevik Coup
For the allies the autumn and winter of 1917–18 proved the most

depressing and anxious time of the entire war. The Americans were coming but their mobilisation had been delayed by the collapse of the American rail network, and massive jams at America's east coast ports. News from Russia in the later summer was increasingly patchy, though not alarming. In mid-September *The Times*'s Moscow correspondent Robert Wilton was so sure nothing was about to happen that he returned to London on leave. Amazed disbelief greeted the news of 7 November 1917, that the Bolsheviks, led by Lenin, had seized the Winter Palace in Petrograd, defended only by a women's battalion. It was widely assumed that this was an urban coup which would quickly be crushed, like that of the IRB in Dublin 18 months earlier. But three western correspondents remaining in Russia, John Reed, now correspondent for *The Masses*, Philips Price of the *Manchester Guardian*, and Arthur Ransome of the *London Daily News*, all warned that this was not a coup but a deep-rooted revolution. Photographs were rare until January 1918, when pictures of the Russo–German negotiations at Brest Litovsk, which were taking Russia out of the war, were reproduced in British and French papers. Suddenly Lenin and Trotsky became familiar faces. As Russia was now out of the war, and the new Bolshevik regime seen as little more than a tool of the German secret service, British and French censors allowed the publication of extraordinary photographs from German journals of wholesale surrenders of Russian troops. The message was clear – this is what Bolshevism does to an army and this is why it must be stopped. In the summer of 1918, with the announcement of the death of the Tsar and his family, western papers showed the last photographs of the

Romanovs, a family group, Nicholas II bearing an uncanny resemblance to King George V, and his daughters still looking young and pretty.

During this dark time newspapers concentrated on bringing good news from other fronts. There was precious little comfort from Italy, where an Austro-German offensive had cracked the Italian line at Caparetto, necessitating the despatch of British and French troops from the hard-pressed Western Front to the line of the Piave. The news from Mesopotamia, where a British expeditionary force had been fighting the Turks, was better. The British had taken Baghdad in March 1917 and had then pressed northwards to the Mosul oilfields. It was in Palestine, however, where Britain could celebrate its greatest victory. On 31 October 1917 the Australian Light Horse had charged and overrun Turkish defences at Beersheba, unhinging the Turkish front line. Five weeks later the British commander, General Allenby, walked into Jerusalem, the first time the city had been in the hands of a Christian power for 800 years. It was a momentous event, but unfortunately officialdom prevented a truly memorable image. The cameraman was kept so far away that his picture lost much of its dramatic impact.

The Arab Revolt

Another campaign in the Middle East was going well, but the British high command gave it little publicity. Since 1916 Colonel T. E. Lawrence had been co-ordinating and then leading an Arab guerrilla war against the Turks in the Hejaz. On 6 July 1917 Lawrence's forces captured Aqaba, which made direct communications with Egypt very much easier. Lawrence, an inveterate photographer, supplied Cairo with dozens of pictures of his successful operations. But his high command decided against using them, in part because he was still engaged in a clandestine operation, in part because the British did not want to add legitimacy to any Arab post-war claims. In time Lawrence would win widespread publicity, thanks to the American journalist Lowell Thomas, but not until war was over.

'Lafayette, we have come!'

At the beginning of 1918 the situation on the Western Front was critical. Now free of the Russians, the Germans redeployed their forces for one last knock-out blow, to be delivered against the British. They struck on 21 March. The British line buckled and gave way, formations falling back more than 40 miles in a few weeks, but the line did not break. The Germans struck again and again between April and early July, each time getting a little weaker. A year earlier General Pershing, the commander of US forces, had arrived in France with the words 'Lafayette, we have come!', a reference to the debt America owed to the Marquis de Lafayette and his French troops during their own War of Independence. Since then nearly two million Americans had arrived in France, and were anxious to get into action. On 28 May the US 1st Division attacked the Germans at Cantigny. On 30 May the US 2nd and 3rd Divisions smashed into the spearhead of the German thrust along the Marne, and held them at Chateau-Thierry and at Belleau Wood. On 9 June a Franco-American offensive held the Germans at Noyon-Montdidier, and five weeks later the US 3rd Division held them west of Reims. And then on 18 July the Allies counter-attacked, ten American divisions providing the *elan* which French formations had last seen in 1914. The Americans were not skilful – they suffered casualties on a scale not seen on the Western Front since 1916 – but this prodigality alone served to convince the Germans that their time had run out. Unlike earlier wars there were few American civilian photographers to cover their operations – Jimmy Hare, for example, was in Italy – but nearly 500 photographers of the US Army Signals Corps made up for the deficiency.

A black day

The British, Australians and Canadians struck on 8 August at Amiens, and in the next 72 hours advanced 11 miles, overran for the first time ever a German corps headquarters, and took more than 30,000 prisoners. It was a marvellous photo opportunity, and cameramen recorded a sea of faces, arranged *en masse* to convince the Allied public that the Germans really were on the point of collapse. Ludendorf remarked in front of subordinates that 8 August was a black day for the German army. The British broke the Hindenburg Line at the end of September, and crossed the St Quentin Canal. One of the assault battalions celebrated this victory by posing for its own group photo perched precariously up the canal's steep cutting. On 29 October Germany, like Russia before it, collapsed into revolution. The fleet mutinied, the Kaiser fled to Holland and a provisional civilian government negotiated and signed the armistice on 11 November.

The war to end wars?

In allied countries there was rejoicing. Propagandists had told the armies they were fighting 'the war to end wars', and the apparent cause of war, the militarism of Prussia, seemed at an end. But fighting was going on in the streets of Berlin and other cities, as the Communist Spartacist militias battled for control with Frei Korps returning from the front. There was also a civil war in Russia, as Tsarist generals attempted to extinguish the revolution, supported by intervention forces from Britain, France, Japan and the United States. Photographers were present in Petrograd, Moscow and Berlin, taking pictures of the street fighting. The Great War was over, but there was as much as ever to cover.

The Golden Age
1919–39

With the armistice, photo-journalists were free again. As though
to make the point, the Moscow-based correspondent of the
Daily News raced from Moscow to Berlin to be the first British
correspondent to enter the enemy's capital. As Germany, Austria-
Hungary and Turkey collapsed into revolution, the apparatus of
state control disappeared, leaving the correspondent free to
photograph what he liked, as long as he was willing to risk being
shot. The term 'inter-war years' is a misnomer, because the
twenty-year hiatus between the two conflicts was anything but
peaceful, and so there was much to photograph.

There was, too, a new camera. In 1925 the 35mm Leica came on
the market, a compact camera with an automatic range finder,
which vastly increased the possibilities of capturing a fleeting
image. And there was also a seemingly limitless market for

photographs. The first steps were taken in the early 1920s with the publication of *Time and Tide* in London, *Time Magazine* in New York, and in Germany the *Illustrierte Zeitungs* of Berlin and Munich. In the 1930s the format became larger, with new magazines now devoted entirely to pictures and captions. The French led the way with the foundation of *Paris Match* in 1934, followed by *Life* published in the USA in 1936 and *Picture Post* in England in 1938.

Chaos first

The journals of 1919 carried pictures of cheering crowds, returning soldiers, the surrender of the German fleet, and statesmen at conference tables. But they also traced the collapse of empires. Bolshevism, a radical social doctrine sometimes allied to resurgent nationalism, had driven many parts of the world into revolutionary fervour. In Berlin photographers captured the fighting between the radical Spartacist militias and the Frei Korps, which stopped revolution in its tracks. In Russia the West now had newsmen with the armies of intervention, but the Bolsheviks also had their own cameramen, who, despite only intermittent film supplies, managed to create a photographic record of part of the revolution. As the White Armies closed on Moscow, and the western press daily predicted the end of Bolshevik Russia, pictures of Trotsky rallying the Soviet forces became increasingly common. At this stage Trotsky, rather than Lenin, personified the revolution. Trotsky's innate military genius, and the fact that his forces were operating on classic interior lines, allowed him to defeat each of the White Armies in turn. Soviet forces then moved on Warsaw, only to be defeated by a revitalised Polish army. Dimitri Kassell, a young Bolshevik photographer, lost his camera in this campaign – a commissar smashed it over his head as he tried to take a picture of the bodies of Polish prisoners freshly murdered by the Reds. Most villages of Eastern Europe yielded equally harrowing pictures since the breakdown of the distribution system had produced widespread famine. Lenin finally decided that publicity might prick the conscience of the West and produce food aid rather than armies of intervention. In 1921 the *Chicago Tribune's* Floyd Gibbons, a one-eyed swashbuckler in the Jack London tradition sporting a piratical eye-patch, was allowed free access to most of the famine-stricken areas. Gibbons's coverage, supported by pictures of skeletal children, produced a comprehensive Anglo-American aid package, triggered equally by Lenin's announcement of the liberalisation of the Russian economy.

The Turkish empire also had disintegrated. On 15 May 1919 Greece, believing Turkey stricken, landed an army on the Anatolian coast at Smyrna, to enforce a Greek claim to the Hellenic settlements along the Aegean coast. Simultaneously Armenian columns struck into eastern Anatolia, avenging themselves on the Turkish population for the massacres of 1915–16. Assailed on all sides, a group of Turkish officers rallied around Mustapha Kemal, formed a national government, revitalised the army and struck back against the invaders. Photos of them massacring Armenians as they struck east caused a clamour for intervention in Britain and France. Film crews were too far off to capture their subsequent massacre of the Greeks

when the Turks finally drove them into the sea at Smyrna. But
their simultaneous campaign to drive the Greeks from Thrace
was recorded by Ernest Hemingway, then acting as a roving
reporter for diverse US journals.

Ireland again

The British Empire also proved vulnerable to the force of
radical nationalism, which tore at both her oldest and richest
possessions. In Ireland the execution of 15 of the leaders of the
April 1916 uprising had created the very force the British had
hoped to suppress. On 21 January 1919 Sinn Fein declared Ireland
independent, and its MPs who had been elected to Westminster in
the General Election of 1918 refused to take their seats in the
British House of Commons. When the British refused to
recognise Irish independence, the military wing of Sinn Fein,
the Irish Republican Army (IRA), launched a campaign of
assassination and bombing against what they regarded as an
illegitimate occupation force. At first it had great success. By the
spring of 1920 British rule had ceased to exist through many
rural areas in the south. In County Cork, for example, the Royal
Irish Constabulary abandoned 31 police stations, which were
subsequently burnt down by the IRA. Aware of the problem of
fighting terrorists with a conventional army, the British decided
to play the IRA at its own game, raising a force of irregulars from
amongst ex-servicemen, who from their khaki uniforms and
black webbing became known as the Black and Tans. When the
IRA murdered 14 British officers in their beds in Dublin at dawn
on 21 November 1920, the Black and Tans exacted revenge later in

the day, shooting dead 12 spectators at an Irish football match at Dublin's Craig Park and shooting two more suspects near Dublin Castle later in the evening. The British knew they could rely on sympathetic coverage from their own press, but Ireland was being covered by Americans, amongst whom Floyd Gibbons was most prominent, and their position became increasingly supportive of Sinn Fein. Pictures of tanks in the streets of Dublin, or of British soldiers using barbed wire to corral civilians, allowed the American press to argue that Britain was indeed an unpopular occupying power, and Sinn Fein to assert that they were engaged in an Anglo-Irish War. Unwilling to hold the south by force indefinitely the British negotiated a compromise peace, and on 6 December 1921 the Irish Free State came into existence, minus the six predominantly protestant counties of Northern Ireland.

Saviour of the Raj?

Equally problematic was the situation in India. The usual frontier wars continued in Waziristan and Afghanistan, where the British had first experimented with mustard gas in 1919 as a means of dealing with dissident tribesmen, but within India there was now an increasingly coherent nationalist movement which aimed to secure independence for India. Early in April 1919 the most respected of the nationalist leaders, Mahatma Gandhi, organised an India-wide strike against legislation which severely curbed civil liberties. Gandhi had visualised mass non-violent protest, but in many areas rioting broke out, with attacks on isolated Europeans. The revolutionary storm then sweeping around the world like a forest fire, reinforced by folk-memories of the

Mutiny, made the British extremely nervous. Nowhere was the tension greater than in Amritsar, the capital of the Punjab, a province which had sent a half-million men to fight for the British Empire between 1914 and 1918. With the cities crowded with these now-demobilised veterans, the head of the Punjab government, Sir Michael O'Dwyer, authorised the army commander, Major General Reginald Dyer, to react vigorously if faced with a breakdown of law and order. On 13 April Dyer ordered his troops to open fire into a large crowd gathered in Amritsar's Jallianwala Bagh. In a few minutes his men discharged 1,650 rounds at point-blank range into a mass of terrified men, women and children, killing 400 and wounding another 1,200. Until his dying day, Dyer believed that he had saved the Raj; in fact no single act did more to hasten its end. In Britain a storm of criticism soon subsided, but in India nationalism had been reinvigorated. A propaganda campaign, built around grisly images of the British suppression of the Mutiny, served to remind Indians of past injustices and stimulated a widespread campaign of terrorist bombings.

Chaos in China

The journals of the inter-war period were filled from time to time with images of conflict in Europe, in the Middle East and southern Asia. But the largest and longest wars of this period were fought in China. In the 1920s Shanghai and Hong Kong teemed with western correspondents, like Edward Abend, Thomas Milland and Edgar Snow, who were joined in the early 1930s by heavyweights like Sir Percival Phillips and Floyd Gibbons.

In addition western businessmen, and more particularly western missionaries, including several thousand proselytising for various American Christian denominations, all took cameras deep into the interior of China.

China in the inter-war period was very similar in many ways to the Balkans in the 1990s, though on a much larger scale. In 1911 the Manchu dynasty had collapsed into revolutionary chaos, with large areas of China falling under the control of warlords. By the early 1920s the Kuo Min-tang, a nationalist party, supported by China's infant Communist movement, had its own armies in the field, gradually consolidating power. Tearing itself to pieces, China was at the mercy of rapacious westerners, who had carved out large economic concessions for themselves in the coastal regions, and had actually established an internationally controlled district in Shanghai, where the writ of the Chinese government did not run.

In the mid- and late 1920s a wave of anti-foreign violence swept the Yangtse valley and Shanghai, which British troops suppressed, firing into Chinese mobs. Simultaneously the Nationalist movement began to fragment. Throughout urban areas Communists attempted the type of coup which in very different conditions had worked for Lenin in Petrograd 1917. But it didn't work in China. Nationalists and their henchmen, often crime bosses commanding well-armed gangs, sealed off disaffected areas, and worked their way through the cities street by street, systematically killing all dissidents. On arriving in Shanghai in 1928, the young Edgar Snow was confronted by scenes of severed heads on telegraph poles and heads in baskets.

The Manchuria Incident

A more potent threat came from Japan. On 19 September 1931 Japan's Kwantung Army, which had established extra-territorial rights in Manchuria, used an alleged terrorist plot to blow up the Port Arthur–Mukden railway line as an excuse to occupy key points in Manchuria. It was virtually bloodless, but Floyd Gibbons got a scoop, photographing the Japanese commander, and then interviewing him on radio for direct transmission to the United States. China retaliated with an economic boycott, which led to the Japanese landing a 70,000-strong army in Shanghai on 28 January 1932. The Kuo Min-tang resisted fiercely and for a month held the Japanese at the waterfront. Amongst the foreigners in the International Settlement making forays into the war zone was Edgar Snow, whose pictures graphically portrayed the brutalities of the Japanese.

The Long March

To the Nationalist leader Chiang Kai-shek, the Japanese were a disease of the body, whereas the Communists were a disease of the spirit. On 4 March 1932 he lifted the boycott, so that he could concentrate on his war with the Communists. The Nationalists had already waged extermination campaigns against an increasingly successful rural-based Communist insurgency in south central China in 1930 and 1931, and were to send three more expeditions against the Communists in 1932, 1933 and 1934. At the heart of the insurgency lay Kiangsi province, where Communist leader Mao Tse-tung had succeeded in politicising and organising barely literate peasants into an effective guerrilla army. By the autumn of 1934 the Nationalists, advised by officers on loan from the Reichswehr, had penned Mao and his followers into an increasingly small area. Faced with inevitable defeat, in October Mao and 100,000 Communists set off on a strategic withdrawal. A year and 6,000 miles later they reached Shensi province in China's remote north-west, far enough away from the nationalist armies to ensure their survival.

During this period little direct information reached the coastal cities, though rumours abounded. In June 1936, armed with a letter of introduction to Mao Tse-tung written in invisible ink, Snow set off for the remote north-western city of Sian, where he made contact with the Communist underground. Travelling to Paoan, deep in the Loess hills in the heart of Shensi, Snow met and photographed Mao and paid him the ultimate accolade. Mao was 'a gaunt, rather Lincolnesque figure, above average height for a Chinese ... He was plain-speaking and combined curious qualities of naïveté with incisive wit and worldly sophistication.' Snow stayed in Paoan for four months, deeply impressed with what he saw. He photographed a revolution in action, from cheering Communist cadets to happy peasants, now working for the collective good rather than rapacious landlords. Returning to Shanghai in mid-October 1936, Snow wrote *Red Star Over China*, which on publication in 1937 introduced the world to the revolutionary theories of Mao Tse-tung and the new world he was creating in Shensi. It was to inspire would-be revolutionaries for the rest of the century.

Abyssinian interlude

As Mao and his followers were trudging into Shensi, the focal point of international media attention shifted to Africa. In the summer of 1935 growing tensions along the border between Abyssinia and the Italian colonies of Somaliland and Eritrea saw an influx of journalists to the region. When Italian armies crossed the frontiers on 2 October 1935, the high command took great pains to ensure that journalists were kept away from the front, so that they did not witness actual fighting. The media image they wished to portray was of a bloodless victory, with Ethiopians either welcoming the Italians as liberators, or surrendering in droves. Most Italian journalists toed the military's line, but Americans like the *New York Times* correspondent Herbert Matthews, and Joe Caneva, a photographer for AP, had returned to their freewheeling days. At the beginning of the campaign Caneva got a major scoop when he brought the motorcade of the Eritrean front commander, Field Marshal Badoglio, to a halt by placing himself in the centre of the road and holding up his hand. Matthews later recalled the scene:

'General,' said Joe, 'I'm an American photographer and I'd like to take your picture.' Badoglio chuckled and smiled half-sheepishly at his officers as he got out and shook hands. 'Now,' said Joe, 'you stand over here. No, turn this way. Put your hat back a little. Hold that! One more! Now, I wish you'd get some field-glasses. That's the idea! Hold them up to your chest. No! Lower. That's it! Steady!'

Such opportunities were rare. The official Italian *Luce*

photographers who were attached to various formations found that action took place at such long ranges that they rarely got anything more than a puff of smoke. Much more common were pictures of Italian soldiers marching along mountain tracks, building roads or resting by rivers. Matthews teamed up with Luigi Barzini, the son of the Luigi Barzini who was now a member of the Italian senate, and together they survived an Abyssinian ambush of an Italian column in Ende Gorge. Matthews used up his last remaining film pack without seeing a single Ethiopian, 'despite the continuous firing and hand-to-hand attacks at various points only a few hundred yards from me.'

Addis Ababa, the Abyssinian capital, attracted many more international correspondents, including the *Daily Telegraph*'s Sir Jocelyn Phillips, the up-and-coming novelist Evelyn Waugh, the Australian Noel Monks and the young 'Bill' Deedes, who was going to become a Fleet Street legend. Like the South African republics 35 years earlier, the Abyssinian emperor, Haile Selassie, was anxious that the world's press portray his domain as a proper state which was rapidly modernising. Like Lincoln and Bismarck and many lesser rulers, Haile Selassie was well aware of the power of *The Times*, and assiduously cultivated that paper's correspondent, George Steer, a 26-year-old English-educated South African. The authorities provided suitable photo-opportunities, such as Ethiopia's five modern aircraft, a newly constructed military academy with cadets on parade, and the reasonably well-equipped imperial guard. It didn't really work. Steer recorded seeing members of the imperial guard using their rifles as shooting sticks, their barrels stuck in the mud.

Photographers were much more interested in filming exotic tribesmen in chain-mail, armed with shields and swords.

Steer, unlike most correspondents, was allowed a limited degree of travel. He first went to the southern front in the Ogaden and photographed the aftermath of the fighting. A handful of Italian tanks had been captured, but some troops had fled. The leader of one detachment, Simu, who had surrendered, was publicly flogged. In the meantime the emperor had moved his headquarters north to Dessye, a strategically important town on the main route from Eritrea to Addis Ababa. On 6 December 1935 a heavy Italian air raid hit a Red Cross Dressing Station as well as the town, killing and wounding more than 250. Haile Selassie manned an anti-aircraft gun throughout the attack, and then gave journalists the photograph of a lifetime, by posing with his foot on a large unexploded bomb. Steer arrived in Dessye at the emperor's request on 22 December. On the same day Badoglio, his northern attack bogged down in the area of Adowa, ordered the use of mustard gas against the Ethiopian defenders, commanded by Imru. Steer witnessed the results, and sent off an emotional if historically inaccurate despatch. 'For the first time in the history of the world, a people supposedly white used poison gas upon a people supposedly savage ... Some were blinded ... others saw the burns spread upon their arms and legs and felt the increasing pain, whose source and end they could not understand and for whose cure they had no medicine.'

Both sides could claim to be victims of atrocities. A few days later Lieutenant Tito Manietti was captured in south-eastern Abyssinia, when his aircraft was forced down by engine trouble.

His captors dragged him to a village he had just strafed. First they cut off his fingers, then, pulling down his trousers, they cut off his testicles, and finally, forcing him to kneel in the village square, they beheaded him. They then carried his head in a leather bag from village to village as a talisman of Ethiopian victory. The Italian press gave extensive coverage to the Manietti story, though when his head was eventually recovered, it was considered too gruesome to photograph. *Luce* cameramen were less squeamish about digging up recently interred corpses, to photograph the horrific wounds made by Ethiopian rounds, which seemed to indicate that the enemy was using dumdum bullets. Herbert Matthews knew they were the result of soft lead bullets the Ethiopians used in their ancient rifles, but the Italians weren't interested in his explanation. It was a war fought with increasing barbarity on both sides. The Ethiopians took only five Italian prisoners, while the Italians literally gassed their way into Addis Ababa early in the summer of 1936.

Spain

When Haile Selassie addressed the League of Nations on 30 June he muttered a prophetic warning, 'Me today … you tomorrow.' The world did not have long to wait. On 18 July military garrisons in 12 cities in Spain and five in Spanish Morocco revolted. Troops loyal to the left-wing government of the Republic managed to suppress the uprisings in Barcelona and in Madrid, where enthusiastic Communist militiamen massacred rebels in the Montana Barracks, leaving their bodies lying in the courtyard. In Toledo, cadets of the military academy also rose in revolt, and

survived by holding the Alcazar fortress for more than two
months, in the face of increasingly desperate Republican attacks.

The military revolt would almost certainly have been crushed
had it not been for the intervention of the Luftwaffe, whose JU 52
transport aircraft carried General Francesco Franco and 14,000
troops from Spanish Morocco to Algeciras and La Linea.
Reinforced from local garrisons Franco's army struck north-east
towards Madrid, taking the government-controlled city of
Badajoz on 15 August and slaughtering the Republican defenders.
Pictures of the Montana Barracks and Badajoz massacres filled
the world's press during the summer of 1936, reinforcing
ideological preconceptions and allowing the rapid demonisation
of the enemy. Germany and Italy rushed aid to Franco's
Nationalists, the Soviet Union transported smaller amounts to
the Republic, while Britain and France declared their neutrality.
So great were the passions roused worldwide, that individuals
travelled to Spain in their thousands to fight in foreign volunteer
units, a relatively small number for the Nationalist Carlists, and
at least a strong division's worth to serve in the Republic's
International Brigade.

Because of the intense interest, and because Spain was easy
to reach, correspondents flooded in, including leading literary
figures of the day like Ernest Hemingway and John Dos Passos.
For others it was a baptism of fire, like Eric Blair, later to change
his name to George Orwell, and Andrei Friedmann, a 23-year-old
Hungarian who had studied journalism in Berlin, who a year
earlier had changed his name to Robert Capa. Armed with a 1925
Leica, Capa freelanced for a number of European and American

journals. In October 1936 the *Paris Vu* published what was going to be the most famous picture of the conflict, and one of the most controversial pictures ever taken. 'The Falling Soldier' captured the actual moment a bullet smashed into the head of a Republican militiaman. A sub-genre of photographic studies evolved around it, and arguments as to its authenticity continued to rage until the soldier was identified by name and medical evidence which conclusively proved the picture portrayed his death put the controversy to rest. It was a brilliant image and Capa quickly emerged as a photographer whose genius was widely acknowledged. His pictures were both artistic and newsworthy, and after his lover Gerda Taro, a photographer for *Life* Magazine, had been crushed to death by a tank in July 1937, were infused with pain and passion. Those taken during the siege of Madrid of anxious men and women looking skyward as German bombers circled overhead were a priceless gift to the Republican cause.

George Steer was another journalist for whom personal tragedy became intertwined with the larger tragedy of the Civil War. In the summer and autumn of 1936 he was in northern Spain on a working honeymoon with his new wife, Margarita de Herrero, an Anglo-Spanish journalist working for *Le Journal*, whom he had met and married in Addis Ababa just before the Italians entered the city. In January 1937 the heavily pregnant Margarita returned to England to give birth, but complications set in and she died, leaving a bereft husband to lose himself in the cause of the Basque independence. Steer's opportunity came on 26 April, when he and his cameraman sifted through the burning ruins of what had been the town of Guernica, destroyed the previous day in a sophisticated incendiary raid by the German Condor Legion. Steer and his photographer were too busy helping the injured to take pictures at first, but Steer took notes and on 28 April 1937 his devastating article 'The Tragedy of Guernica' appeared in *The Times*. The Franco regime took fright, denied it had been their allies, and claimed that the town had been burnt by the Basques or the Republicans themselves, an assertion generally supported by the right wing in Britain.

Meanwhile on the battle fronts Republican armies had done surprisingly well against the much better equipped Nationalists, and had smashed successive Italian offensives. Fearing a stalemate, Germany and Italy stepped up aid to Franco, but no such help was offered to the Republic. Simultaneously the various factions which formed the Republican movement began falling out. The first weeks of May 1937 saw Barcelona devastated by fighting between anarchists and Communists, which created fissures throughout the Republican movement. Divided and poorly equipped, the Republicans eventually accepted an understanding with the Nationalists in 1938 that all foreign forces would be repatriated. Barcelona said farewell to the International Brigade in scenes of enormous emotional intensity, because their presence had been a symbol of worldwide support, and their departure meant that the Republican cause was now doomed.

The China 'incident'

The nationalists entered Barcelona on 26 January 1939, and took Madrid two months later. By that time media attention had shifted back to China once again. On 7 July 1937 Japan had launched a full-scale invasion of northern China, with heavy fighting once again in Shanghai. Wong Hai-sheng, a Chinese newsreel cameraman working for the Hearst chain, captured an unforgettable image of a solitary baby crying in the rubble of a bombed-out Shanghai railway station. In 1938 *Life* magazine estimated that the still Wong took at the same time had been seen by 136,000,000 people. Conscious of the picture's power, the Japanese and their apologists claimed it was a fake, and controversy has swirled around the picture ever since. The Nationalists had their best forces in Shanghai, but sympathetic photographers like Edgar Snow chose to depict the battle as one of the Chinese people fighting a sophisticated military machine. In December the Japanese broke Chinese resistance and surged up the Yangtse to Nanking, where their army ran amok in an orgy of rape, looting and murder. Western cameramen photographed the aftermath which shocked the world, accelerating the process by which the Japanese came to be seen as brutal savages, and then as something less than human. By contrast the Chinese became for a time the embodiment of heroic fortitude. A photograph of a wounded Chinese soldier on the retreat from Nanking to Hangkow, taken by Robert Capa in 1938, said it all – China was badly damaged but she wasn't beaten. By 1939 a generation of photographers had honed their skills in Spain and China – they had the techniques, the technology, the publishing outlets and, in September, they got yet another war.

The Second World War

In the years before 1914 there had been widespread enthusiasm for war. Conversely, during the late 1930s the prospect of war was regarded with intense anxiety. The British, French and Germans expected a war to begin with devastating air raids, like those depicted in films like *Idiot's Delight* (1931) and *Things to Come* (1936), and confirmed in photographs and film from Abyssinia, Spain and China. In the autumn of 1938 Europe had seemed to stand on the brink of catastrophe over Hitler's demand that the German-speaking Sudatenland be incorporated into the Reich. At the very last minute British Prime Minister Neville Chamberlain had flown to Munich and returned with an agreement signed by Hitler, that the Sudetenland was positively the German Chancellor's last territorial demand in Europe. A picture taken at Hendon airport of the Prime Minister holding up the Munich

Agreement was flashed around the world by the new technique of radiophotography. George Gallup's new polling organisation found that Chamberlain's approval rating had gone off their scale. For a short time he was the most popular leader in the world, receiving nearly 60,000 telegrams of congratulation, while the local constituency association tried on several occasions during the winter to deselect their member, the Prime Minister's greatest critic, Winston Churchill.

The following March Hitler occupied the rest of Czechoslovakia, and proceeded to make demands on Poland, namely the return to Germany of the port of Danzig and adjoining territory, which had been given to Poland under the terms of the Treaty of Versailles in 1919. Britain and France now gave guarantees of support to Poland and many other countries in Eastern Europe, but it was too late. On 23 August Germany and the USSR signed a non-aggression pact, which was taken as a signal that war was now inevitable. *Picture* magazine in both London and Berlin carried stories told in photographs of how the crisis had developed. The German view was that their nation had been saved from a Bolshevik–Jewish conspiracy by the election of Adolf Hitler and the National Socialist Party in 1933, from which time things had started to improve. The Jews had been forced from the economy and encouraged to emigrate, unemployment had fallen, home-ownership had increased and autobahns were being built. Hitler merely wished to wipe out the stain of Versailles, and have German people living under alien rule incorporated into the Reich. Magazines like *Picture Post* in Britain had a different take. Its photograph essays showed Nazi gangs smashing Jewish shops and burning synagogues, while factories geared up for war production. Hitler's territorial moves – the remilitarisation of the Rhineland, the annexation of Austria, the occupation of Czechoslovakia and the demands on Poland all showed that Germany was bent on European – perhaps world – conquest.

'Blitzkrieg'

On 1 September three German Army groups, attacking from East Prussia and Slovakia, enveloped Poland and struck towards Warsaw. Two days later Britain and her Commonwealth declared war, followed by France. Unlike the *ad hoc* arrangements of 1914 the Wehrmacht, thanks to a suggestion in 1938 by the Minister of Propaganda and Public Enlightenment, Dr Joseph Goebbels, had conscripted experienced cameramen, eventually more than 1,000, into a propaganda division under Major General Hasso von Wedel. Operating in detachments which became known as Propaganda Kompanien (PK), their role was 'to influence the course of the war by psychological control of the mood at home, abroad, at the Front, and in enemy territory'. In their coverage of the Polish campaign PK photographers established the main themes of their early work. The emphasis was on the superiority of high technology – speed, power and modernity – over masses of poorly led infantry. The pictures showed JU 87B Stuka dive-bombers supporting columns of speeding tanks and half-tracks, a war in which the maintenance of momentum would bring victory without having to fight. In mid-September a correspondent for *Time* magazine coined a German word – 'Blitzkrieg' – for what he had seen, a term which the Germans soon adopted themselves, albeit unofficially.

On 17 September the USSR invaded Poland from the east, meeting the Germans on a pre-arranged demarcation line running through Brest-Litovsk. Not to be outdone by Hitler, on 30 November Stalin sent his armoured formations rolling into Finland, in what was intended to be a three-week campaign. But in a maze of lakes and forests, and against skilfully constructed positions, the Soviets met defeat after defeat. Some of the finest photographers in the world descended on Helsinki to record a classic David v. Goliath conflict. Amongst them was Carl Mydans, whose pictures of Russian corpses frozen in grotesque attitudes, and of Finnish ski troops gliding through the forests, graced the pages of *Life* magazine. The Soviets eventually crushed the Finns through sheer weight of numbers the following spring, but their performance had been inept in the extreme, something which the German high command had observed closely.

The French and the British had been slow to get their own information ministries off the ground, and both had conscripted photographers into official photographic units, as well as having specially accredited civilian correspondents. In contrast to the dynamism of the Germans, French photographic essays were passive, concentrating on the impregnability of the Maginot Line. British coverage reassured the public that their version of the Maginot Line, their front-line air defences, were sound, though extensive coverage of the evacuation of children from urban areas was designed to make assurance double-sure. As in the First World War, the British also needed to assert their domination of the seas, particularly after some embarrassing early losses to u-boats. This came with the scuttling of the German raider *Graf Spee* in Montevideo harbour, in front of the world's press in December 1939.

In the spring of 1940 the Wehrmacht established *Signal*, its own photographic magazine. It was inspired by *Life*; but under the direction of Fritz Solm, a journalist of considerable talent, it leapt ahead in the sophistication of its layout. *Signal* was lavishly funded – its salary bill alone for 1940–41 came to two and a half million US dollars – and it printed extensively in colour. *Signal*'s editorial staff of about 15 had first call of the thousands of photographs from the PKs which passed through its offices. It was printed in virtually every European language, and had a fairly large English language edition which circulated in the United States until December 1941 and in the Irish Free State throughout the war.

Signal's photo-essays on the Norwegian campaign of April 1940 showed that the British had behaved with near-criminal ineptitude. British readers might have been tempted to dismiss this as German propaganda, but for the fact that the coverage corresponded with that of neutral American pressmen in Norway. In Britain a political storm brewed up, which swept away Neville Chamberlain and brought in Winston Churchill as Prime Minister, just in time. On 10 May 1940 the Wehrmacht struck in the West, cleverly drawing the French 1st Army group into Belgium, while Panzer formations struck through the Ardennes and cut north to the Channel coast at Abbeville, trapping Anglo-French forces in a pocket along the Franco-Belgian frontier. The evacuation of a third of a million Allied troops through Dunkirk was a major disaster, but the few photographs taken, some by soldiers with their own cameras, others by the civilians in the small boats who had come to rescue them, were skilfully turned by the Ministry of Information into a propaganda triumph. They showed an army cleverly avoiding a trap as it was about to be sprung. In Paris the mood was less sanguine. The French regarded Dunkirk as a betrayal, and although they fought well when the Germans struck west again on 9 June, they no longer had sufficient forces to maintain a coherent front, and capitulated on 22 June.

Britain alone

A month later the Luftwaffe began its air assaults on shipping in the Channel, and on adjacent airfields – the opening phase of what came to be called the Battle of Britain. German photographers were keen to cover this high-technology warfare, filming from bombers passing over British bases and later over London. Photographers in Britain, who now included a growing number of American newsmen such as CBS bureau chief Ed Murrow, had two audiences in mind: the British population, whose morale had to be maintained, and the people of the still-neutral United States. Pictures of the battle emphasised the humanity of the British. Robert Capa, for example, concentrated on the pilots – handsome young men waiting to climb into the cockpits of their reassuringly effective fighters – and of the stoicism of the British people under a rain of bombs. On 23 September 1940 *Life* magazine devoted its front cover to a heavily bandaged British toddler lying in a hospital bed.

The same edition devoted a story to Frederick Harrison, a six-year-old East Ender resembling a potential heavy-weight boxer, who glared pugnaciously at the camera while he described how he had rescued his three-year-old sister from their bombed tenement. Here was the bulldog breed personified, a reassuringly tough little boy who could take anything the Luftwaffe could drop on him: the junior counterpart to a belligerent-looking Winston Churchill who was photographed on several occasions climbing over piles of rubble in bombed areas, acknowledging the cheers of his undefeated people. On 29 December, during one of the heaviest raids thus far, Bill Brandt managed to take a shot of the dome of St Paul's Cathedral rising above the smoke and flames of the surrounding districts, which appeared in the papers just two days later, captioned 'The Finest Picture of the War'. If not the finest, it was certainly one of the finest, an iconic image of British endurance.

During this period the British searched desperately for good news from other fronts. Right on cue between December 1940 and February 1941 came a series of spectacular victories over the Italians, won by British and Australian forces in Libya. Frank Hurley took pictures of long columns of Italian prisoners, though his concern with photography as an art form led to increasing conflict with younger Australian cameramen like Damien Parer who saw their purpose as getting out a news story. The Libyan victories were only a short interlude. The Afrika Korps under Erwin Rommel counterattacked and drove the British back to the Egyptian frontier, but could not advance further because the Australians held the port of Tobruk, once more photographed by

Hurley. Spectacular German success in Greece and Crete, with the PK photographers giving free reign to airborne and airlanding forces, was followed by success at sea, when *Bismarck* and *Prinz Eugen* destroyed *Hood*, in their brief North Atlantic foray. Three days later the *Bismarck*'s short career ended in a mid-Atlantic gun duel with a large British task force. The Royal Navy released pictures of the end of the *Bismarck* within 48 hours, as this was about the only good news Britain could offer its people and the world in the summer of 1941.

Barbarossa

For Hitler, campaigns in North Africa, the Balkans and in the Atlantic were of secondary importance to Operation Barbarossa, the invasion of the USSR which the German high command had been planning since July 1940. At dawn on Sunday 22 June 1941 three million German troops surged across the common frontier. For the first weeks photographs were almost exclusively the preserve of the various PKs, who presented the campaign in overtly ideological and racial terms. Pictures were published showing small numbers of tall blond soldiers herding vast numbers of semi-Asiatic prisoners into holding areas, which dwarfed pictures taken in Poland and France, along with acres of smashed and captured Soviet equipment. After eight weeks of campaigning the coverage shifted. Now the German public saw tired men sleeping over the handlebars of motor bikes, or columns trudging eastward through nearly impenetrable clouds of dust against a vast, seemingly limitless, horizon. By early October, with the Wehrmacht within striking distance of Moscow,

Executed Indians, photographed by Felice Beato in the spring of 1858. Subsequent generations have seen this picture as an example of ruthless British repression, but at the time it was seen to epitomise British restraint. Beato could have taken pictures of trees festooned with corpses, and of Indians being flogged and humiliated before they were hanged. But he exercised remarkable self-censorship.

Hulton Archive

Boers and British communicate via graffiti. Before abandoning a farm, the Boers had written, 'Don't forget Majuba, Boys', a reference to a famous Boer victory over the British in 1881. 'No fear, Boers, no fear,' replied the British.

Hulton Archive

The result of the bomb which shredded Grand Duke Sergei, the Tsar's brother, on 17 February 1905. In the 1860s the development of dynamite and associated explosives produced a quantum leap in the killing power of the lone assassin. By 1900 terrorist bombings were an almost-daily occurrence, a trend which was to continue without abeyance throughout the twentieth century.

Hulton Archive

The 'shot heard around the world'. Princip and his fellow conspirators were members of the Bosnian Serb 'Black-Hand' organisation which was supported by the War Ministry in Belgrade. While the Archduke and his wife were on their way to the town hall, terrorists had thrown a bomb into the Archduke's car, which he picked up and threw back on to the road where it detonated, injuring the occupants of the following car. On the return journey from the reception the driver, having lost his way, slowed down to reverse directly in front of Princip.

Hulton Archive

Too good to be true. A heavily cropped photograph, which originally included a trench manned by Germans firing at the attacking French at point-blank range. There are two problems. First, the weight of German fire would have been so great that the French would not have got so close. Second, the angle from which the photograph was taken suggests that the camera was on a tripod. The picture was probably posed but this does not detract from its emotional power. In the cropped version the officer dies heroically at the head of his men, who continue to press home the attack. In the uncropped version, the futility of the gesture can be fully grasped. The French attack is brave, but superior German firepower has condemned it to failure.

Hulton-Deutsch Collection/Corbis

On the second day of the Passchendaele Battle, 1 August 1917, British official photographer John Warwick Brooke snapped what was to become an iconic photograph of the First World War. After a night of torrential rain the mud was already deep, and the stretcher party was having difficulty. It took seven men to carry this stretcher. Later in the battle men who slipped from duck-boards into the quagmire had little chance of survival. Personal accounts abound of them pleading with their comrades to shoot them, as they sank out of sight.

Hulton Archive

In house-to-house fighting in Shanghai, the Japanese took few prisoners, beheading or bayoneting most who fell into their hands. Japanese junior officers believed that such pictures would serve to intimidate their enemy – hence their remarkable willingness to allow western newsmen to photograph them at work, little understanding the impact that such photographs would have on Japan's standing in London and New York. *The Edgar Snow Collection*

The most famous picture of the Civil War, Robert Capa's 'The Falling Soldier', captured a bullet smashing into the head of a Republican militiaman. Was it a forgery? Later forensic examination determined that the body posture could only have resulted from sudden and massive brain damage. Historians discovered that the only man killed on 5 September 1937 was Federico Borrell Garcia. His widow identified the 'falling soldier' as her husband. This unique photograph testifies to a rare window of opportunity and a genius behind the camera lens.
Robert Capa/Magnum Photos

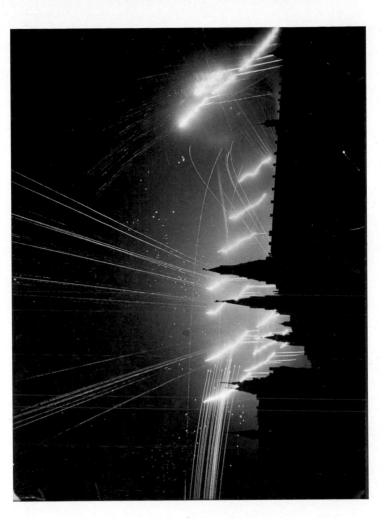

The Luftwaffe attacks Moscow, Summer 1941. *Life* magazine photographer Margaret Bourke White was on assignment in Russia doing a story on economic development when the Germans attacked on 22 June. She did everything in her power to get to the front, but was consistently thwarted by an extremely nervous Soviet bureaucracy, who were terrified that she would photograph what was turning into a disorderly rout. Fortunately the Germans came to her, bombing Moscow on a regular basis during the summer. *Time Life Pictures/Getty Images*

US Marines raise the Stars and Stripes on Mount Suribachi. Joe Rosenthal actually posed the picture that was to make him famous – Marines had already raised a much smaller flag about half an hour earlier. Rosenthal's picture, published all over the world, was celebrated on us postage stamps, and was used as the basis of the Marine Corps monument in Washington. In the aftermath of 9/11, New York firemen raised the Stars and Stripes on the mountain of smouldering rubble, an attempt to draw on the spiritual power of Rosenthal's image.

Corbis

West meets East in the streets of Inchon, September 1950. A typical Bert Hardy composition, artfully arranged to question the role of the United States in Korea. For Hardy and Cameron, the encounter between the American Marine and the small Korean child epitomised the disparity between an impoverished Asian country and the world's pre-eminent power. This subtle questioning of the us role irritated MacArthur far more than the allegation that us forces had killed civilians. The juxtaposition of American strength with Korean weakness suggested the us was a bullying aggressor, whereas MacArthur believed America had a sacred mission to save the people from Communism.
Hulton-Deutsch Collection/Corbis

'The Price of Victory', *Newsweek*, 9 October 1950. Signal Corps photographer Sergeant Al Chang photographed the GI hugging his buddy after a friend had been killed in fighting in the Hoktong Ni area on 8 August 1950. Although later generations viewed the photo as anti-war, Americans who had just emerged from the Second World War read it differently. The poignant embrace epitomised the selflessness, sacrifice and brotherhood with which victory is bought. A reader wrote to *Newsweek* that the picture 'should take its place in the annals of history alongside that other immortal classic, "The Marines plant the American flag on Suribachi"', which came out of the Second World War. Like millions of other Americans the author knew that grieving was an essential part of war – it made victory meaningful. *Corbis*

Cold-blooded murder?

Tet, 1 February 1968. Eddie Adams'
famous picture belies a complex
situation. That morning Brigadier
General Nguyen Ngoc Loan had
just learned that the entire family of
one of his officers had been
massacred by the Viet Cong. He
carried out a summary execution of
a captured guerrilla brought to him.
Adams claimed he had no idea of
what was about to happen. 'It was
common to hold a pistol to the head
of prisoners during questioning ...
The man just pulled a pistol out of
his holster and raised it to the vc's
head and shot him in the temple.
I made a picture at the same time.'
Associated Press, AP

Troops of the Royal Anglian Regiment charge in the Bogside, 1971. Don McCullin knew that there were likely to be photo opportunities in Derry's Bogside on Saturday afternoons when the pubs closed. Gangs of youths would start throwing stones, and some might hurl Molotov cocktails, forcing the army to retaliate. McCullin thought the Royal Anglians 'appeared like Bushido warriors' burdened with medieval armour.

Contact Press/Don McCullin

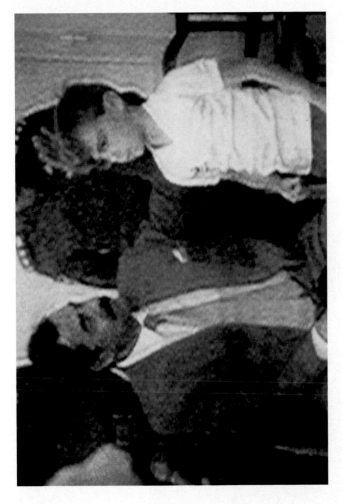

Nine-year-old Stewart Lockwood tenses at Saddam's touch – Baghdad, 23 August 1990. On 17 August Saddam had announced that all 'visitors' to Iraq would be moved to strategic sites to act as human shields to deter attacks. General Norman Schwarzkopf, setting up his headquarters at Riyadh, said he 'was sick to his stomach at the news'. At a televised news conference designed to appease international condemnation, Saddam tried to display his benign intentions to his Baghdad 'visitors'. The move backfired when the newspapers published this sinister still, hinting at the Iraqi leader's deplorable human rights record.

Rex

War comes to America – a second aircraft plunges towards the north tower, New York, 11 September 2001. Everyone knew about Pearl Harbor, and now it was happening again. The target this time was even more significant: the symbolic and actual heart of the economy, both domestic and worldwide. While the attack was under way, news came through that the Pentagon had also been hit, and that a fourth aircraft had crashed in Pennsylvania. In the words of Admiral Yamamoto after Pearl Harbor, the terrorists 'had succeeded only in waking a sleeping giant'.

Associated Press, AP

the rains came. Now the emphasis was on mud, as the PK were unconsciously preparing an excuse for failure. By mid-November it was snow and ice. Troops were still moving towards Moscow, but they were having to improvise, starting their trucks by lighting fires under them. And then the impossible happened. On 5 December the Soviets counterattacked, and now the theme of the PKs' pictures was Germanic endurance in the face of impossible conditions against a savage Mongol enemy. People at home were soon fully involved, donating boots, rugs and furs to make up for shortfalls in German logistic planning.

Soviet coverage of the first weeks of the war was as poor as their military performance. The most spectacular pictures were obtained by Margaret Bourke White, *Life* magazine reporter, who was in the USSR doing a special feature when the Germans attacked. Prevented from leaving Moscow by the Soviet authorities who wished to keep from the world the extent of the disaster that had overwhelmed their forces, she was able to photograph German air raids on Moscow from the roof of the American embassy. A little later she was allowed to do a spread on Joseph Stalin, showing his kindly, avuncular side, which prepared the American people for the possibility of an alliance. Soviet coverage was at a discount until 7 November 1941, the twenty-fourth anniversary of the revolution, when photographers were out in force to cover a review of the arrival of fresh divisions from Siberia, a reminder of the sheer depth of Soviet strength.

Meanwhile tension between Japan and the United States had been building, over Tokyo's attempts to expand south into Indo-China at the expense of the now stricken French. In July

1941 the United States imposed an embargo on oil exports to Japan, soon joined by Britain and the Dutch government in exile, which still had control of the oil-rich Dutch East Indies. When Japan attempted to negotiate her way out of a strait-jacket, the Americans demanded that she evacuate not just Indo-China, but China as well, which was too much of a humiliation for Tokyo to stomach. During the latter part of 1941 British and American magazines carried extensive picture essays on the strength of their forces in the Pacific – the US battle-fleet at Pearl Harbor in Hawaii, the B-17 bombers beginning to reach General Douglas MacArthur's command in the Philippines, the immense fortifications of Singapore Island and the voyage of the battleship *Prince of Wales* and 'other heavy units' to the Far East to bolster British power.

End of Empire

The Japanese struck simultaneously across one quarter of the earth's surface, from the Gulf of Siam [Thailand] to Pearl Harbor, on 7–8 December 1941. In Hawaii they left much of the American battlefleet smouldering scrap-iron; in the Philippines they destroyed or damaged most of MacArthur's B-17s on the ground; and two days later their bombers sent *Prince of Wales* and *Repulse* to the bottom of the Gulf of Siam, as their troops surged remorselessly down the western coast of the Malay Peninsula. Japanese photographers recorded success upon success, their troops liberating Hong Kong, Manila and Kuala Lumpur. The shock effect produced by Japan's advance was captured in the increasingly terse telegrams that Ian Morrison, *The Times*'s man in Singapore, transmitted back to London. On 26 January Morrison informed his office: 'Events moving so swiftly and in such fashion South Pacific am increasingly doubtful of wisdom moving Javawards both regards Telegraphic communications and continued personal mobility. Stop. Would you approve my going Burmawards instead if this should later seem wiser move?' The Japanese crossed the Johore Straits on to Singapore Island on 9 February 1942, and four days later the British surrendered. On 1 March the Japanese landed in Java, and seven days later Morrison cabled London, 'Obliged leave Java Australiawards.' Rangoon fell the same day, and by the beginning of May Japanese armies had reached the borders of India.

Of the many photographs the Japanese had taken during their triumphant surge, the ones with the greatest impact were those of the surrender of Singapore on 14 February 1942. Flashed around the world was the image of a nervous and exhausted British commander, General Arthur Percival, looking like a startled rabbit, surrendering the bastion of the British Empire to a tough-looking General Yamashita. Soon 40,000 of the 45,000 Indian troops who had surrendered in Singapore had joined the Japanese-sponsored Indian National Army. Throughout the Raj, British rule was shaken to its core by widespread rioting, disturbances which soon spread to Egypt, where young officers, including Abdul Nasser and Anwar Sadat, attempted a pro-Axis coup.

The moment of triumph, however, was also the moment of nemesis. Though a total ban was placed at first on the publication of pictures of Pearl Harbor in the United States, *Life* magazine devoted an edition to printing portrait photographs of those who had died. In the absence of visual confirmation the public assumed the worst. Opposition to America's entry into the war disappeared overnight, with recruiting depots jammed with young men literally fighting each other to enlist. In the Philippines General Douglas MacArthur's own news organisation, ably created and run by Mydans and Jacoby, supplied the pictures America craved of the handsome general defying the Japanese from the Bataan Peninsula and the island fortress of Corregidor. It sent of a wave of MacArthur mania through the United States, with elements of the Republican Party seriously considering nominating the general as a presidential candidate to run against Roosevelt in 1944.

The US and Australian navies blunted Japan's thrust in the Battle of the Coral Sea in May 1942. The US claimed two Japanese carriers sunk (in fact it was only one) and therefore allowed the publication of a photograph of the sinking of the USS *Lexington*, the major American casualty of the battle. A month later US journals carried spectacular pictures of the destruction of Japanese carriers and heavy cruisers in the Battle of Midway in the Central Pacific. Meanwhile the Australians had stopped a Japanese advance across the eastern part of the island of Papua New Guinea on the Kokoda Track, a gruelling ordeal filmed and photographed by Damien Parer, who won a Pulitzer Prize for this work in 1943. At the same time the US 1st Marine Division landed on Guadalcanal for a six months' attritional battle fought on land, sea and in the air. In December the Australian and American army forces converged on Buna, Gona and Sanananda on the north coast of Papua, where fighting bogged down in a slogging match in which heavy casualties were taken on both sides. With the initial crisis in the Pacific now averted, in December 1942 the US censors allowed the publication of photographs of Pearl Harbor on 7 December 1941, as a means of reminding the American people why they were at war.

In the Middle East and Russia, Germany was in the ascendant during the first ten months of 1942. PKs photographed the capture of Tobruk from the British at the end of June, the defeat of the Anglo-landing at Dieppe on 18 August, and the drive through the Ukraine to the outskirts of Stalingrad at the end of August. It was now that the tide began to turn. On 31 August Rommel, who had been turned by the German media into a superstar (a status also accorded him by the Allies), tried to manoeuvre his way from El Alamein to Cairo, only 60 miles distant. He was stopped on Alam Halfa Ridge by the British Eighth Army, now under the command of a new commander, General Bernard Montgomery. Like Rommel, Montgomery fostered a personality cult, giving cameramen every possible photo-opportunity to present him in a heroic light. The subsequent battle of El Alamein was depicted as a duel between Montgomery and Rommel, with the superior general winning, though the odds were stacked heavily in Montgomery's favour. Four days after Rommel began his retreat from the El Alamein position, Anglo–American forces landed in French North Africa, and advanced to the borders of Tunisia before meeting significant resistance.

Three weeks later Soviet forces attacked north and south of

Stalingrad, cutting off General Paulus's 6th Army in the ruins of the city. At first the situation did not seem too serious. German formations had been cut off on many occasions, and had always been rescued, or had become the focal points of counter-attacks which had bested the Soviets. An army under von Manstein tried to break through just before Christmas but, after some progress, bogged down. The Luftwaffe tried to maintain an air-lift but by mid-January 1943 the beleaguered 6th Army was running short of munitions, and many were starving. Inside Stalingrad the men of PK Hackl, particularly Lieutenant Benno Wundshammer, continued to send out photographs until the last airfield was overrun early on 22 January 1943. Goebbels did nothing to diminish the disaster of Paulus's surrender on 2 February. Instead picture essays heroised the defenders with comparisons to Leonidas's Spartans at Thermopylae and the Nationalist Spanish cadets at the Alcazar.

Year of endurance

For the allies 1943 began promisingly, but soon became a year of endurance. Meeting at Casablanca in January, Roosevelt and Churchill had sought to reassure Stalin of their solidarity by issuing a declaration that peace would only be made with the Axis on the basis of unconditional surrender. The Germans in particular took the western Allies at their word, Goebbels promising a meeting of cheering Gauleiters at the Berlin Sportzplatz a few days later that the Reich would now gear itself for total war. The Allied advance in North Africa bogged down in the winter rains so that Tunis was not taken until May. The campaign in Sicily in high summer was so badly handled that most of the defenders escaped to the Italian mainland, and the invasion of Italy itself ended up stalled against the formidable Gothic Line, which incorporated the monastery of Monte Cassino. The Soviets, too, had a hard time. An offensive after Stalingrad was bloodily smashed in a brilliant counter-attack by Erich von Manstein in March, a huge attritional battle was fought at Kursk in July and, though offensives in the autumn made ground, at the end of the year the Germans were still on Soviet soil. In the Pacific the Japanese imposed bloody battles on the allies for each step taken. By the year's end it seemed that Tokyo would never be reached. And in Burma the British began the year with a humiliating defeat in the Arakan, redeemed only by the exploits of Orde Wingate's Chindit raiding column. This particular operation suffered huge losses for very little gain, though it was given immense media attention, in the effort to prove that the British could operate just as effectively in the jungle as could the Japanese. Worried that the American public would lose its initial enthusiasm for the war, in September President Roosevelt decreed that, for the first time since 1898, *News* magazine could publish photographs of dead American soldiers. On 20 September 1943 *Life* magazine printed a photograph of three American bodies lying on the beach at Buna in January. It provoked ill-considered outrage, which *Life* editorials deftly turned to advantage.

Amongst the most difficult and dangerous assignments for photographers was the coverage of the Battle of the Atlantic and the bomber campaign. Anti-submarine patrols were gruelling and tedious while, by the summer of 1943, photographers in a u-boat had a less than one-in-two chance of surviving. Most photographs of sinking ships were taken by crewmen of other ships of the convoy, or by destroyer crews as their ships raced by to depth-charge the enemy. With the increasing effectiveness of Allied anti-submarine measures, the German media concentrated on picture stories of the life of u-boat crews, mainly photographed in St Nazaire or one of the other Atlantic bases.

The British bomber campaign had began in earnest in the spring of 1942 with the area bombing of German cities, referred to euphemistically as 'de-housing'. Because the British flew at night, pictures of actual operations were at a premium, particularly when they showed the white glow of a burning German city. The exception was the raid by 617 Squadron in May 1943 against the Roer dams, with pictures of the breached walls and the emptying dams appearing over the following days. The Americans flew during the day, so that operations of the us Eighth Air Force were well covered, though casualties were very heavy until the introduction of long-range P-51 fighters in December 1943. The Americans then engaged in a war of attrition with the Germans. Relatively little damage was done to German industry, but the Luftwaffe was slowly shot out of the sky, though at huge cost. For their part, the Germans published pictures showing mountains of wrecked aircraft and dead Allied air crew, and of resolute German civilians putting their lives together after yet another British terror raid.

D-Day

If 1943 was the year of endurance, then 1944 was to prove the year of victory. The Allies' media concentrated on projecting images of overwhelming strength – the build-up codenamed Bolero – while the German media ran specials on the construction of the Atlantic Wall, with reassuring pictures of Rommel, now Inspector General of Fortifications. On the evening of 5 June Allied supreme commander, General Dwight D. Eisenhower, drove to Greenham Common to wish the paratroopers of the 101st Airborne well. The photographer caught his face in the evening light as he spoke to the young soldiers, a mask of pain, concern and strain. Eisenhower well understood how important it was that the public of a democracy engaged in total war should be kept involved; this was the correspondent's job. He had written that journalists 'should be allowed to talk freely with officers and enlisted personnel and to see the machinery of war in operation in order to visualise and transmit to the public the conditions under which men from their countries are waging war against the enemy'.

Despite the fact that he believed the landings rested on a knife's edge, 558 correspondents, many of them photo-journalists, went in with the airborne forces just after midnight, or landed with the first amphibious waves just after dawn. It was Robert Capa's fate to land at the very worst place, Omaha Beach. He lay in the surf taking pictures of men huddling behind the tetrahedrons, images that came to exemplify the terror of that morning. Normandy turned into an attritional slogging match:

it took the Allies 11 weeks from the day of landing to liberate Paris, where snipers had remained behind to disrupt de Gaulle's entry. The Germans were now in full retreat for the frontier, with the Allies in hot pursuit, but logistics gave way. Given time to recover, the Germans were able to defeat Operation Market Garden, Montgomery's attempt to advance an armoured corps into the heart of the Reich along a corridor seized by airborne forces. And then on 16 December they counter-attacked through the Ardennes, driving the Americans back some 40 miles. To make matters worse, since 10 June, v1s, and then in September, v2s, had been crashing down on London, killing and injuring dozens each day. Early in January a depressed General Marshall, US Army Chief of Staff, wrote a memo in which he expressed doubt that the Allies had the strength to conquer Germany in the immediate future.

In the Pacific two great thrusts – MacArthur from New Guinea and Nimitz from Hawaii – converged on the Philippines and Formosa. US Navy cameramen were amongst the best in the world and in June captured the destruction of Japanese naval aviation in the Battle of the Philippine Sea, and paved the way for the capture of Saipan and Tinian, and more effective B-29 bombing of Japan. In October Douglas MacArthur returned to the Philippines, choosing to wade ashore, to give Carl Mydans a chance for a dramatic shot. By January the Americans were on Luzon again, and by the beginning of March had fought their way into Manila, though the city was virtually destroyed and 100,000 of its inhabitants killed. In the same month US Marines landed on Iwo Jima, where, by a stroke of luck, photographer Joe Rosenthal managed to snap a group of Marines in the process of raising the 'Stars and Stripes' on top of Mount Suribachi. This image was to prove one of the most famous pictures of war – of any war – yet taken. The capture of Iwo Jima had cost the Marines 7,000 dead, but thanks to its airstrip, the lives of many airmen were saved as they nursed their crippled B-29s back from Tokyo. In April the Americans landed on Okinawa, and encountered the full fury of the Kamikaze attacks, many of which were captured on camera.

Red Storm

In January, while the western Allies were still recovering from the German ardennes offensive, the Soviets launched a massive attack which carried their forces across the frozen plains of Poland from the Vistula to the Oder River, at a point only about 60 miles from Berlin. While the Soviets regrouped and resupplied, the western Allies fought their way slowly to the Rhine. Helped greatly by the capture of an undemolished railway bridge at Remegan, on 21 March they crossed in strength and, after breaking through a thin crust of resistance, struck into the heart of Germany. It was here they learned about the true nature of the Nazi regime, as they stumbled across concentration camps containing the pitiful remnants of European Jewry, the survivors of the extermination camps of the east. Many harrowing pictures were taken, but Margaret Bourke White's photograph of Buchenwald has an almost cinematic horror. The Russians already knew the true nature of the Nazi regime from first-hand experience. On 16 April Zhukov and Koniev launched their offensives towards Berlin.

Zhukov's initial onslaught was bloodily repulsed for three days on the Seelow Heights to the east overlooking the floodplain of the Oder, an indication that the Germans were still capable of extremely effective resistance. But Koniev's tanks, smashing in from the south-east, cracked the last defences. The Soviet thrusts met to the west of the city on 25 April, cutting it off from outside support, while infantry fought their way into the centre, street by street. On 30 April, the day Hitler killed himself, Russian soldiers climbed to the top of the Reichstag to hang a huge improvised Soviet flag over the city, a moment captured by TASS photographer Yevgeny Khaldei. In the basement the 5,000 German troops were still resisting fiercely, and would not surrender for another 48 hours, but it was vital the picture was in Moscow for the celebrations of 1 May.

The war had ended in Europe, but it was expected to go on in the Pacific until at least the end of 1946. After an attritional struggle along the India–Burma border General Bill Slim's XIV Army had outmanoeuvred and destroyed Japanese forces in central Burma and taken Rangoon on 3 May 1945. British forces in the Far East now prepared to land on the coast of Malaya in mid-September, while the Soviets had promised to strike into Manchuria at about the same time. Meanwhile American forces were preparing for a landing on Kyushu, the southernmost of Japan's home islands, in December, to be followed by another landing on Honshu in April 1946. Allied casualties in these operations were placed at more than one million, but even worse were projected Japanese civilian casualties, which were expected to be as high as ten million. By July 1945 American submarines had virtually cut Japan off from the outside world, while B-29s were immolating her cities in firestorms, but despite some tentative approaches through the still-neutral USSR there was no indication that the Japanese government was prepared to accept Allied terms.

The Basic Power of the Universe

Back in June 1943 *New York Times* science correspondent William L. Laurence had received a letter from the US Federal Office of Censorship requesting that he stop writing speculative articles about the possibilities of explosive devices from uranium. Laurence knew from that point on that the United States was developing an atomic bomb. As one of the few reporters who understood the process, on 16 July 1945 he was invited to witness the detonation of the first experimental bomb near Alamogordo in New Mexico. No reporter was allowed to fly in the *Enola Gay* on 6 August – the pictures of the Hiroshima bomb were taken by the B-29's tail gunner – but on 9 August he flew in one of the aircraft which observed *The Great Artiste* drop its bomb on Nagasaki. The news of the second bomb was received in Tokyo a short time later, at almost exactly the same time that high command in Manchuria reported massive Soviet attacks across the border. It was a combination of these events that broke the will of Japan's governing class. The following day the emperor accepted that surrender was now inevitable.

The Second World War was fought in an age before the

widespread availability of television, but magazines such as *Life*, *Picture Post* and *Signal* served a similar function. The war itself had called such magazines into existence: and they in turn bequeathed for posterity lasting images of the war. Far more than the newsreels, the images captured by photo-journalists created the reference points for future generations – from the dome of St Paul's rising above the ruins of London to the US Marines raising Old Glory on Iwo Jima.

Hot Spots in the Cold War
1946–62

The Bomb

In 1945 the most important news story was the atomic bomb –
a world-changing invention. Although the Americans had relied
on British help to build the bomb, they secured a monopoly on
it by rushing an act through Congress forbidding further
collaboration. Both the British and the Soviets then raced to
develop their own bombs. On 19 September 1949 an agitated
President Truman announced the detection of the first Russian
A-bomb test. The British finally detonated their own bomb in
the Monte Bello islands off the coast of Western Australia on 3
October 1952. By this time the United States had been working on
the development of a thermo-nuclear weapon, a hydrogen bomb,
for two years and detonated it on Eniwetok Atoll on 1 November
1952. Equivalent to 50 times the explosion that destroyed

Hiroshima, the blast atomised the island. America's lead was short-lived – on 12 August 1953 the Soviets also detonated an H-bomb. Prototypes of the American B-52 and the British Victor and Vulcan long-range bombers had already flown, and were joined in 1954 by the Soviets' long-range Tupolev TU 16 Badger Bomber. Over subsequent decades the western alliance and the Soviet bloc refined and developed increasingly sophisticated missile systems.

Many people now believed that the next war, the inevitable clash between the American and Soviet 'empires', would be an all-out nuclear war which might bring life on earth to an end. Yet analysts gradually realised that nuclear capability might prove a deterrent, rather than a stimulus, to war. The United States and the Soviet Union would fight by proxy through client states – a so-called 'Cold War' – and if they became directly involved in a conflict, they would consciously fight well below the threshold of their capabilities. There were to be no total wars, but at any one time a dozen or so limited wars caused by the interaction of Cold War tensions with the break-up of the colonial empires.

The photo-journalists of this generation were collectively the most experienced ever to cover conflict. Most had started in Abyssinia, Spain and China ten years earlier, and had then had the six years of the Second World War to hone their skills. They were used to wearing uniforms, and having military rank and military friends. They were men and women used to exercising self-censorship, which explains the curious quality of photo-journalism during this period – technically brilliant, but with a reluctance to follow up stories that might prove embarrassing to their close officer friends.

But they were more than ready to investigate the activities of other armies. American journalists were fascinated by the disintegrating British Empire. AP's Max Desfor photographed massacres in the Indian subcontinent and riots in Burma. The story that got the greatest coverage was the three-sided war being waged in Palestine, where the British were endeavouring to keep Jews and Arabs from each others' throats. On 22 July 1946 the Stern Gang, a Zionist terrorist organisation, blew up the King David Hotel, British military headquarters in Jerusalem, killing 91 and injuring 56, many of whom were hideously disfigured. It was the single worst terrorist act carried out against the British army, their wives and children and was followed by more bombings, reprisals, executions and murders. Stories from the *Herald Tribune*'s Homer Bigart, and pictures by Pulitzer prizewinner Frank E. 'Pappy' Noel of Jewish girls being marched under arrest by British soldiers, and of a pitched battle fought to prevent Jewish refugees disembarking from the American-crewed *Exodus*, turned American opinion against Britain, and hastened her decision to hand her mandate over to the United Nations. When Palestine was partitioned in January 1948, six Arab armies attacked the new state of Israel. Robert Capa was on hand to record what he believed might be a second Masada, the final stand of the Israelites against the Romans in AD 73. Yet Israel triumphed, thanks to a courage born of desperation, and a poorly trained Arab army.

American attention was also focused on China. In 1945 Theodore White resigned as China correspondent for *Time* after realising that its proprietor Henry Luce would never accept his analysis that Mao Tse-tung and his Communists were destined to supplant the Nationalists. Jack Beldon's 'China Shakes the World' confirmed White's views. Australian Wilfred Burchett, covering the Civil War from the Communist side, added his own incisive analysis, while Carl Mydans kept *Life* magazine supplied with photographs detailing the collapse of Nationalist forces. Despite the warnings, many Americans were shocked by Mao's triumph in 1949, fearing him as a tool of Russian Soviet imperialism.

Korea

When North Korean forces struck into South Korea on 25 June 1950, America and the West believed that a part of the Cold War had suddenly turned hot. Foremost among them was General Douglas MacArthur, commander of Allied occupation forces in Japan, a right-wing Republican dismayed by the Truman administration's abandonment of Chiang Kai-shek and Nationalist China to Mao Tse-tung's Communists. Knowing that Truman would be reluctant to send troops to Korea, on 27 June MacArthur flew to the front lines, accompanied by a planeload of reporters. MacArthur gave his entourage ideal photo-opportunities. He posed on a hilltop with shells landing in the distance as lines of retreating troops passed by – the hero General standing alone between the free world and the Communist hordes. MacArthur, who had spent two years as press liaison officer in Washington, knew what press photographers wanted. To firm up America's commitment to a ground war in Korea, MacArthur encouraged *Life* and *Newsweek* to print photos of the bodies of GIS who had been murdered by the North Koreans during their advance. Washington was aghast, cabling 'due to decidedly unfavourable public reaction to recent atrocity pictures and pictures of wounded men in battle areas, strongly recommend no release of this type of picture in battle area'. But MacArthur understood the American public. *Life* and *Newsweek* were inundated with letters complaining that the Truman administration had been caught by surprise, and now had to fight the war properly. As one bereaved father wrote, 'Our sons were not given a fair fighting chance for their lives.'

MacArthur refused to impose censorship on reporters in Korea, trusting their experience and judgement. But within weeks there were more than 300 of them, not all willing to support his position. *Picture Post* sent left-wing commentator James Cameron and photographer Bert Hardy, who had distinguished himself during the London blitz. The British in Korea began ferreting out some embarrassing stories. As they advanced the North Koreans infiltrated guerrillas into columns of refugees. Rumours persisted that panicky GIS had opened fire on them, also killing civilians. Cameron and Hardy photographed the aftermath, and American caption writers tried to impose blame on North Koreans. MacArthur clamped down on Cameron and Hardy (both left the peninsula before the end of the year) but allowed 'trustworthy' correspondents great latitude. Two years later Margaret Bourke White covered a counter-insurgency campaign well behind the front line, involving torture and summary executions, but exercised self-censorship. It was not until 1990, the fortieth anniversary of the outbreak of the conflict, that

American veterans came forward to confess to shooting people they knew were civilians.

By 5 August 1950 US forces had been pushed back to a small perimeter around the port of Pusan in south-east Korea, but reinforcements were beginning to arrive – not just from the United States but from Britain, Australia, Canada and other UN members. Throughout August and early September UN forces fought off North Korean attempts to eliminate the Pusan pocket, while MacArthur prepared his counter-stroke. At dawn on 15 September landing craft piloted by Japanese sailors ferried the US 1st Marine Division through the treacherous currents and reefs of the west coast of Korea to the high sea wall at the port of Inchon, 150 miles north of the battlefront, and only 20 miles from Seoul. Surprise was total – even the United States navy had deep misgivings about the feasibility of the operation. In the landing craft photographers snapped Marines scaling rope ladders up the sea wall. Marguerite Higgins, correspondent for the *Herald Tribune*, came ashore with the fifth wave. In her best-selling *War in Korea*, published in 1951, she wrote, 'We struck the sea wall hard at a place where it crumbled into a canyon. The bullets were whining persistently, spattering the water around us. We clambered over the high steel sides of the boat.' The 1st Marine Division struck north for Kimpo airfield, while 7th Division troops, who had followed the Marines ashore, secured Inchon and headed south.

Meanwhile 150 miles south, US 8th Army broke out of the Pusan perimeter, the 1st Cavalry Division driving north to meet up with the troops advancing inland from Inchon. On

26 September the Americans entered Seoul, the capital of South Korea, and rolled north of the 38th parallel, the old demarcation line. They took Pyongyang, North Korea's capital, on 20 October, and reached the Yalu River, the border between Korea and Manchuria, on 26 October. In the midst of an American triumph *Newsweek* published a photograph showing a grief-stricken GI whose buddy had just been killed, being comforted by a friend. It had been taken two months earlier by Signal Corps photographer Sergeant Al Chang, when US forces were reeling back to the Pusan perimeter. The picture served to remind the Americans just how far they had come, but it also had a much deeper resonance with a generation which had had more direct experience of war than any other Americans of the 20th century.

During the advance north MacArthur received intelligence that if his forces approached the Yalu River, the Chinese would attack. MacArthur thought Mao was bluffing, and so did the CIA. But on 25 November 180,000 Chinese troops hit the right flank of the 8th Army, threatening to envelop it. Simultaneously 120,000 Chinese troops attacked and surrounded the US 1st Marine Division, up in the north-east of Korea near the Chosin reservoir. The Marines' only hope was to conduct a withdrawal south to Hungnam. Commander of the division, Major General Oliver Smith, told his troops they were not retreating but 'attacking in another direction'. Another Marine told a correspondent, 'Remember, whatever you write, that this was no retreat. All that happened was we found more Chinese behind us than in front of us. So we about-faced and attacked.'

David Douglas Duncan, a photographer who had covered the

1st Marine Division during the Second World War, managed to hitch a lift on a supply flight to Chosin, and once more attached himself to the division. With temperatures dropping to minus 34 degrees centigrade, Duncan had to hold the camera next to his body to thaw it out before taking pictures. Despite constant Communist harassment, the Marines trudged into Hungnam in the second week of December, in time for Duncan's photographs to be published in *Life*'s Christmas issue, in a spread entitled 'This is War!'. Duncan, celebrating the Marines' retreat as an epic event, wrote: 'As they moved down the road the wounded and frozen got to ride. The dead also rode – tied upon trucks and trailers. Behind them – the shuffle of their feet following the rising and falling beat of a tragic rhythm – walked the living.'

The retreat finally ended about 30 miles south of Seoul on 25 January 1951. MacArthur attacked again in March and April, driving Communist forces back to the 38th parallel. With the enemy on the run again, he could not resist the chance to dictate foreign policy to the White House. Out of step with Cold War politics, he continued to think in traditional American crusading total war terms, announcing to a senator that 'in war there is no substitute for victory'. When MacArthur unilaterally demanded the surrender of the Chinese Communist commander, and hinted that the United States might be about to use atomic bombs, President Truman had to sack him. For a time it looked like the end of Harry Truman – it was widely assumed that MacArthur would easily secure the nomination as presidential candidate for the Republican Party in the elections of 1952. In the event the Republicans selected Dwight D. Eisenhower,

MacArthur's former chief-of-staff. The war settled down into a stalemate, the belligerents eventually opting for a safe compromise in July 1953, with a division of the peninsula into North and South Korea.

Indo-China

Conventional war had become too dangerous a game, at least for super-powers, but Mao's revolutionary approach was now inspiring guerrilla insurgencies throughout the world. Western governments responded with varying degrees of success. In Indo-China the Viet Minh, a coalition of Vietnamese nationalists and communists led by Mao protégé Ho Chi Minh, had started to wage a clandestine war against the Japanese when they occupied the French Colony in 1941. When the French returned in 1945 Ho looked to the Americans for support, taking their anti-European imperialist rhetoric at face value. Disappointed, the Viet Minh began a campaign against the French. It began to have real success once the Communists had taken power in China and could begin supplying the Viet Minh directly across the border.

By 1953 the French still held the cities and the main communication routes, at least in daytime, but had been unable to bring the Viet Minh to battle in the open. In November 1953 paratroopers of the French Foreign Legion, supported by some indigenous troops, set up a base around an airfield at Dien Bien Phu on the Laotian border, right in the middle of Viet Minh supply lines. The French hoped to bring on a pitched battle, and they succeeded, but the Viet Minh won. On 7 May 1954, 10,000 survivors surrendered, half of whom were wounded. Another

5,000 lay in graves around the airfield. They still held most of Indo-China, and had nearly 300,000 troops in the field, but morale in Paris collapsed.

On 25 May, 50 miles to the east at Nam Dinh in the Red River valley, Robert Capa and *Time–Life* correspondent John Mecklin went visiting outposts with a French colonial patrol. Just before 15:00 hours the patrol made contact with the Viet Minh near Doai Than, exchanging some desultory fire. Capa was bored. He climbed up on the road saying, 'I'm going up the road a little bit. Look for me when you get started again.' A few minutes later there was firing and an explosion, and then a lieutenant said, 'Le photographe est mort.' Mecklin raced ahead and at a bend in the road found Capa on his back, the stump of his shattered left leg about a foot from a hole blown in the earth by the explosion, a gaping hole in his chest, and a camera clutched in his left hand. He had taken his last picture a few minutes earlier.

Algeria

The defeat at Dien Bien Phu led to a French withdrawal from Indo-China, and the division of the three Vietnamese provinces of Tonking, Annam and Cochin China into two new states, North and South Vietnam. In Algeria, which France ruled as part of metropolitan France, the Front de Libération Nationale (FLN) began a revolutionary insurgency, inspired by the example of both Mao and Ho Chi Minh. The French had learned hard lessons in Indo-China. They sealed the borders with Morocco and Tunisia, divided the countryside up into the 'quadrillage' – killing zones demarcated by bloc-houses and barbed-wire fences – and set up quick-reaction helicopter-borne forces. It took the deployment of about half the French army, leaving some 10,000 French and 70,000 Algerian dead, but by 1958 the activities of the FLN in the countryside had been severely curtailed. Forced out of the countryside, the FLN began a terror campaign in Algiers, bombing night clubs and restaurants, and killing *pieds noirs* (Algerians of French descent) at random. The 10th Colonial Parachute Division took over security in the city, and at the orders of its commander, General Massu, rounded up thousands of suspects, who were then subjected to intensive interrogation, including torture. About 3,000 Algerians arrested by the Foreign Legion Paratroopers simply disappeared.

In a purely military sense the policy worked – the incidence of bombing declined rapidly – but the conscience of the West was becoming uneasy. The American correspondent Georgette 'Dickey' Chapelle, who had covered Iwo Jima and Okinawa with the US Marines, managed to make contact with the FLN, and travelled to Algeria dressed as a veiled Muslim woman. She took pictures of the results of French air raids, one which killed 18 shepherds including an infant boy, and gave faces and names to the Algerians. Investigative journalism of this sort – the French Left was also asking questions – led to the collapse of the Fourth Republic and the emergence of Charles de Gaulle, who offered Algeria self-determination by referendum.

The Savage Wars of Peace

The French lost their wars in Indo-China and Algeria, in part because they were outfought, in part because they didn't really understand the media's power to shape public attitudes. The British fought much smaller wars during this period, but were generally more successful. Between 1948 and 1960 they faced an insurgency amongst the Chinese squatter population in Perak, which soon spread to other parts of Malaya. Initial police attempts to round up 'bandits' failed, in large part because the police consisted of three distinct elements – the Malayan Police, who had been utterly demoralised by three and a half years of Japanese internment, and the Indian and Palestine police, who had been drafted in to help restore the situation in Malaya.

It was not until the arrival of Arthur Young, a former head of the Metropolitan Police, and the appointment of Brigadier Douglas Henchley as his chief of staff, that the three elements were forced into co-operation. At Henchley's urging, a fast promotion scheme was established for young Chinese policemen to rise rapidly to the rank of inspector. Once the British had a substantial Chinese police force, the flow of intelligence on the activities of the Communist guerrillas improved remarkably. This information enabled a more discriminatory use of force. The population was moved from the most disaffected areas and resettled in new villages, and the now-isolated guerrillas could be hunted down with less fear of civilian casualties.

The new Supremo, General Gerald Templar, claimed that Britain had simply reversed Mao's doctrine and was winning back 'hearts and minds'. Military operations were supported by a sophisticated media campaign which showed the Communist guerrillas being pushed further and further into the jungles of the central highlands, where they were hunted down by long-range patrols, including the SAS. Had the media been less co-operative the campaign might have been derailed. Templar's 'hearts and minds' did not mean being nice to people at all costs. If Chinese or Malays were discovered smuggling ammunition, for example, they were tried and sentenced to death by hanging. It was a fate meted out to several hundred Communist sympathisers, some of them idealistic young women who had agreed to smuggle grenades under their sarongs. And once the British had pushed the guerrillas into the jungle, they forcibly removed the Aboriginal tribes to camps on the coast, where they concentrated them. In a replay of the events in South Africa 50 years earlier, about 10,000 of the 100,000 deportees died of simple communicable diseases within a few months. Templar was lucky – there was no Dickey Chapelle in Malaya.

Britain also faced an insurgency in Kenya, where the Mau Mau society, a terrorist organisation recruited mainly from the Kikuyu tribe, began murdering other Africans and a much smaller number of European farmers. The Mau Mau frequently hacked their victims to death with machetes, killing entire families, which made it easy for British journalists to demonise them. By 1955 Britain had deployed 10,000 troops, pushing the Mau Mau into the Aberdare Forest and the Mt Kenya region. Britain had killed about 10,000 terrorists in battle, but had another 24,000 Kikuyu concentrated in camps, where there were frequent violent disturbances. In addition, the British rigorously imposed the death penalty for possession of firearms. Some 1,200 Kikuyu went to the scaffold, sometimes several at once. Questions were asked in the British parliament about British counter-insurgency operations in Kenya but the Mau Mau had no real sympathisers in the West.

In Malaya and Kenya the British had been lucky, fighting against easily identifiable minorities like the Chinese squatters or the Kikuyu. In Cyprus they had to protect a Turkish minority, about 20 per cent of the population, from the Greek majority, virtually all of whom wanted 'enosis' (union) with Greece. Penetration of the Greek Cypriot community proved impossible. In desperation, some British soldiers used excessive violence to interrogate suspects, stories which soon reached the British press. The situation in Cyprus showed that there were limits to the British approach to countering an insurgency, particularly when the insurgency had widespread popular support.

Suez

In autumn 1956 the French and British joined forces to strike a killer blow to Arab nationalism, a force undermining their positions in the Middle East. Israel, working in co-operation with Britain and France, attacked into the Sinai on 29 October, which elicited an Anglo-French ultimatum to both Israel and Egypt. When the Egyptians refused the ceasefire, Anglo-French warships and aircraft began bombarding Egyptian air bases and other military installations. It went on for five days, enough time for American opinion to harden and threaten Britain and France with economic collapse if they went ahead. Thinking the Americans were bluffing, Anglo-French forces landed at Port Said on 5 November, and within 48 hours discovered that the United States had pulled the plug on the pound and the franc.

Both nations were forced into a humiliating withdrawal, acknowledging at last that they really were living in the American century.

If the French and British empires were having problems, so too were the Russians. For nearly a decade Voice of America had been beaming promises to the people of Eastern Europe that if they rose up to throw off Soviet chains, America would help them. On 23 October 1953 Hungary did precisely that. Crowds tore down statues of Stalin, and stormed the barracks of the secret police, killing many. On 25 October a pro-western government was formed by Imre Nagy, and western journalists, including Dickey Chapelle, flooded in. Soviet forces – some 200,000 troops and 2,500 tanks – surrounded Budapest and attacked on 1 November. Fighting raged through the city for four days, in which 7,000 Russians and 25,000 Hungarians were killed. The Soviets arrested Dickey Chapelle and held her for three months, but not before she was able to get her best photographs into the West.

Cuba

The United States was having problems, too. In December 1956 a ragtag band of would-be Maoist revolutionaries led by two young upper-class lawyers, Fidel and Raul Castro, and an Argentine doctor they had met in Mexico, Che Guevara, landed in the south of Cuba. Fidel Castro knew the area. The Sierra Mastre mountains were nearby, and he intended these to become his Shansi Province. But Castro would not slavishly follow Mao. He knew that Cuba's 1896 revolution had been achieved largely by the manipulation of American power, and he knew that Cuban dictator Batista, though supported by the American Mafia, had few friends in the United States. Using contacts in Havana, in February 1957 Castro offered exclusive rights to the *New York Times* for the coverage of his revolution. This proved so successful that soon American television companies were sending teams into the Sierra Mastre to film documentaries. With long hair and beards, the Castro boys and Che appeared wildly romantic, and soon their faces filled the photo magazines of the West. More than 3,000 idealistic American college students travelled down to Cuba to join Castro's growing bands. Spanish-language stations in Florida carried stories about the Castros, which could be picked up in Cuba, only 90 miles away. In desperation Batista sent more and more troops into the Sierra Mastre and fewer and fewer came back – they simply defected *en masse* to the revolution. On 1 January 1959 the revolutionary army entered Havana, two years after landing in Cuba and about 30 years before Castro had thought it possible.

The Cuban revolution was a clear demonstration of the power of photographic images to motivate people to bring an unpopular regime crashing to the ground. People did die, but not in large numbers, and the atmosphere was almost light-hearted. In its aftermath Che Guevara developed the Foco Theory of revolution, the idea that throughout the world there were regimes tottering to collapse, which required little more than a gentle push from a small band of revolutionaries who would act as the focal point for all the forces of discontent in a society. The new American president, John F. Kennedy, believed him, established the Peace Corps and Green Berets Special Forces, and set forth to do battle with Focoists and other revolutionaries throughout the world.

The Americans also decided that the Castro regime was like a Communist cancer cell in the western hemisphere which had to be eliminated. An economic blockade and a ludicrous American-backed invasion by Cuban exiles in 1961 forced Castro into the arms of the Soviet Union. In October 1962 a photograph from a U2 spy plane showing the construction of Soviet intermediate-range missile sites in Cuba pushed the United States and Russia to the brink of nuclear war. It was only by good luck, not by good management, that the world survived. The United States and the USSR remained locked in combat, but now remembered it would have to be by proxy.

From Vietnam to Afghanistan
1963–89

Just after 9am on 11 June 1963 Malcolm Browne, the 32-year-old
head of the AP's Saigon Bureau, waited at the intersection of
Phan Dinh Phung and Le Van Duyet streets, near the city's main
Buddhist pagoda. During the previous months South Vietnam
had been rocked by Buddhist demonstrations protesting the rule
of President Diem, which had culminated on 8 May in the South
Vietnamese police quelling a demonstration in Hue by shooting
eight Buddhists. Browne's Buddhist contacts had promised him a
unique photo-opportunity. At about 9.20 he was in exactly the
right spot to photograph the self-immolation of Tich Quang Duc,
an old Buddhist priest who hoped that his death would be the
catalyst for change. He would not have been disappointed. When
Madam Nhu, Diem's cruelly beautiful sister-in-law, saw the

pictures, she said she would welcome more Buddhist 'barbecues'. 'Let them burn, and we shall clap our hands,' she said. Browne's picture was also seen by President Kennedy who told Henry Cabot Lodge, US Ambassador to Saigon, that America 'would have to do something about that regime'. On 1 November Diem was killed in a CIA-organised coup, but instead of a stable military regime emerging, South Vietnam plunged into chaos, exacerbated by the activities of the Viet Cong, Communist insurgents who already controlled much of the heavily populated Mekong Delta.

Nearly three years earlier the secretary of the Soviet Communist Party, Nikita Khrushchev, had flung down a gauntlet to the United States declaring that 'the USSR and its allies would support just wars of liberation and popular uprising', and President Kennedy had picked it up. He saw South Vietnam as the chosen field of battle; Kennedy was preparing to reinforce the 16,000 advisers already in Vietnam when he was assassinated on 22 November 1963. His successor, President Lyndon Johnson, accelerated the build-up after an apparent naval clash in the Gulf of Tonkin in August 1964, and a Viet Cong attack on a base at Pleiku on 7 February 1965. The following day American warplanes bombed North Vietnam, the beginning of 'Rolling Thunder'. For the next eight years – at times intermittently – the USAF was to drop more bombs on the North than had been dropped by all the belligerents in the Second World War. Both sides developed media campaigns: the Americans attempted to portray themselves as very much stronger and more effective than they actually were, while the VC pretended to be hapless victims.

Escalation

The air campaign was the prelude to massive reinforcement. First in were the Marines, who landed at Da Nang in the north of South Vietnam on 8 March 1965. Journalists who had covered the Second World War and Korea saw Vietnam in much the same terms as the earlier conflicts. David Douglas Duncan, who, though now in his early fifties, covered the war for *Life*, wrote of one battle that the Marines viewed it 'in the same light as Tarawa and Iwo Jima and are proud and happy to have held this hillock in a remote land'. Dickey Chapelle also arrived in Da Nang, and covered five operations with the Marines before she was killed by a land-mine on 18 October 1965, the first American woman photographer to be killed in action. Some of the best action footage was taken by Larry Burrows, a British photographer, who as an 18-year-old laboratory assistant had on 7 June 1944 inadvertently destroyed most of Robert Capa's D-Day pictures. In the spring of 1965 Burrows came close to matching his hero's exploits in a picture essay for *Life*, 'One Ride with Yankee Papa 13', the story of the unsuccessful attempt of a Marine helicopter crew to rescue the crew of a downed helicopter.

Remembering the good relationship that had existed between the military and journalists in Korea, the American army made no attempt to impose censorship in South Vietnam. It would not have been legally possible. Instead, the US military made press accreditation to South Vietnam almost ludicrously easy, and then provided transport and protection once in theatre. Simultaneously picture agencies and magazines were offering substantial premiums for good war photographs. A much younger generation of photo-journalists was soon flooding into Vietnam, people born in the 1930s and 40s who had no direct experience of war, and sometimes very little experience as journalists. Significantly there was also a large number of young women, some of whom had come to Vietnam following boyfriends, and who started freelancing for various agencies. Driven by cut-throat competition for sensational pictures, some of this new generation concentrated on the one per cent of war which is unadulterated horror, removing it from the context of boredom, comradeship and humour – sometimes black – which forms the backdrop of any conflict.

There were several different wars going on in Vietnam simultaneously. Battles in the lightly populated central high-lands against regular Viet Cong units, and units of the North Vietnamese Army, became very much like battles on Okinawa or Iwo Jima, where American firepower was brought to bear against heavily entrenched Vietnamese positions. But counter-guerrilla operations in heavily populated areas like the Mekong Delta or the provinces around Saigon invariably produced civilian casualties, and pictures of dead women and children were soon commonplace. These images were not solely responsible for undermining domestic support for the war, but they contributed to the process. Much more significant were announcements in late 1967 that the war was as good as won, and that the next couple of years would be devoted to mopping-up operations.

Tet Offensive

In January 1968 VC units struck the Americans and their allies simultaneously, from the citadel of Hue to the US embassy compound in Saigon. For a few days it seemed they might overrun the country, but then American firepower began turning the tide. It was a bloodbath, a massive tactical defeat for the VC who were virtually wiped out in some areas. But at the strategic level, Tet was a massive Communist victory, for it broke the will of the Americans to carry on. On 1 February 1968 Eddie Adams, a 35-year-old AP correspondent, joined an NBC camera team to follow South Vietnamese soldiers marching a captured VC guerrilla down a street. Adams kept photographing the prisoner 'in case someone were to take a swing at him or he fell or whatever … when some guy walked over and pulled a pistol out.' Adams pressed the shutter and caught the instant Brigadier General Nguyen Ngoc Loan, commander of the Vietnam National Police, shot the prisoner dead. The picture – a middle-aged general killing the young suspect, whose hands were tied behind his back – had an immense impact. It seemed wanton cold-blooded murder and won Adams a Pulitzer prize.

The Long Goodbye

Deciding not to run for the presidency in 1968, Johnson devoted his efforts to negotiating an honourable peace, an effort the new American president in 1969, Richard Nixon, was going to continue. Protests in America were now widespread, with opposition to the war reaching fever pitch with the *Cleveland Plain Dealer*'s publication on 20 November 1969 of Ronald L. Haeberle's pictures of women and children about to be gunned down by troops of Lt Calley's detachment at My Lai, on 16 May 1968.

The only strategy seemed to be a withdrawal linked to the creation of a more effective indigenous army for South Vietnam, a process known as Vietnamization. In an effort to buy time, on 30 April 1970 the Americans struck across the border into Cambodia, wrecking VC logistic bases. It made perfect military sense, but in the colleges of the United States it provoked widespread protests, which culminated on 4 May with the Ohio National Guard opening fire on some 600 demonstrating students, killing four, at last giving credence to the protestors' aim of repatriating the war.

In 1965 the United States had committed a very good army to Vietnam, but by the early 1970s the war had taken its toll. Discipline was breaking down, drug-taking was increasing, and the Army relied almost entirely on firepower, now directed with very little discrimination. However, the most striking image of the latter part of the conflict was not the result of American firepower, but of Vietnamization, when South Vietnamese aircraft mistakenly napalmed the village of Trang Bang on 8 June 1972, sending children with their flesh alight running for their lives. After so many dead and maimed it was surprising that the picture had the impact it did, one American newsman announcing to the American public that his heart was about to break. Nine months later the last US combat soldiers left Vietnam, Nixon and Kissinger having, through negotiation, backed by the heavy bombing of Hanoi, secured North Vietnam's agreement to a compromise peace. After 12 years the war was once again a largely Vietnamese affair.

Israeli Blitzkrieg

While the United States was mired in Vietnam, the Middle East had erupted in conflict. At 8am on 5 June 1967 Israeli warplanes had swept down on Egyptian air bases, destroying much of the Egyptian airforce on the ground. The Israelis refuelled and re-armed, and hit airfields in Jordan, Syria and western Iraq. Three Israeli armoured divisions then struck into the Sinai, bypassing Egyptian defensive positions, to inflict a crushing defeat on the Egyptian armoured reserve in central Sinai. Meanwhile, after a hard fight, Israeli paratroopers captured the old city of Jerusalem from Jordan's Arab Legion, while other Israeli columns drove Jordanian forces from all Arab territory on the west bank of the Jordan. On 9 June the Israelis struck again, heliborne forces supported by ground attack aircraft overrunning the 3,000-foot-high Golan Heights from which Syrian artillery had dominated much of northern Israel. War had come so suddenly that most journalists did not reach Israel until 7–8 June, and Israeli forces moved so rapidly that few were able to catch up with them. The world's press relied on Israeli images, which were oddly reminiscent of the way German photographers had portrayed the Wehrmacht's 1940 campaign. One image above all others came to symbolise Israel's new-found reputation for military excellence: the defence minister Moshe Dayan, whose piratical black patch helped convey the sense that he was an experienced warrior.

Terrorists and Freedom Fighters

For a short time Israel believed it had at last attained security, but within months the Popular Front for the Liberation of Palestine

(PFLP), a breakaway group from the Palestinian Liberation Organisation, had launched a worldwide terror campaign against Israeli interests. El Al aircraft were highjacked and attacks made on Israeli airports, but the incident which gained the most attention was Black September's kidnapping of the Israeli team at the Munich Olympics on 5 September 1972. Very much against their better judgement the West Germans launched a hurriedly planned and under-rehearsed rescue operation, which resulted in five terrorists and nine athletes dead.

Yom Kippur

Israel now concentrated its intelligence efforts on combating terrorism, so much so that it failed to detect Egyptian and Syrian moves to avenge the defeat of 1967. On 6 October 1973 at just after 2pm, 2,000 Egyptian guns opened fire on the Bar Lev line, the Israeli positions along the east bank of the Suez Canal. Simultaneously five Syrian divisions attacked the Israelis on the Golan Heights. Israeli aircraft counter-attacked, only to be shot out of the sky by sophisticated anti-aircraft missiles which the Soviet Union had tested in North Vietnam, and then supplied to its Arab friends. Israeli tanks, too, were knocked out or disabled by new anti-tank missiles, particularly the wire-guided Sagger. By 9 October, with Israel's situation looking increasingly desperate, the prime minister, Mrs Golda Meir, gave the order to assemble and activate Israel's nuclear weapons at Diamona in the Negev, a decision which was leaked to the USA. The prospect of the war going nuclear had the desired effect. Over the next two weeks giant C141 and C5 transports conducted the largest airlift of military hardware the world had so far seen, allowing Israel to counter-attack and redress the balance. An uneasy peace with Egypt was eventually negotiated, with an Israeli withdrawal from the Sinai, but the problem of Palestine remained unsolved.

Defeat in South-East Asia

In saving Israel the United States had used up much of its reserves of material and munitions, and stocks were at an all-time low when in March 1975 the North Vietnamese Army launched what was intended to be a limited offensive into the northern part of South Vietnam. To its surprise South Vietnamese resistance evaporated and on 30 March North Vietnamese tanks rolled into Da Nang. The Saigon government pleaded for American support, but without a reserve supply of munitions, and with public opinion making direct involvement impossible, nothing could be done. Capitalising on this unexpected victory, in mid-April North Vietnam launched an all-out offensive to eradicate the south.

Meanwhile the Khmer Rouge had closed around Phnom Penh, the Cambodian capital. On 17 April, amidst scenes of panic, the Khmer Rouge entered Phnom Penh, western journalists, who had remained behind photographing semi-hysterical fanatics, ordering the population out of the city. Cambodia had been wracked by civil war since the American incursion in 1970, but now the country was going to descend into a nightmare as the Khmer Rouge returned the population to the year zero, so that a new and pure society could be built. Thirteen days later the North Vietnamese Army rolled into Saigon, as Vietnamese who had served with or been employed by the Americans fought to break into the compound of the American embassy for a place on the last evacuation helicopters.

America in the mid-1970s was in a state of shock. Defeated in South-East Asia, it also faced threats in the western hemisphere. In 1967 the Bolivian army, with the assistance of American special forces, had run Che Guevara to earth, but in the process had turned him into a revolutionary saint. In 1973 the CIA had snuffed out what looked like a left-wing takeover in Chile, supporting a military coup which toppled President Allende. Unfortunately Allende had been democratically elected and a journalist had been able to take one last photograph showing a bravely determined president wearing a helmet and carrying an automatic rifle, preparing to go down fighting in defence of democratic freedoms. Together Che and Allende inspired a generation of insurgents in Latin and South America, which the United States attempted to fight, sometimes enlisting some unsavoury allies.

Revolution in Iran

The main challenge continued to come from the Middle East. The linchpin of American power in the Middle East was oil-rich Iran, ruled by a pro-American Shah who had been attempting to westernise and modernise his country. But the programme had gone too quickly for some and not quickly enough for others. His regime faced threats from both Islamic fundamentalists and left-wing radicals, which the Shah suppressed. In 1979, when the army refused to fire on vast street demonstrations, the Shah and his entourage fled, and was replaced by the violently anti-western theocracy of fundamentalist Ayatollahs. Early the following year revolutionary students stormed the US embassy, and held hostage some 400 embassy personnel. In April the United States launched a clandestine mission to snatch the hostages from under the noses of the revolutionary guards in the heart of Tehran. It ended in bloody failure at a secret landing strip in the Iranian desert, when a C-130 collided with a helicopter. The first the world knew of the operation were pictures from Iran, showing bearded Ayatollahs grinning with satisfaction as they picked through the wreckage. It was another major humiliation for the United States, and spelled the end of Jimmy Carter's presidency.

Early in 1981 America's new president, Ronald Reagan, embarked on a programme of rebuilding the United States armed forces, but the miasma of Vietnam seemed to bedevil all efforts. On 6 June 1982, in an effort to be free of continuing cross-border incursions, Israel had struck into Lebanon, increasingly the home of Palestinian terrorist groups. It had taken Israeli armour only six days to get to Beirut, but a prolonged siege ensued, in which pictures of the Israeli bombardment began to turn world opinion in favour of the Arab cause. An Israeli withdrawal was eventually brokered, with an international peace-keeping force drawn from the USA, France, Italy and Britain entering Beirut. On 23 October 1983 a member of the Iranian-backed Hezbollah (Party of God) drove a truck loaded with 2,000 pounds of explosives directly at US Marine Corps HQ at Beirut airport, killing 241 and seriously injuring 71. The French were hit at the same time, incurring 73 dead and wounded, but it was photographs of the American disaster which flashed around the world.

Operation Urgent Fury

Forty-eight hours later US forces landed on the Caribbean island of Grenada, which US intelligence believed was being taken over by revolutionary Marxists, supported by Cubans. The ostensible objective was to rescue US students at an American campus on the island, although commentators believed that the Beirut bomb had accelerated the operation. As this was the first major US operational deployment since Vietnam, the press was tightly controlled. The US deployed overwhelming strength against an enemy which numbered about 500, armed only with light weapons. With the exception of the landing of the Marines on the eastern side of the island, the operation was a fiasco, with special forces losing seven Black Hawk helicopters, while the Rangers and 82nd Airborne were pinned down by a handful of Cuban construction workers. But it took more than three years for the full story to seep out. At the time photographs approved for publication showed 'Urgent Fury' as an outstanding success, though the ground commander in Grenada, Major General Norman Schwarzkopf, knew that the US military had not yet recovered from Vietnam.

Britain struggles back

In the early 1980s, when some American generals despaired of ever seeing a US military renaissance, a few took heart from the British experience. In Beirut on 23 October 1983, for example, the British base had been attacked as well, but alert British sentries had shot the truck bomber dead and then deactivated the explosives, events which had been kept very quiet. But Britain's own military reputation had stood at a low ebb at Suez, just 27 years earlier, and it had been a long climb back. In the 1960s and 70s Britain had steadily withdrawn from commitments, sometimes very hastily, as in Aden, and had refused to take any on, even when the moral case was overwhelming, as when former colonies collapsed into chaos. In Africa, for example, when Nigeria had fallen into civil war in 1967, the British government ignored a well-orchestrated press campaign to help the stricken breakaway province of Biafra, which the federal government proceeded to starve into submission. Nor did the British do more than offer their good offices to the feuding successors to the Raj, India and Pakistan, who fought short but intense wars in 1965 and 1971.

The Troubles

By the early 1970s Britain seemed to have slipped back into the role of a peripheral and declining European state, beset by its own domestic difficulties. In Northern Ireland the forces of Irish nationalism had re-emerged, with an urban-guerrilla splinter group of the IRA, the Provisional IRA, conducting increasingly effective operations, including a bombing campaign. British troops, who had been sent to the province in 1969 to protect Catholics from Protestants, soon found themselves the target of attack, and responded in a heavy-handed way which made the situation worse. During the long war in Northern Ireland the British army honed its military skills, from small unit actions (section and platoon attacks), force security, special force operations and media management. By the early 1980s, over a quarter of a million troops had passed through Northern Ireland, which was providing excellent training, but which passed relatively unnoticed by the world outside.

The Falklands

In 1980, within days of the failure of Operation Eagle's Claw, Britain's shadowy Special Air Service (SAS) came momentarily into the limelight, ending a terrorist siege of the Iranian embassy at London's Prince's Gate in a spectacular but coldly efficient fashion. It was the first time most of the public had ever heard of, let alone seen, the SAS and it sent a ripple of excitement through a public which had had very little to be proud of, at least in a military sense, for nearly a generation. It might have been a passing blip, but for the Argentine invasion of the Falkland Islands on 2 April 1982. Overjoyed with the success of the operation, Argentine cameramen photographed Royal Marine prisoners being forced by gun-waving Argentine special forces to lie on their stomachs on the road outside Government House in Port Stanley. When the photograph was published in Britain, it provoked outrage, ending any real possibility of a negotiated peace. In the ensuing conflict, the press were kept tightly controlled, in part an inevitable response to the lessons of Vietnam, in part the sheer impossibility of it being otherwise, given that they were utterly dependent on the British armed forces 8,000 miles from home. The Falklands was a clean campaign. There were only 2,000 civilians on the islands, and by and large the Argentinians behaved correctly. Only three islanders were killed, when the British accidentally dropped a shell on to Stanley. The land battles were mainly fought at night, and so the photographs tended to be before and after shots of combat, in which the tough professionalism of the British shone through. They were tired, wet, dirty, cold and hungry, but their eyes and faces were not those of demoralised and defeated men. Even the pictures of ships sinking and exploding were taken as indications of British resilience, and an almost-welcome reminder that the war was by no means a walk-over. In Britain the victory was like a collective tonic to an ailing nation. It seemed to indicate that the decline might not be inexorable, that the bottom had been reached and that from now on the country was bouncing back.

Afghanistan

Many Americans were irritated with the British for placing so much store on reclaiming such distant possessions when the Cold War seemed to be entering yet another critical phase. In December 1979, taking advantage of the chaos caused by the Iranian revolution, the USSR invaded Afghanistan, to bolster a reformist Marxist government. The United States and Britain both trained and armed insurgents of the Mujaheddin, ultra-conservative Muslims, and ensured that the USSR would not be able to secure an early peace. Taking advantage of an apparent power vacuum, in September 1980 Saddam Hussein, the secular president of Iraq, had invaded oil-rich Arabistan, the south-westernmost province of Iran. Instead of collapsing, the Iranians fought back effectively, tying Iraq into a war of attrition. The United States, Britain, and other western nations, now kept Iraq in the field supplying Saddam with modern technology. The Iraqis used mustard gas to blunt Iranian attacks in the mid-1980s, and also employed gas against disaffected Kurdish regions in the north, photographs of which were slowly passed to the West. In addition, the West set up naval patrols in the Gulf, to ensure the free passage of oil tankers. It was a small sea area and very crowded, and inevitably accidents happened. The Iraqis inadvertently fired an Exocet at the USS *Stark*, and the USS *Vincennes* shot down an Iranian airliner, believing it to be an attacking aircraft. In the tragic aftermath, some believe that the Iranians avenged their dead by seeking the help of Libya's Colonel Gadaffi in placing a bomb on a Pan American flight, which blew up over the small Scottish town of Lockerbie just before Christmas 1988.

Mired in Afghanistan, the USSR faced yet other pressures. President Reagan's 'Star Wars' programme, a plan for a space-based anti-ballistic missile system, was designed in part to place unsupportable economic strain on the USSR, but the danger was that if it succeeded the Soviets might lash out in a death spasm. There were also signs that Soviet control in Eastern Europe was unravelling, particularly in Poland, where there were strikes and demonstrations. Like Johnson and Nixon when confronted with Vietnam, the new Soviet premier Mikhail Gorbachev adopted a policy of 'Afghanistanisation', and began to withdraw in March 1988. But the attempt to reduce Soviet over-stretch and to liberalise the Soviet regime had come too late. On 15 March 1989 crowds took to the streets in Budapest demanding democracy and national independence, and then it spread like a bush-fire.

In Eastern Europe governments generally caved in to popular demands, though in Beijing's Tiananmen Square on 3 June tanks of the People's Army crushed about 2,000 pro-democracy demonstrators. Watched throughout the world, this brutal repression acted like petrol being poured on flames. A non-Communist government was elected in Poland; Latvia, Lithuania and Estonia announced their intention to seek independence from the USSR; and on 18 October East German president Erich Honecker resigned in the face of mounting disorder. On 9 November the border between East and West Germany was opened for the first time since 1961. The following night crowds in both East and West Berlin, armed with sledge-hammers and pick-axes, began demolishing the wall.

In the West, particularly in Washington and London, there was a moment of self-congratulation. The Cold War had ended in outright victory, Communist regimes tottering almost by the day. It was an article of faith that the competition between the USA and the USSR had been at the root of global instability. Now the danger of nuclear war had evaporated and the world would enter the 'broad, peaceful uplands' once envisaged by Winston Churchill, at the very darkest period of the twentieth century.

Back to the future
1989–2003

The New World Order?

On 2 August 1990 the world was stunned by the news that Iraq had invaded and overrun Kuwait. Previous threats by Iraq's dictator Saddam Hussein had been dismissed as a strategy to pressurise the Al Sabahs, Kuwait's ruling family, to concede oilfield rights. The West had supported Saddam in his long war with Iran and he judged it inconceivable that it would now turn on him, particularly as he offered the United States long-term stable oil supplies at prices below those of the OPEC cartel. Yet he invaded Kuwait on the very day that Britain's Prime Minister Margaret Thatcher was visiting President George Bush at Aspen, Colorado, both at some distance from their foreign policy advisers. Thatcher had no doubt what had to be done. 'George, this is not a time to go wobbly,' she said. To the consternation of many Arabists in both countries, the United States and Britain determined on a course which would lead to war.

To reassure the West of his essential decency, Saddam made a point of treating airline passengers and ex-patriots trapped in Kuwait as honoured guests, and his media people laid on photo-opportunities. He made the mistake of allowing himself to be photographed with a nine-year-old English boy, Stuart Lockwood, who looked pale and terrified. Flashed around the world, the avuncular brutality of the image spoke tellingly of Saddam's regime. The large and wealthy Kuwaiti community in the West also used the media, but to greater effect. Kuwaitis in the United States hired Hill and Knowlton, a well-known public relations firm, to spread stories about the brutal behaviour of the Iraqi occupation forces. Most were subsequently disproved, but they corresponded to popular preconceptions.

It took several weeks for the United States and Britain to stitch together a coalition, and nearly six months for forces and equipment to be shipped to Saudi Arabia. For the first six weeks of the crisis, from 2 August until about 20 September, the Americans lacked forces in place to stop an Iraqi strike south to the ports of Al Jybal and Dhahran. During this period photographs and television footage of the Coalition Commander, General Norman Schwarzkopf, were projected around the world to create the illusion of overwhelming power, in the absence of its actuality. Schwarzkopf might have come from Hollywood Central Casting; known variously as 'Stormin' Norman' or 'The Bear', the growling, six-foot three-inch, 17-stone general looked as though he could have stopped an Iraqi armoured column single-handedly.

The deployment was the largest the Americans had undertaken since Vietnam, and the largest for the British since Suez 44 years earlier. Vietnam had shown them the dangers of free roving journalists, and both forces took steps to control journalist activity. The American media plan Annex Foxtrot, later leaked to the *New York Times*, stated that journalists in the war zone would be 'escorted at all times. Repeat, at all times'. The Americans alone accredited more than 1,400 journalists and there were hundreds more from Britain and France but, with the exception of an independent handful, most were fed information in a media pool at Dhahran. Unsurprisingly the Iraqis did the same, concentrating journalists in a few major hotels in Baghdad, from where they were able to film the beginning of the air campaign on 16 January 1991.

Obsessed with partly learned 'lessons' from Vietnam, the Coalition high command contrived to present the air campaign as 'high-tech' and relatively bloodless. In fact only seven per cent of the ordnance were so-called 'smart' weapons; the remainder used the same technology employed in Vietnam, Korea and the Second World War. And even 'smart' weapons could kill large numbers of people if they landed in the wrong place. Peter Arnett, a New Zealander working for CNN in Baghdad, earned the Coalition's wrath when he reported from the smouldering ruins of an air-raid shelter in which hundreds of women and children had been sheltering, described in a military briefing as a command and control shelter. When the ground attack began, the Coalition minders discovered that even escorted photo-journalists could capture profoundly disturbing images. One, a picture of the charred but still recognisably human form of an Iraqi tank commander, still in the turret of his tank, was pulled from the AP wire because it was considered too horrific. The London *Observer* published it anyway, provoking a storm of controversy in the liberal media. When photo-journalists and television crews reached the Mutla Ridge, and began filming the carnage that was produced when Coalition air-power had massacred the retreating Iraqis at a choke-point, President Bush decided the time had come to halt military operations, reaffirming the power of an image to influence behaviour.

In March 1991 all the hopes of 1989 seemed to be coming to fruition. For the first time in its history the United Nations had performed in the way its founders had intended, providing the framework for the international community to resist aggression. On 19 August there was a frightening blip, when Communist hardliners in Moscow led by Gennady Yanayev took advantage of reforming premier Mikhail Gorbachev's absence in the Crimea to stage a coup. For 48 hours it seemed that the old order was about to reassert itself, but the hour found its man. On 21 August the world thrilled to the image of Boris Yeltsin, the flamboyant President of the Russian Federation, rallying Muscovites in front of the White House, the Russian Parliament building. The coup collapsed, and then events moved with astonishing rapidity. On 29 August the Russian Parliament suspended the Communist Party, seized its assets and disbanded the KGB. And on 1 January 1992 the Soviet Union ceased to exist. President Bush's determination to create a 'New World Order' at last seemed achievable.

Or the New World Disorder?

In the winter of 1991–92 armed forces throughout the West, like the armies of the old Soviet bloc, were being reduced in size. But in the midst of the euphoria there were indications that the celebrations were premature. Far from being the cause of instability it was becoming apparent that the Cold War had subsumed a variety of ethnic, religious and territorial tensions into an over-arching ideological struggle. In many areas of the world long-established patterns of historical evolution had been frozen for more than a generation. With the thaw the evolutionary rivers began flowing once again. The collapse of Communism had not seen the end of history – it had brought history back to life. Nowhere was this more apparent than in the Balkans, where by 1991 the disintegration of Yugoslavia had led to fighting between Serbia and the newly independent republics of Croatia and Slovenia. The former Yugoslavia in the early 1990s allowed journalists the same freedoms but exposed them to even greater dangers than Vietnam in the 1960s or Spain in the 1930s. Would-be Robert Capas and Margaret Bourke Whites, festooned with Nikons, swarmed into the war zone. Some were going to die, many were going to go back to 'proper' jobs, but a few would make it.

The wars of Yugoslavian disintegration, 1991–99

One of the first to reach the Balkans was a 26-year-old New Yorker, Ron Haviv, who had taken up photography as a hobby while a student at New York University. None of those involved in the Balkan bloodletting had a particularly sophisticated awareness of the power of the media, but the Bosnian Serbs were particularly inept. Local warlord Zelijko Raznatovic, known as Arkan, was delighted when Haviv offered to photograph him. Backed by his sinisterly hooded men, holding their AK-47s, Arkan stared menacingly at the camera, holding a sub-machine gun in his right hand and a tiger-cub in his left.

After the first clashes in Slovenia and Croatia, on 25 September 1991 the United Nations imposed a mandatory arms embargo on Yugoslavia, which hurt everyone but the well-equipped Serbs, who had inherited most of the old federal army. By the spring of 1992 civil war had broken out in Bosnia, with Bosnian Serbs supported by federal forces blockading and shelling Sarajevo, Bosnia's capital. In predominantly Serb areas tens of thousands of Muslims and Croats were on the move, their lives threatened and their homes burnt. Where they resisted they were massacred. No one knows exactly how many died in 1992, the worst year in the Balkans, but the United Nations estimated that it was at least 130,000. Young men of military age who were not killed were herded into concentration camps, where they were left to die of starvation. That summer Ron Haviv discovered one such camp at Trnopolje and his pictures appalled the world.

The pictures pouring in from the Balkans provoked action, but it proved inadequate. The United Nations' new protection force (UNPROFOR), tasked with providing humanitarian relief, amounted to only 23,000. Bosnian Muslims and Croats soon came to see UNPROFOR as another enemy. The United Nations declared certain towns 'safe areas' under UN protection, but then failed to protect them. UN humiliation seemed inevitable. On 11 July 1995 a Bosnian Serb army overran Srebrenica, one of the larger safe areas. Oblivious to the presence of the world's press, they systematically killed 8,000 unarmed male Muslims, ranging from boys to old men.

The destruction of Srebrenica effectively ended the United Nations mission, but the United States had already embarked on a different policy. On 11 November 1994 it had abandoned the arms embargo in order to arm Muslims and Croats, believing a balance of military capability might restore peace. In early August 1995 a re-equipped and well-trained Croatian army, supported by NATO (American) air power, launched Operation Storm. This succeeded in breaking Serbian resistance in the Krajina, and sent a flood of 250,000 Serbs fleeing east towards Belgrade. On 30 August another heavy air bombardment on Serb positions around Sarajevo finally forced them to accept an agreement negotiated and signed in Dayton, Ohio on 25 November 1995. Bosnia was now to become a military protectorate of the international community. The situation could not last, but at least the killing had stopped.

Less than six months later, fighting flared up in Kosovo, Serbia's southernmost province, the now predominantly Albanian core of the former medieval Serbian state. The Kosovo Liberation Army (KLA) initially comprised a few gangs, but in 1997 as Albania itself slipped into disintegration, arms and trained men flooded across the border. By 1998 the KLA's demands for Kosovan independence increased the danger of a general conflagration in the southern Balkans also involving Macedonia, Bulgaria, Greece and possibly Turkey. On 24 March 1999 after Serbia refused to admit NATO forces, NATO launched an extensive bombing campaign, which hardened rather than weakened Serbian resolve. Serbian forces drove tens of thousands of Kosovar Albanians across the frontier into Macedonia.

The bombing went on until the second week in June. NATO lacked sufficient ground forces to invade. Serb resolve was weakened when Boris Yeltsin, accepting an American offer of 30 billion dollars in credits to Russia, withdrew traditional Russian military support for Serbia. The NATO commander in Macedonia, General Mike Jackson, managed to negotiate a peaceful withdrawal of the Serbian army, but at the last minute a small Russian column from Bosnia raced down to Pristina, the predominantly Serb capital of Kosovo, where they were treated as heroes. Ordered by NATO commander General Wesley Clark to helicopter forces to Pristina to face down the Russians, Jackson refused, saying, 'General, I'm not going to start World War III for you.'

Heart of darkness

During the 1990s many areas of the world slipped into chaos. In Africa the mood was at first optimistic. South Africa avoided the long-predicted blood-bath, experiencing a relatively peaceful transition from white minority to black majority rule. In December 1992 the United States landed marines at Mogadishu in Somalia, their mission to feed the population. There was a moment of high farce when they came ashore ready for combat, and were dazzled by the flash-bulbs of a mob of photographers and television teams waiting for them, but Christmas 1992 saw President George Bush mobbed by cheering crowds as he made a triumphal procession through Mogadishu. The incoming Clinton administration expanded the mission from humanitarian relief to the rebuilding of the Somali nation, a noble but horrendously difficult task. In an attempt to eliminate one source of instability, on 3 October 1993, 400 US Rangers descended by helicopter into central Mogadishu on a cordon-and-search operation to arrest Mohammed Aidid, the most powerful of the Somali warlords. The warlike Somalis gave the Rangers a hot reception; in seven hours of fighting they shot down two Black Hawk helicopters and inflicted 95 casualties on the Rangers, 18 of whom were killed. A photographer from the *Toronto Star* took pictures of Somali mobs dragging the mutilated bodies of naked Rangers through the streets, images which induced the Clinton administration to abandon the mission.

After Somalia the mood in Washington changed – henceforth the US gave up any pretence to global policing. On 12 April 1994, six days after the Hutus of Rwanda turned on their Tutsi neighbours in a frenzy of bloodletting, American reporter Donatella Lorche entered Kigali in a Red Cross medical convoy from Burundi. She reported that the roads were clogged with fleeing refugees. 'Bodies lay everywhere. Several truckloads of frenzied screaming men waving machetes and screwdrivers drove by. At night, screams followed by automatic gunfire could be heard from the churches in Kigali.' Yet these horrific pictures failed to move the US administration. European countries were no keener to get involved. Western media coverage of Hutus fleeing from vengeful Tutsis led to a belated humanitarian effort, with France sending forces to protect refugees from a danger already past. The response to the Rwanda massacres established a pattern for western involvement in Africa. They would intervene to resolve relatively small problems (the British in Sierra Leone in 1999, France in the Ivory Coast in 2002 and the United States in Liberia in 2003) but were reluctant to tackle the vast and unpredictable.

The mid- and late 1990s saw a mood of neo-isolationism sweeping over the United States. The world's only remaining superpower proved reluctant to shoulder the burdens its status demanded. It remained happy to continue operating as a regional power, policing the western hemisphere in ways which Theodore Roosevelt and Woodrow Wilson would have understood. On 20 December 1989, 27,000 US troops had swept into Panama, forcing General Noriega, Panama's self-appointed 'Maximum Leader', to seek refuge in the Papal Nunciatura, the sovereign territory of the Vatican. Here he was forced to surrender on 3 January 1990 by the Americans playing heavy metal rock music through loudspeakers, non-stop. On 19 September 1994 American forces landed in Haiti to restore order. And throughout this period America gave covert support to counter-insurgency campaigns in Central and South America. Occasionally a stunning success was achieved – the arrest and incarceration of Guzman, leader of Peru's Shining Path Guerrillas. But it was mainly an unglamorous and low-key war fought in the shadows, typified by the struggle with Columbian cocaine barons.

Russia, too, concentrated on problems close to home. On 4 October 1993 world TV cameras and photo-journalists assembled outside the Russian Parliament building in Moscow.

They captured the assault by pro-Yeltsin forces to end a rebellion by the followers of Vice Presdient Rutskoi. Russia was very far from being a stable liberal-democracy. Nor was the Russian Federation particularly stable. On 11 December 1994 Russian armoured columns invaded the breakaway republic of Chechenya in the Caucasus, and were smashed to pieces in a Chechen ambush in the streets of Grozny. A major urban battle developed, and Grozny, a large city of high-rise reinforced-concrete buildings, soon resembled Stalingrad. Western newsmen, infiltrating the city through Chechen lines, kept the papers of New York and London filled with images of burning Russian armour amidst mountains of rubble. Chechen terrorists carried the war into Russia, bombing government buildings, barracks and hospitals. In the spring of 2003 they seized the Moscow State Theatre, prompting a bloodily inept rescue operation being carried out by the police and army.

With the exception of Africa and the fringes of the Russian federation, as the 20th century came to an end the mood of optimistic self-congratulation which had characterised 1989 began to return. Many problems seemed on the wane: there was a real prospect of peace in Northern Ireland; the Balkans appeared quiet; and in Cambodia in 1993 and East Timor in 1999, UN interventions, underwritten by the power of the United States, had brought a degree of stability to two of Asia's trouble-spots.

Clash of cultures

Yet peace was far from imminent in the Muslim world, the vast swathe of territory running from Morocco on the Atlantic to the

Philippines in the Pacific. In 1998 Harvard Professor Samuel Huntington had argued that whereas conflict in the 20th century had been driven by competing ideologies, in the 21st century it would involve a clash of cultures and civilisations between the West and Islam. His analysis provoked a storm of criticism – the 'West' came in many forms, as did Islam – but there was much evidence to support it. In 1979 Islamic theocracy triumphed in Iran, a reaction to a process of enforced westernisation; and in 1989 the Soviets, bent on modernising and secularising, had been driven from Afghanistan. In December 1991 the people of Algeria elected a radical Islamic government, only to have the army conduct a coup and establish a military dictatorship with the tacit consent of the West. Everywhere Islam saw itself beleaguered, whether in Bosnia, in the disputed province of Kashmir or in the southern Philippines. Israel's occupation since 1967 of the territories on the West Bank of the Jordan River had in the 1980s created the *Intifada* (the 'shaking off'), with its crowds of stone-flinging children. Under intense American pressure Israel conceded a limited degree of autonomy to a Palestinian entity: but this created enclaves from where terrorist bombers and suicide bombers could easily operate.

Throughout the decade there had been worrying indications that extremist Islamic groups would hit targets well beyond Israel. On 26 February 1993 a large bomb was detonated in the parking lot under the 110-storey New York World Trade Center, a symbol of western economic dominance. British journalists, used to covering IRA outrages, were convinced that the terrorists had intended to bring the entire structure crashing down. This time

New Yorkers were lucky; only six of the 50,000 people were killed, though about 1,000 were injured. The bombers were quickly traced and arrested. All from the Middle East, they were small fry, acting under the direction of Ramzi Ahmed Yousef, a lieutenant of Osama bin Laden, a wealthy Saudi Arabian who in the 1980s had been one of the principal recruiters and fundraisers for the fundamentalist Mujaheddin. Following the Soviet withdrawal from Afghanistan he had formed an organisation called al-Qaeda ('the base'), ostensibly to provide support for redundant guerrillas, including the funding of a massive multi-volume official history of the war in Afghanistan, which included helpful hints on guerrilla operations, and which became a best-seller in Pakistan and Iran. Proud of their defeat of the Soviets (the first Muslim victory over Europeans since the Turks drove the Greeks into the sea at Smyrna in 1923), al-Qaeda decided to wage war against the United States, and the regimes it supported.

Operating first from the Sudan and then from Afghanistan, bin Laden orchestrated a world-wide terror campaign. Attempts to assassinate Crown Prince Abdullah of Jordan in June 1993 and President Mubarak of Egypt in June 1995 were followed on 25 June 1996 by a truck bomb at the Al Khobar Towers in Saudi Arabia, which killed 19 and wounded 385 US service personnel. On 7 August 1998 al-Qaeda blew up US embassies in Dar es Salaam and Nairobi, killing more than 200 and injuring about 4,000, which provoked the US into an ineffectual cruise-missile attack on suspected al-Qaeda bases in Afghanistan on 20 August 1998. By the late 1990s intelligence services throughout western countries with Islamic populations were reporting an unusually large movement of young Muslim men to Pakistan and possibly Afghanistan. Britain's MI5 estimated that as many as 2,000 British Muslims had left to spend time in training camps in Afghanistan in 1998 alone. Events like the suicide bombing of the USS *Cole* in Aden harbour on 12 October 2000 served to stimulate recruitment further.

9/11

Yet the United States remained in a fool's paradise, its intelligence agencies misinterpreting the growing wealth of information pointing to something imminent and spectacular. James Nachtwey, a contract photographer for *Time* magazine, arrived back in New York from an assignment in Europe on 10 September 2001. He had a good view of the World Trade Center from his apartment and heard the first explosion quite clearly. Grabbing his camera, he headed into an area from which everyone else was fleeing. He recalled: 'I was two blocks from the first tower when it collapsed and I photographed the cloud of debris as it boiled through the canyons of lower Manhattan. I made my way through the smoke to photograph the skyscraper where it lay in ruins in the street ... Then I heard what sounded like a huge waterfall in the sky. I looked up and saw the second tower falling straight down at me.' Nachtwey realised there wasn't time to take a picture – he ran, and he survived. War correspondent Bill Biggart was also taking pictures and couldn't resist the shot of a lifetime. His camera, miraculously undamaged, was found lying near his body a day later, the final frame an image of the second tower as it began to implode.

The attack on the World Trade Center, and the simultaneous attack on the Pentagon, cost 3,000 lives, more than were lost at Pearl Harbor. Like that event, 9/11 (as it soon became known) roused the American population to a righteous anger, but it also dangerously polarised the world. What came to be called the Anglosphere – at its core the United States, Britain and Australia – closed ranks. In October 2001 American special forces, supported particularly by troops from Britain and Australia, arrived in Afghanistan to co-ordinate the employment of massive American airstrikes in support of the Northern Alliance, a coalition of clans and tribes who had been waging war against the Taliban for nearly ten years. Kabul was taken with surprising ease, but the core of al-Qaeda had already fled. Western journalists combed Pakistan, hoping for a lead to Osama bin Laden, and some got too lucky. On 23 January 2002 Wall Street Journal correspondent Daniel Pearl was kidnapped by Islamic militants, who killed him eight days later.

During the spring several other soft targets were hit around the world, particularly western tourists in Islamic countries. By the summer of 2002 a number of nations who had initially supported the American-led campaign began to distance themselves from further operations, leaving the Anglosphere looking isolated, though when asked whether this worried him the Australian Prime Minister John Howard replied, 'No – it was the same in 1942.' The drawing together of the Anglosphere was confirmed by a car bomb outside a Bali nightclub in October 2002, which killed more than 200 and maimed hundreds more, the great majority British and Australians, many of them young women.

The attacks of 9/11, and the subsequent outrages, brought into sharp relief the likelihood – indeed, the certainty – that terrorist groups would soon acquire nuclear weapons, and biological and chemical weapons only slightly less terrifying in their effect. Since the early 1990s desperate efforts (not entirely successful) had been made to monitor the disposal of the vast nuclear arsenal of the Soviet Union, but there was also the danger posed by so-called rogue states, who might fund the private development of weapons of mass destruction, or might launch their own programme of development. Foremost amongst these states was Iraq. In tandem with an information campaign designed to prepare public opinion, from September 2002 to March 2003 some 250,000 US personnel, joined by 47,000 British and 2,000 Australians, deployed to Kuwait. On 20 March, supported by massive air attacks, the British struck towards Basra, the Americans attacked directly into central Iraq, while American special forces, accompanied by the Australians, cut Iraq's communications with Syria to the West. American forces were differently structured from those which had fought under Schwarzkopf. They were much lighter and much more dependent on air support, and on a few occasions they were held up by surprisingly determined resistance, but by 9 April US Marines were in Iraq and cheering Shiites were tearing down statues of Saddam Hussein. On 14 April American forces entered Tikrit, Saddam's home town, and centre of his power, and on 1 May President Bush declared major combat operations at an end.

It was premature. Iraqi divisions had collapsed too quickly, and a power vacuum had been created. As the situation slipped into guerrilla war, observers began making comparisons with Vietnam, but they were wrong. They were in a situation which William Howard Russell, Felice Beato and John Burke would have understood only too well. As Russell had once said of the British, the Americans and their friends were now 'empiring it around the world'. No one in Washington had planned this, just as no one in London had quite planned the expansion of the British Empire.

At the dawn of the new century opportunities for the war photographers – those who wish to understand and record the complexities of combat – and photographers of war – those who dwell on the consequences – were never greater.

Biographies

Adams, Edward 'Eddie' T. (1933–)

Associated Press correspondent Adams was on his third
tour to Vietnam in early 1968, when he captured one of the
defining moments of the conflict, the summary execution of
a Viet Cong suspect by Brigadier General Nguyen Ngoc Loan,
commander of the South Vietnam National Police. The
picture suggested straightforward murder but belied a more
complex reality. That morning Loan had just learned that the
entire family of one of his officers had been massacred by the
Viet Cong. When Saigon fell in April 1975, Loan escaped to
America, where he opened a Vietnamese restaurant in
Virginia.

Barzini, Luigi (1874–1947)

The most famous Italian photo-journalist of the first quarter of the 20th century, Barzini joined the staff of Milan's *Corriere della Sera* in 1900, the largest newspaper in Italy. He rose to prominence thanks to the grisly scenes of executions that he took during the suppression of the Boxer Rebellion in the late summer of 1900. Four years later, he was one of the few correspondents allowed by the Japanese to cover their side of the Russo-Japanese War, and as a result had a ring-side seat for the Battle of Mukden, about which he wrote a book, predicting in large measure the true nature of modern industrial war. Barzini also covered the Mexican Revolution, and the first and second Balkan Wars. Widely respected for his objectivity, during Italy's invasion of Libya in 1911 Barzini allowed his patriotism to colour reportage, when he protested vigorously against aspects of the British press coverage, and attempted to have hostile British newsmen expelled from the area of operations.

Bean, Charles Edwin Woodrow (1879–1968)

Born in Bathurst in New South Wales, in 1908 Bean abandoned his career as a lawyer to become a journalist on the *Sydney Morning Herald*. With the outbreak of war in 1914, Bean was appointed official correspondent to the Australian Imperial Force (AIF), the expedition the young country sent to the Middle East. Bean was one of a handful of correspondents to cover the disastrous Gallipoli campaign, where he began compiling a detailed diary and a photographic record, not for immediate publication, but to celebrate the troops and their exploits after the war. Arriving at the Western Front in 1916, Bean continued his compilation so that by the armistice he had 120 hand-written diaries and thousands of photographs. This material provided him with the basis of a six-volume official history of Australia in the war, which he completed in 1942, and the foundation for a collection which was going to grow into the massive Australian War Memorial in the new national capital of Canberra.

Beato, Felice (1820–1903)

Born in Venice, Beato pioneered landscape photography in Italy and the Mediterranean, before entering into a partnership with British photographer James Robertson in 1852, to form Robertson, Beato and Company. In 1855 Beato, now established as an architectural photographer, travelled to the Crimea with Robertson, where they continued the work begun by Roger Fenton. Beato's photographs of the Sebastopol fortifications, detailing the destruction wrought by Allied siege batteries, alerted the Royal Engineers of the British army to the wider uses of photography, particularly as a means of accurately recording the impact of different types of ordnance against a variety of defensive systems. It has been argued that the science of operational analysis began at this point. Beato subsequently photographed the results of the siege of Lucknow (1857) and the bombardment of the Taku forts (1860). From China, Beato went to Japan, where in 1864 he photographed the French landing at Akama Fort, part of an operation by a western international coalition to destroy the resistance of the conservative Choshu clan to European and American penetration. In the latter part of the century, Beato documented the spread of western influence around the globe, capturing the landing of American Marines on a punitive expedition to Korea in May 1871, the British expedition up the Nile to rescue the besieged Gordon in Khartoum (1884–85), and the expedition up the Irrawaddy to occupy Ava, the capital of Burma (1885).

Biggart, Bill (1948–2001)

Born in Berlin to US Army parents, Biggart grew up in New York, and worked for 20 years as a freelance photographer for New York City's Impact Visuals photo agency. Though based in Greenwich Village, Biggart travelled widely, covering Northern Ireland, Gaza and the Gulf War. On 11 September 2001 he happened to be right there, ready for the scoop of a lifetime. Biggart went towards the stricken World Trade Center with New York firemen, and kept shooting with his camera as the towers collapsed. He was too close. Two days later his body was recovered from the debris, with his cameras, which had miraculously survived intact, containing the pictures of the falling buildings he had given his life to photograph.

Bourke White, Margaret (1906–1971)

Joining the staff of *Life* magazine at its inception in 1935, Bourke White achieved her first scoop as a war photographer when she was sent to the USSR early in the summer of 1941, to do a feature on Stalin and the industrialisation of Russia. Still in Moscow when the Germans attacked on 22 June, she managed to get some spectacular pictures of German air raids over the Kremlin, though strict Soviet controls prevented her from covering the front. On her return to the United States she found the American authorities equally reluctant to grant her permission to report from war zones, and the bureaucratic battles she fought and won opened the way for a new generation of women war reporters. Finally given permission to cross the Atlantic, when her ship was torpedoed Bourke White kept snapping pictures, providing her with a remarkable scoop. With her credentials as a combat photographer now established, on 22 January 1943 Bourke White became the first woman to fly on an American combat mission. She covered the North-West Europe campaign, and was one of the first photographers to enter the concentration camps in April 1945, her pictures of heaped bodies in Buchenwald having an immense political effect. Margaret Bourke White went on to cover the early stages of the Korean War. Now at the height of her powers, the most famous woman war photographer in the world, she noticed the first symptoms of Parkinson's disease, which effectively put an end to her career, though she developed another as a writer and went on to author six books.

Brady, Matthew B. (1823–1896)

The founder of American war photography, Brady began his career taking daguerreotype portraits of New York's social elite in 1844. By 1860 he was regarded as New York's top society photographer, a position which was confirmed when presidential candidate Abraham Lincoln chose Brady to take his portrait for the election campaign. With Lincoln's election and the outbreak of war, Brady sought at first to emulate Roger Fenton, and other photographers of the Crimea, but the Battle of Bull Run convinced him that it was going to be a long conflict, in which the whole of the Union and the Confederacy would be mobilised. Believing there was money to be made, and also believing that it was his duty to record such a titanic conflict, Brady borrowed heavily and expanded his firm, until he employed up to 20 photographers who covered 35 bases of operation in three states. Brady was an entrepreneur and organiser; only a very small number of the thousands of photographs of the war ascribed to Brady were actually taken by him. Ferocious competition from other photographers, many of whom had started with Brady, reduced profit margins, and by 1865 Brady was facing financial ruin. Congress rejected his offer to sell his collection to the nation for $100,000, eventually buying a much-reduced collection for an absurd $2,840, thousands of images having been sold at knock-down prices to cover debts. Brady died in a paupers' ward of a New York hospital on 15 January, a victim of alcoholism and associated diseases.

Browne, Malcolm W. (1931–)

Educated as a chemist, New York-born Browne stumbled into photo-journalism by accident, when he was drafted into the US Army during the Korean War and assigned to the staff of 'Stars and Stripes'. In 1963, Browne, now Vietnam bureau chief for the Associated Press, got the greatest scoop of his career when he photographed the self-immolation of a monk in Saigon. Browne's picture reportedly led President Kennedy to authorise the coup which overthrew South Vietnam's President Ngo Dinh Diem on 1 November 1963. Although he was to become increasingly disillusioned with the war, Browne stayed in Vietnam, working for the *New York Times* until April 1975.

Burke, John (dates unknown)

Burke was one of a number of photographers who set up business in India and other parts of the Empire from the 1860s onwards, and who specialised in taking portraits of the growing number of British army officers and colonial office agents and their families. Early in the autumn of 1878 Burke was hired by the government of India to accompany Major General Sir Frederick Roberts's expedition to Kabul, which was tasked with removing Sher Ali, the pro-Russian ruler of Afghanistan. After defeating Sher Ali at Peiwar Kotal on 2 December 1878, the British occupied and wintered in Kabul, Burke busying himself with the production of a fine photograph record of the occupation. One of the last photographs he took before the column left Kabul in May

1879, that of British envoy Sir Louis Cavagnari seated with ferocious-looking Afghan leaders, was destined to give Burke fleeting fame, when Cavagnari was murdered four months later. Woodcuts based on Burke's photograph filled the British press, while a war artist produced a sketch of Burke, which appeared in the *Graphic*. Burke went again to Afghanistan with Roberts's punitive expedition (October 1879–October 1881), his unusually fine photographs eventually adorning the messes of the regiments involved, while his numerous studies of Roberts appeared as woodcuts in British illustrated papers, and helped establish the general as a national hero.

Burrows, Larry (1926–1971)

Born in England, Burrows was working as a laboratory assistant in *Life* magazine's London offices in June 1944, when he managed to destroy most of Robert Capa's D-Day photographs by applying too much heat to the negatives. From this very unpromising beginning, Burrows went on to become one of *Life*'s most distinguished photo-journalists, covering conflicts in Africa and the Middle East as well as Vietnam. A picture essay in 1966 of an airborne attempt to rescue the crew of a downed helicopter in Vietnam earned him the Overseas Press Club's Robert Capa Award. In all, Burrows spent nine years covering Vietnam. He was killed on 10 February 1971, when the helicopter in which he was travelling was shot down over Laos.

Capa, Robert (1913–1954)

Born Andrei Friedmann in Budapest, he changed his name to Capa in 1935, after he had begun working as a freelance photojournalist for *Life* magazine, on the assumption that more contracts would come his way if commissioning editors thought he was an American. In 1936 Capa went to Spain to cover the civil war from the loyalist side, accompanied by his lover, Gerda Taro, a photographer for *Life* magazine. Their partnership was brought to an end in July 1937, when Gerda was crushed to death under a loyalist tank during confused fighting. Profoundly affected by her death, Capa now lived only for his art, in pursuit of which he now took the most extraordinary chances, constantly exposing himself to hostile fire. On 5 September 1937 Capa snapped the moment a bullet smashed into the head of Federico Borrell Garcia, a loyalist militiaman, a photograph which was published around the world under the title 'The Falling Soldier'. Overnight Capa became famous, but detractors were soon arguing that the picture had been faked, leading to one of the longest-lasting and best-known controversies in the history of photography, until Garcia's widow positively identified the man in the photograph as her husband, who had been killed on the day Capa had always said he had taken the picture. Capa went to China in 1938, to cover the Japanese offensive up the Yangtse, and in the summer and autumn of 1940 he was in England to photograph the Battle of Britain and the London blitz.

When America was propelled into the war in December 1941, Capa found himself classified as an enemy alien and forbidden to travel beyond New York City. Reclassified in March 1943, Capa made up for lost time, covering the Italian campaign, and then Normandy, for *Life* magazine. On 6 June 1944 Capa went ashore with the first assault waves on Omaha Beach. Lying in the surf under intense fire he took 106 pictures, of which only 11 survived the attempts of *Life* magazine's laboratory assistant Larry Burrows to speed up the drying of the negatives by placing them in an airing cabinet under hot-air blowers. Capa continued to produce action photographs of extraordinary quality. He was almost killed twice, first during the German Ardennes offensive of December 1944, and four months later when he parachuted across the Rhine with American airborne troops. In 1948 Capa went to Palestine to cover the first of the Arab-Israeli wars, joining Israeli troops in heavy fighting in Jerusalem. Six years later, while covering the French Indo-China War, Capa's extraordinary run of luck (he had been risking his life for more than 18 years) finally ran out when he was killed by a landmine as he went towards the sound of fighting. Once asked to explain his success, Capa replied, 'if your pictures aren't good, you aren't close enough.' Capa lived and died by this dictum. In his short life he established standards to which all cameramen aspire, and is widely regarded as the patron saint of combat photography.

Chapelle, Georgette 'Dickey' (1918–1965)

A publicist working for Trans World Airways, in early 1945 Chapelle was given the chance to employ her skills as a combat photographer when she was assigned to do a story on a hospital ship bound for Iwo Jima. One of her pictures, a snap of a seriously wounded Marine being lifted aboard the ship, was published under the caption 'The Dying Marine', and was to become the focal point for US blood donor drives for the rest of the war. With her credentials established by photographing Japanese Kamikaze attacks off Okinawa, Chapelle was employed on a variety of dangerous assignments by *Life* magazine after the war. She covered the Hungarian uprising in the autumn of 1956, and was jailed by the Soviets for three months. Violently anti-Communist, Chapelle was equally opposed to European colonialism, producing a devastating photo-essay on French counter-insurgency operations in Algeria in 1958, which she took from the side of the FLN guerrillas. Beginning in 1961, she became a regular visitor to Vietnam; she was killed by a booby-trap on her fifth assignment in November 1965, the first American woman correspondent to die in action.

Davis, Richard Harding (1864–1916)

The leading war correspondent in the English-speaking world in the late 19th and early 20th century, Davis got a taste for action when he covered US cavalry anti-bandit patrols along the Rio Grande in the early 1890s for *Harper's Weekly*. Hired by William Randolph Hearst in 1896 to cover the insurrection against Spanish rule in Cuba, Davis resigned when Hearst altered one of his despatches. Davis returned to Cuba in 1898 with the American invasion force, covering the assault on San

Juan Hill, and heroising the role of Theodore Roosevelt. The following year he covered the Boer War from both sides, and from 1904–05 the Russo-Japanese War. Returning to the United States, Davis again covered operations along the Rio Grande, this time against Pancho Villa. With the outbreak of the European war, Davis, although an Anglophile, attempted, as in the Boer War, to cover the war from both sides, almost being shot by the Germans as a British spy. In 1916 Davis went back to the United States to campaign for American entry into the war, but the exertions proved too much and he died from a heart attack.

Dinwiddie, William (1867–1934)

One of the first photo-journalists, Dinwiddie covered the Spanish-American War for *Harper's Weekly*, taking an action photograph of American artillery firing on the Spanish during the battle of El Caney. Hired by the *New York Herald*, Dinwiddie photographed American counter-insurgency operations in the Philippines, British operations in the Boer War, and the Japanese assault on the Russians in Manchuria in 1904. Not as persistent as Barzini, or as lucky as London, Dinwiddie left when frustrated by Japanese censorship.

Duncan, David Douglas (1916–)

Employed as a photographer by the American Museum of Natural History in 1940, three years later Duncan enlisted in the United States Marine Corps, and covered the campaign in the Pacific, including the battle for Okinawa and the official

Japanese surrender aboard the USS *Missouri* in 1945. Joining
Life magazine on his return to the USA, Duncan achieved his
greatest scoop in Korea in 1950, when he photographed the
retreat of the 1st US Marine Division from Chosin Reservoir,
which later formed the basis of a best-selling picture essay,
This Is War!. Duncan went to Vietnam in 1967, where he was
bitterly critical of what he saw as overly emotional and
unbalanced coverage by young and inexperienced
photographers.

Fiorillo, Luigi (dates unknown)

One of a growing number of photographers based in
Egypt, Fiorillo specialised in providing images of Egyptian
antiquities for the growing tourist market. On 1 February 1881,
Egypt was plunged into chaos when the army, led by Arabi
Pasha, overthrew Sultan Tewfik. Mobs of Islamic
fundamentalists attacked Western interests, murdered
Europeans, and soon turned on Egypt's Coptic Christian
minority. At considerable risk to his own life, Fiorillo
abandoned the tourist industry, concentrating instead on
Egypt's slide into anarchy. Unwilling to tolerate disorder
near the Suez Canal, its lifeline to India, on 11 July 1882 the
Royal Navy bombarded Alexandria, as a preliminary to the
landing of an expeditionary force. The British claimed the
bombardment was designed to hit purely military targets, and
printed official photographs, showing the damage inflicted
on Alexandria's forts. In fact the bombardment had also
devastated residential districts of Alexandria, damage which

Fiorillo catalogued in a collection of photographs 'Album Souvenir d'Alexandrie: Ruines'. After failing to be accepted as photographer to Wolsely's 1884 expedition up the Nile (the task went to fellow Italian Felice Beato), Fiorillo photographed the Italian punitive expedition to Abyssinia, following the massacre of an Italian column at Dogali on 26 January 1887.

Gardner, Alexander (1821–1882)

Born in Scotland, Gardner worked as a jeweller's apprentice and as a reporter on the *Glasgow Sentinel* before emigrating to the United States in 1856. Employed as an assistant to Matthew Brady, in 1858 he took over the management of Brady's Washington studio, and soon came to be known by the capital's élite. In 1862 Gardner broke with Brady, using his political contacts to secure his appointment as official photographer to the Army of the Potomac. Emulating Brady, Gardner set up teams of photographers, often poaching his erstwhile employer's best cameramen. In 1866 Gardner published *Sketch Book of the War*, comprising 100 photographs which traced the course of the conflict, and which became the best-known and most frequently utilised source of pictures of the conflict. In 1867 Gardner became the official photographer to the Union Pacific Railroad, and devoted his remaining years to recording America's ever-receding frontier.

Gibbons, Floyd (1887–1939)

A reporter for the *Chicago Tribune*, Gibbons first rose to prominence when he formed a friendship with Mexican bandit and revolutionary Pancho Villa, during the border clashes of 1916. The following year Gibbons got the scoop of a lifetime, when the ss *Laconia*, the liner on which he was travelling to Europe, was torpedoed by a U-boat 200 miles off the coast of Ireland. He photographed the stricken liner from a lifeboat, and then lived on his accounts of the attack for many months. Arriving on the Western Front, Gibbons joined the United States Marine Corps attack in Belleau Wood, where he was shot in the head, and lost an eye. Thereafter Gibbons sported a piratical eye patch. In the inter-war years Gibbons was to be found wherever the action was hottest – in Ireland in 1919, on the Russo-Polish border in 1920, in the midst of famine-stricken Russia in 1921, in Morocco at the height of the Riff War in the mid-1920s, and in China, Manchuria, Ethiopia and Spain in the 1930s. Gibbons died of a heart attack on 24 September 1939, while preparing to cover the German invasion of Poland.

Hardy, Albert 'Bert' (1913–1995)

Born in London, Hardy joined the new *Picture Post* in 1938. In 1940 and 1941 he covered the London Blitz, risking his life night after night to get close to the action, and establishing for himself a reputation as a photographer of the first rank. Hardy accompanied the Canadians and Commandos on the disastrous Dieppe raid of August 1942, and survived to cover the Normandy landings, the liberation of Paris, and the crossing of the Rhine. Pushed by experience ever to the left of the political spectrum, Hardy gave sympathetic coverage

to the Communists in the Greek Civil War and the Malayan
Emergency, a bias which became overt in the picture essays
he produced in Korea. The massacre of civilians he laid
exclusively at the door of the USA, reinforcing his contention
by producing images which contrasted American strength
with Korean weakness. The proprietor of *Picture Post*, Sir
Edward Hulton, refused to allow publication, which led the
editor to resign in defence of freedom of the press, though
Hardy remained with the magazine until 1957.

Hare, James H. 'Jimmy' (1856–1946)

An English-born freelance photographer, Hare shot to
prominence when he photographed the wreck of the USS
Maine in Havana harbour in 1898 for New York's *Collier's
Weekly*. Hare subsequently used his status as a correspondent
to carry messages from US invasion forces to Maximo Gomez,
leader of the Cuban guerrilla movement, a mission which
enhanced his carefully constructed image as a swashbuckler.
Over the next 22 years Hare photographed conflicts around
the world. He was frustrated by the censorship of the Japanese
in their conflict with Russia (1904–05), and of the Bulgarians
in the Balkan Wars, but had free rein in Mexico, covering
fighting along the Rio Grande and at Vera Cruz from the front
lines. So dramatic were some of Hare's photographs that
Collier's warned him he would be no good to them 'if dead or
wounded'. Though now in his late fifties, Hare covered
fighting on the Western Front after 1914, and of the fighting in
Italy and north of Salonika. He was famous for his spectacular

scoops; he rushed to Ireland in May 1915 to photograph the bodies of the victims of the *Lusitania*'s sinking being brought ashore, was lucky enough to be back in North America in December 1917 so that he could cover the devastating ammunition explosion which devastated Halifax, Nova Scotia, and in the summer of 1920 managed to get to Warsaw to cover the Polish defeat of the Red Army's advance. Now 64 years old, Hare decided on a quieter life, spending the next 26 years managing newspapers and writing.

Haviv, Ron (1964–)

Born in New York, Haviv's career as a freelance photo-journalist received an enormous boost when a visit to Panama in December 1989 happened to coincide with the US invasion and the removal of Panamanian dictator President Noreiga. Haviv's pictures were published in the major New York magazines, making it easy for him to get backing for a visit to the Balkans in 1991. Once again Haviv was in the right place to make full use of his skills. Over the next few years he catalogued the disintegration of Yugoslavia, his pictures of starving prisoners in concentration camps awakening the conscience of the West, and paving the way for effective intervention.

Hurley, James Francis 'Frank' (1885–1962)

Born in Sydney, by 1916 Hurley was Australia's best-known photographer, thanks to the pictures he brought back from Antarctica of Sir Ernest Shackleton's ill-fated expedition.

In 1917 he was appointed official photographer to the Australian Imperial Force and travelled to France. Despairing of capturing the immensity and violence of the battlefield in a single photograph, he experimented with montages and even altered photographs to produce what he considered a more realistic image, though fellow Australian war correspondent Charles Bean accused him of putting a desire for artistic effect above the obligation to record the truth. Despite the disagreement, Bean still included several of Hurley's montages in the collection of the new Australian War Memorial. At the outbreak of the Second World War, Hurley was appointed head of the Australian Imperial Photographic Unit, covering the campaigns of the 2nd AIF in the Middle East in 1941 and early 1942.

Khaldei, Yevgeni (1916–1996)

Employed by the TASS agency in the mid-1930s, Ukrainian-born Khaldei covered the Soviet army's 1936 Kiev manoeuvres, producing pictures of high-quality and dramatic intensity. The photographs, showing masses of tanks, paratroopers and low-flying ground-attack aircraft, were freely made available to western embassies and the Western media, in order to convince the capitalist world that the USSR was now too strong to attack. From the summer of 1941, Khaldei photographed real military operations on the Ukranian front, retreating to the Volga by the summer of 1942, and then covering the remorseless Soviet advance in 1943 and 1944, liberating the Ukraine, and then invading the Balkans. Khaldei's greatest scoop came on 1 May 1945, when he snapped Soviet soldiers raising a large red flag (actually a tablecloth with a hammer and sickle sewn on) on top of the Reichstag. The photograph had to be retouched before publication because the right arm of the man supporting the flag-bearer was festooned with wrist-watches, clear evidence of looting.

London, John 'Jack' (1876–1916)

The quintessential American man of action-turned-writer, London rose to fame both as a commentator on social conditions in American and British cities, and for adventure stories based at least partly on his own life. When the chance came to report on the Russo-Japanese War, London grasped it eagerly. Unlike many correspondents who complained bitterly about Japanese censorship, but allowed it to control their activities, London wandered the rear areas without permission, gaining a series of scoops by a combination of bluff and sheer good fortune. Conscious of his image, London refused to co-operate with the Japanese, on one occasion assaulting a Japanese officer, which led to threats of a firing squad. A tall, well-built man, London died unexpectedly in 1914 from dysentery while accompanying US Marines who were about to occupy Vera Cruz.

Matthews, Herbert Lionel (1900–1977)

Born in New York, on America's entry into the First World War Matthews lied about his age to serve with the American Expeditionary Force. Resuming his education at Columbia

University after the war, in 1922 Matthews joined the *New York Times*, the paper with which he was to remain for the next 45 years. Matthews covered the 1935 Italian invasion of Abyssinia, earning the hatred of the left throughout the English-speaking world for his generally pro-Italian views, a bias which seemed to be confirmed by Mussolini's award to him of the Italian Croce de Guerra. After covering the Spanish Civil War with rather more objectivity, Matthews ran the *New York Times*'s Rome bureau from 1939 until Mussolini's declaration of war on the USA on 10 December 1941. Repatriated to the United States in exchange for Italian newsmen, Matthews covered the war in the Pacific until July 1943, when he covered the invasion of Sicily, and the subsequent Italian campaign.

The *New York Times*'s most famous war correspondent, Matthews achieved his greatest scoop in February 1957 when he interviewed Fidel Castro and the remnants of his guerrilla band in the Sierra Mastre mountains of southern Cuba. Photographs of Matthews and Castro smoking cigars together, published in the *New York Times*, gave the lie to Cuban dictator Batista's claims to have wiped out the guerrilla band, and precipitated a veritable flood of American newsmen into the Sierra Mastre, all wanting to emulate Matthew's coup. The ironical result was to bring back to life an almost extinguished revolutionary movement, and to pave the way for a Marxist government in Cuba.

McCullin, Don (1935–)

Born in a tough working-class suburb in North London, McCullin's big break came in 1953, when he was drafted into the RAF for his National Service, and was trained in photo-reconnaissance. Taught to use a camera, McCullin managed to get a job as a 'stringer' with the *Observer* in 1958, which became progressively more full-time, as he proved his worth on photographic assignments. In 1964 McCullin covered his first conflict, disturbances between Greeks and Turks on Cyprus, and began a career which spanned 30 years, and was to take him around the world several times, to places like the Congo, Vietnam, Biafra, Northern Ireland and the Middle East.

A photographer of highly developed sensitivity, his ability to continue witnessing horror and folly finally broke when he was attacked by an hysterical woman in Beirut, who had lost her home and her family, and accused him of exploiting her pain. McCullin moved to Somerset, specialising in landscape photography before returning to photo-journalism with powerful stories on the spread of HIV in Africa.

Mydans, Carl (1907–?)

After graduating from Boston University School of Journalism, Mydans joined *Life* magazine in 1936. Three years later he covered the Russo-Finnish War, his photographs helping to establish the heroic status that the formidable Finnish ski-troops soon acquired in Europe and America. Mydans photographed the collapse of France in June 1940, joining refugee columns as they fled westward, his images

forming a poignant picture essay in *Life* magazine. He next
reported on the Sino-Japanese War, before arriving in the
Philippines in time for the Japanese onslaught in December
1941. America's Far Eastern commander, General Douglas
MacArthur, who had served as a press liaison officer early in
his career, well understood the power of the media, and made
sure that Mydans and other journalists accompanied him to
Corrigidor, where they were afforded radio-telephone links
with the United States, so that Mydans's pictures continued to
appear from the beleaguered island fortress. When Corrigidor
finally surrendered in May 1942, Mydans and his wife Shelly,
who also worked for *Life*, were interned in Manila's Santo
Tomas University until they were released in a prisoner
exchange in late 1943. Mydans returned to the Philippines
with MacArthur's invasion force in October 1944, his image
of the General wading ashore on Leyte soon acquiring an
iconic status, and ensuring that MacArthur, already a hero
to many, would become a demi-god. On 2 September 1945
MacArthur expressed his gratitude to Mydans by making sure
he had the best position to cover the Japanese surrender
aboard the USS *Missouri*. Mydans was to cover several more
wars – the Chinese Civil War, Korea and the French Indo-
China War – but he never again achieved such a coup.

Nachtwey, James (1948–)

Born in Syracuse in New York state in 1948, Nachtwey studied
Art History at Dartmouth College, before getting a job on a
New Mexico newspaper in 1976, where he learned the art of

photo-journalism. Returning to New York, Nachtwey pursued a career as a freelancer, which took him to Northern Ireland, El Salvador, Nicaragua, and several other trouble spots, before he joined the staff of *Time* magazine in 1984. On 11 September 2001 he happened to be in the right place at the right time, looking at the New York World Trade Center from the bedroom of his hotel, when the first aircraft hit. His photographs, along with those of Bill Biggart, provided a visual record of the atrocity with appalling clarity.

Rider-Rider, William (1891–?)

Employed as a photographer for the *Daily Mirror* in 1910, Rider-Rider was accredited to the Canadian Army in June 1917 as an official photographer, thanks to the machinations of Canadian Press Magnate, Lord Beaverbrook. Hitherto neglected in press coverage, particularly when compared to the ANZACS, Beaverbrook ensured that Rider-Rider's photographs were widely printed in British newspapers. Rider-Rider covered the ill-fated Passchendaele offensive, some of his photographs, depictions of soldiers wading through a sea of mud, achieving iconic status. In all, Rider-Rider took some 4,000 photographs, which became the basis of a huge collection of memorabilia now housed in the Federal Archives in Ottawa.

Robertson, James (1813–1881)

An engraver by training, James Robertson developed an early interest in photographic processes, seeing the possibility of printing photographs directly on to newsprint. He was working as the chief engraver at the Imperial Mint at Constantinople in the early 1850s when he formed a partnership with Italian landscape photographer, Felice Beato. His first pictures, many of which were reproduced as engravings in the *Illustrated London News*, were of allied troops arriving in Constantinople, on their way to the Crimea. He travelled to the Crimea with Beato in March 1855, photographing scenes which emphasised the efficiency with which the siege was being conducted. Having endeared himself to the British military establishment, in 1857 he was appointed official photographer to the British Army in India, where he covered the latter stages of the suppression of the mutiny.

Rosenthal, Joe (1912–?)

A San Francisco-based photographer who worked for a number of newspapers, Rosenthal tried to enlist after Pearl Harbor, but was rejected because of poor eyesight. For much of the war Rosenthal worked for the Associated Press office in San Francisco until February 1945, when AP asked him to cover the landing of the US Marines on Iwo Jima. Having no experience as a combat photographer, Rosenthal did not land with the assault waves, but came ashore after Mount Suribachi, the peak dominating the island, had already been captured. Having been told that the Marines had already raised a flag on the mountain, Rosenthal climbed to take additional pictures, and came across a group of six Marines taking down a small flag, and preparing to hoist a much larger one in its place. Rosenthal asked the men to pose, and photographed them from a platform he constructed from sandbags taken from a Japanese machine-gun post. It was Rosenthal's first day in a war zone, and his first photograph as a combat cameraman. By a combination of extraordinary luck and very good management, he produced the most famous combat photograph ever taken. It earned Rosenthal the Pulitzer Prize in 1945, was celebrated on US postage stamps, and was used as the basis of the Marine Corps monument in Washington. In the aftermath of 9/11, New York firemen raised the Stars and Stripes on the mountain of smouldering rubble, an attempt to draw on the spiritual power of Rosenthal's image.

Snow, Edgar (1905–1972)

A graduate of Columbia University School of Journalism, in 1928 Snow joined the staff of the Hong Kong-based *China Weekly Review*. Snow quickly demonstrated that he was a daring and skilful photographer, covering the Chinese Nationalist army's suppression of Mao Tse-tung's Communist guerrilla movement in south central China in the late 1920s, and the Japanese attack on Shanghai in 1931. Five years later, thanks to help from China's revolutionary first lady, Madam Sun Yat Sen, Snow got the scoop of a lifetime when he managed to spend four months with Mao Tse-tung and the Communist revolutionary leadership in Yennan in north-west China. Widely published in the late 1930s, Snow's photographs gave the outside world a unique insight into the Chinese

Communist philosophy and the revolution it was sustaining, and probably served to stimulate revolutionary movements in other areas of Asia.

Steer, George Lowther (1909–1944)

Born in South Africa and educated at Oxford, Steer was employed by *The Times* in 1935 to cover the Italian invasion of Abyssinia. As a representative of what was still the world's most influential paper, Steer was fêted by Emperor Haile Selassie, and allowed into areas denied other correspondents. Steer was not a skilled photographer – he referred to his pictures as 'beastly things' – but by taking a large number he made sure that some were of considerable force, particularly his coverage of the aftermath of the Italian employment of mustard gas, which he was the first to announce to the world. In the spring of 1936, as the finally victorious Italian army advanced on Addis Abba and order broke down in the capital, Steer married Margarita de Herrero, an Anglo-Spanish journalist working for *Le Journal*. In the summer of 1936 Steer, accompanied by the now-pregnant Margarita, reported the outbreak of the Spanish Civil War from the Basque country, but the strain proved too much and Margarita died in childbirth in January 1937. A bereft Steer threw himself into the cause of Basque independence, in April 1937 breaking the news of the destruction of Guernica to the world, and making it clear that the German Condor Legion was responsible. When the editor of *The Times*, following the paper's policy of appeasement, attempted to absolve the Germans of responsibility, Steer resigned and joined the *Daily Telegraph*. Steer returned to Abyssinia in 1941 with the British Army, and subsequently served as an intelligence officer in Burma, dying in a road traffic accident on Christmas Day, 1944.

Steichen, Edward Jean (1879–1973)

Emigrating to America with his parents from his native Luxembourg at the age of two, in 1893 Steichen apprenticed himself to a photographer in Wisconsin. Early in his training Steichen showed artistic flair, a talent which he developed in Paris at the turn of the century, where he specialised in portraits. By 1902 Steichen was famous. The rich and powerful, including US President Theodore Roosevelt, clamoured to have Steichen take their pictures. With America's entry into the war in 1917, Steichen enlisted in the US Army Signals Corps, and was soon placed in charge of photographic operations of the American Expeditionary Force. Steichen managed an increasingly large team, but still found time to take his own pictures of the American offensives which brought the war to an end in the autumn of 1918.

Returning to New York, Steichen resumed his role as New York's leading society photographer, until the Japanese attack on Pearl Harbor, when he enlisted once more, this time to serve with the United States Navy. Steichen served throughout the Pacific war, photographing US aircraft carriers under attack, and the aftermath of the fighting on Iwo Jima. Steichen had suffered post-traumatic stress syndrome after the First

World War, and his experiences of the Second World War reawakened the old memories. His photographs from Iwo Jima of dead Japanese emphasised their youth and humanity, but were eclipsed at the time by the adulation heaped on Joe Rosenthal for his triumphal picture of the raising of the 'Stars and Stripes' over the island. After the war, Steichen worked through his trauma by photographing and compiling images capturing the human experiences of birth, courtship, marriage and death throughout the world, an exhibition he entitled 'The Family of Man', and which took New York, and then the world, by storm. The exhibition finally found a permanent home in his native Luxembourg.

Chronology

1850–July 1864	Taiping Rebellion
March 1852–December 1853	Anglo-Burmese War
October 1853–March 1856	**Crimean War**
April–October 1856	Civil war in Kansas between pro-slavery and free-soil guerrillas
October 1856–October 1860	Second Opium War
May 1857–April 1859	Indian Mutiny
August 1858–March 1862	French invasion of Cochin China
April–July 1859	Franco-Austrian War
October 1859	John Brown's Harpers Ferry Raid
October 1859–April 1860	Spanish invasion of Morocco
March 1860–February 1872	Maori Wars
May 1860–March 1861	Garibaldi's invasion of Sicily

April 1861–April 1865	**American Civil War**
December 1861–June 1867	French intervention in Mexico
March–October 1862	Garibaldi's operations against Rome
January 1863–May 1864	Polish uprising against Russia
February to August 1864	Schleswig-Holstein War
June 1863–September 1864	British, French, Dutch and US naval bombardments of Japanese ports
November 1864	US-Indian Wars (Sand River Massacre)
December 1864–March 1870	**War of the Triple Alliance (Lopez War)**
June–August 1866	**The Austro-Prussian War**
December 1866	US-Indian Wars (Fort Phil Kearny)
January–November 1867	Garibaldi's attempt to seize Rome
August 1867	US-Indian Wars (Wagon Box Fight)
1867–May 1868	British expedition to Abyssinia
October 1869–August 1870	Riel Rebellion and British Red River Expedition (Canada)
July 1870–May 1871	**Franco-Prussian War and Paris Commune**
September 1870	Italian occupation of Rome
1872–73	US-Indian Wars (Modoc Campaign)
1873–February 1874	Second Ashanti War
1873–February 1876	Spanish Civil War
1873–1908	Dutch-Atjehenese War
February 1876–January 1877	US-Indian Wars (US v. Sioux and Northern Cheyenne)

April 1877–March 1878	**Russo-Turkish War**
November 1878–1881	Second Afghan War
January 1879–August 1879	Zulu War
1877	US-Indian Wars (Nez Perce Campaign)
February 1879–April 1884	War of the Pacific
January–April 1881	First Boer War
April–May 1881	French invasion of Tunisia
May–September 1882	British invasion of Egypt
1882–83	French invasion of Tongking
1884–1885	Russian conquest of Merv
January 1884–January 1885	Siege of Khartoum
November 1885–January 1886	Third Burmese War
1885–1886	US-Indian Wars (Apache Campaigns)
1885–1886	First Mandingo–French War
March–May 1885	Second Riel Rebellion
1889–1890	First Dahomey-French War
1890–91	US-Indian Wars (Wounded Knee Campaign)
1891–1893	German conquest of Tanganyika
1892	Second Dahomey-French War
1893–94	Third Ashanti War
1894–95	Second Mandingo-French War
June 1894–April 1895	Sino-Japanese War
February 1895–April 1898	Cuban rebellion against Spain
1895–96	Fourth Ashanti War

1895–October 1896	Italo-Abyssinian War
March–October 1896	Matabele War
August 1896	Filipino revolt against Spain
1896–November 1898	British reconquest of the Sudan
1896–1897	Malakand Campaign
April–September 1897	Greco-Turkish War
1897	British conquest of northern Nigeria
1897–1898	Tirah Campaign
1898	Third Mandingo-French War
April–December 1898	Spanish-American War
February 1899–1905	Filipino insurrection against US
October 1899–April 1902	**Second Boer War**
June 1900–September 1901	Boxer Rebellion
1903–September 1904	British invasion of Tibet
February 1904–September 1905	Russo-Japanese War
1904–1908	Herero-German War
December 1905–January 1906	First Russian Revolution
April–June 1910	Turkish suppression of Albanian revolt
May 1911–August 1914	Mexican Revolution
September 1911–October 1912	Italo-Turkish War
October 1911–February 1912	Chinese Revolution
October 1912–May 1913	First Balkan War
May–August 1913	Second Balkan War

August 1914–November 1918	**First World War**
March 1916–February 1917	USA punitive expedition to Mexico
December 1917–October 1922	**Russian Civil War**
May–November 1919	Third Afghan War
November 1919–December 1921	Anglo-Irish Civil War
April–October 1920	Russo-Polish War
July–December 1920	British suppression of Iraqi (Arab) insurrection
December 1920–November 1922	Greco-Turkish War
1921–1924	Spanish-Moroccan (Riff) War
June 1922–July 1924	British suppression of Iraqi (Kurd) insurrection
April 1925–May 1926	Joint Spanish and French operations in Morocco
July 1925–June 1927	French suppression of Druse revolt in Syria
July 1926–July 1927	Nationalist Chinese suppression of warlords
August 1927–December 1949	Nationalist v. Communist Chinese civil war
September 1930–June 1932	British suppression of Kurd revolt (Iraq)
September 1931–February 1932	Japanese invasion of Manchuria
January–March 1932	First battle of Shanghai
June 1932–June 1935	Chaco War
1935–1939	British containment of Arab revolt (Palestine)
October 1935–May 1936	Italian invasion of Abyssinia

July 1936–March 1939	**Spanish Civil War**
July 1937–September 1945	**Sino-Japanese War** (subsumed into Second World War after 7 December 1941)
July–August 1938	Soviet-Japanese Border War
May–September 1939	Soviet-Japanese Border War
September 1939–August 1945	**Second World War**
November 1939–March 1940	Russo-Finnish War
October 1944–1947	Greek Civil War
September–November 1945	British re-establish European control in East Indies
1945–1948	Palestinian insurrection
1945–1949	Dutch-Indonesian War
1946–1949	**Chinese Civil War** (This conflict, begun in 1927, had been interrupted by a brief truce in 1945)
1946–July 1954	**First Indo-China War**
July 1946–August 1947	Indian Partition
1946–1954	Hukabalahap insurgency in Philippines
November 1947–December 1949	Kashmir War
May 1948–January 1949	War of Israeli Independence
1948–1960	Malayan Emergency
March 1948–May 1949	Berlin Airlift
August 1948 (ongoing)	Karen Revolt against Burma
June 1950–July 1953	**Korean War**
October 1950	Chinese invasion of Tibet
October 1952–1960	Mau Mau insurgency

1954–1962	**Algerian War of Independence**
1955–1964	Cyprus insurgency
October–November, 1956	Suez invasion
November 1956	Hungarian uprising
1956–1959	Cuban Revolution
July 1958	Iraqi Military Coup
July–October 1958	American and British occupation of Lebanon and Jordan
March 1959	Chinese suppression of Tibet Revolt
1960–1996	Guatemalan insurgency
July 1960–August 1967	Congo Independence Wars
February 1961–October 1974	Angolan insurgency against Portuguese colonial rule
April 1961	Bay of Pigs invasion of Cuba
July 1961	Bizerta, (French attacks destroy Tunisian attempts to force France from Tunisian bases)
September 1961–March 1971	Kurdish insurgency against Iraq
1961	British deployment to Kuwait thwarts threatened Iraqi invasion
1961–1964	American deployment of advisors to assist South Vietnam fight Viet Cong insurgency
1962–1991	Eritrean War of Independence against Ethiopia
1962–October 1974	Guinea-Bissau insurgency against Portuguese colonial rule

1962–October 1974	Mozambique insurgency against Portuguese colonial rule
1962	Sino-Indian Border War
October 1962	Cuban Missile Crisis
December 1962	British suppression of Indonesian-inspired revolt in Brunei
September 1963–June 1966	Konfrontasi (Malaysian Confrontation)
February 1964	French intervention in Gabon
August 1964	French intervention in Central African Republic
1964–1967	Radfan-Aden War
1964	Renewed Hukbalahap insurgency in Philippines, (ongoing as New People's Army Insurgency)
1964 (ongoing)	FARC Insurgency in Columbia
April 1965	US intervention in Dominican Republic
1965–1980	Rhodesian (Zimbabwe) War of Liberation
September 1965	India-Pakistan War
1965–1975	**Vietnam War (Second Indo-China War)**
1966–1988	SWAPO insurgency against South Africa in Namibia
November 1966–October 1967	Cuban-inspired insurgency in Bolivia
June 1967	**Six-Day War**
1967–1970	Nigerian Civil War

Spring–August 1968	Soviet suppression of reform movement in Czechoslovakia
August 1968 (ongoing)	French intervention in Chad
1969–1974	Tupamoras insurgency in Uruguay
1969 (ongoing)	Northern Ireland 'Troubles'
September 1970	Jordanian suppression of PLO Camps (Black September)
1970–1975	Cambodian Civil War
1970–1975	Dhofar insurgency
March–December 1971	Bangladeshi War of Independence
October 1973	**Yom Kippur War**
1974–1991	Ethiopian civil war
March–September 1974	Portuguese Revolution
July 1974	Turkish invasion of Cyprus
1975–1994	Angolan civil war
1976–1991	Moroccan-Polisaro War for western Sahara
December 1978	Vietnamese invasion of Cambodia
January 1979	Tanzanian invasion of Uganda
February–March 1979	Sino-Vietnamese Border War
January 1979–1980	Iranian Revolution
December 1979–1988	**Soviet-Afghan War**
March 1980 (ongoing)	Peru Sendaro-Luminoso insurgency
March 1980	Syrian Baathist suppression of uprisings in Homs and Aleppo
April 1980	Operation Eagle's Claw (abortive US Special Operation to rescue hostages in Teheran)

1980–1985	Ugandan civil war
September 1980–August 1988	**Iraq-Iran War**
April–June 1982	**Falklands (Malvinas) War**
June 1982	Operation Peace for Galilee (Israeli invasion of Lebanon)
July 1983 (ongoing)	Sri Lankan Tamil insurgency
1983 (ongoing)	Sudanese civil war
October 1983	Operation Urgent Fury (US invasion of Grenada)
1984 (ongoing)	Kurdish insurgency against Turkey
1985–1991	Lebanese civil war
1987	Intifada (ongoing Palestinian uprising against Israeli occupation)
1988–October 1997	Bougainville independence insurgency against Papua-New Guinea
June 1989	Tiananmen Square Massacre
November–December 1989	Collapse of Communist systems in Eastern Europe
December 1989–January 1990	Rumanian uprising
December 1989	Operation Just Cause (US invasion of Panama)
July 1990 (ongoing)	Liberian civil war
August 1990–March 1991	**First Gulf War**
December 1992	Operation Restore Hope (ongoing US and UN intervention in Somalia)
March 1991–June 1999	**Wars of Yugoslavian Disintegration**

August 1991	Attempted hard-line Communist coup in Moscow
December 1991 (ongoing)	Algerian Islamic Salvation Front insurgency
April–August 1994	Rwandan civil war
1994 (ongoing)	Congo civil war
December 1994	Russo-Chechenyan War
1996 (ongoing)	Nepalese Maoist insurgency
1996 (ongoing)	Naxilite (Maoist) insurgency in eastern India
October 1997 (ongoing)	Australian and New Zealand intervention in Bougainville
1998–2002	Second Angolan civil war
1999 (ongoing)	British intervention in Sierra Leone
December 1999	East Timor intervention (Australian-led UN intervention to remove Indonesian militias from East Timor)
11 September 2001	**'9/11' Al Qaeda terrorist attacks on New York and Washington**
December 2001 (ongoing)	US-led invasion of Afghanistan
March 2003 (ongoing)	**Operation Iraqi Freedom (British Operation Telic)**
July 2003 (ongoing)	Australian intervention in Solomon Islands
October 2004 (ongoing)	French intervention in Ivory Coast

Index

L

M

About the type

This book is typeset in FF Nexus, designed by Martin Majoor in 2004. In common with Majoor's earlier typeface Scala, Nexus is a humanistic serif type from which a sans serif version (Nexus Sans) has been derived. However Nexus also has a third dimension: a slab-serif-like design called Nexus Mix (used for the chapter headings in this book). All three designs share the same basic 'skeleton', meaning that they can be used together to provide subtly differing voices. Nexus has been selected as the principal typeface for new Collins books because of its exceptional sense of clarity and openness.

In FF Scala and FF Scala Sans, Martin Majoor (b. 1960) had designed one of the most visible typefaces of the 1990s. In 1994 he designed the typeface Telefont for the Dutch telephone directory, and in 2000 he released FF Seria and FF Seria Sans. The new family FF Nexus confirms Majoor as one of the most refined and original type designers at work today.